Who Killed My Church?

R. James Shupp

Elk Lake
PUBLISHING™

Elk Lake Publishing

Who Killed My Church?

Copyright © 2015 by R. James Shupp

Requests for information should be addressed to:

Elk Lake Publishing, PO Box 4043, Atlanta, GA 30024

Create Space ISBN-13 NUMBER: 978-1-942513-44-5

Cover and graphics design: Anna O'Brien

Editing: Deb Haggerty and Kathi Macias

DEDICATION

To the bride of my youth,
During our evening walks, you encouraged me
to write a story of hope.
This story was imagined step by step, mile after mile.
We laughed and cried over the possibilities,
Dreaming others would too.

ENDORSEMENTS

James Shupp delivers a very compelling story with playful humor, intellectual insights, and spiritual discernment.

Dr. Gary A. Demers, CEO

NotableWriters.com

As a Senior Pastor and avid reader, I digest many books about the Church, her health and growth. Rarely do I find a book that touches me as deeply as did *Who Killed My Church?* I cannot remember the last time I was "moved" emotionally, practically, and spiritually as much as this book did. Almost every page struck a chord (not just a note, a full chord) in my heart. I wept at its truth, rejoiced at its victories, and desire to grow from its influence. In a culture where 80 percent or more of churches are stagnant or dying, this book is a *must read* for every pastor, staff member, leader, and Christ-follower. Without reservation, this may well be the most practical and helpful book you read this year!

Dr. Jerry N. Watts, Senior Pastor

Hueytown, AL

An absolute must read! Powerful, captivating, inspirational, but also very helpful, practical, and informational. Every pastor, church leader, church member, and anyone who desires to make an impact for the Kingdom of God should read this book. God has really given James keen insight about the current challenges every local church faces. Loved it and plan to have my entire staff read it!

Dr. Kevin Hamm, Senior Pastor

Gardendale's First Baptist Church, Gardendale, AL

Having pastored the same church for twenty years, I've seen many phases of church ministry. Until now, no one has explained the process better than James Shupp in his book *Who Killed My Church?* Once I started reading this book, I could not put it down. Way too many pastors use false sensors to determine growth or success as a pastor. This book forced me as a pastor to stop using those sensors and look deep inside at what I called "church." I also had every pastor on my staff read the book. The result was a launching of ministries into our community that has expanded our church like never before. We felt successful in our own eyes; however, this book opened all our eyes to what could happen if we continued doing what we had always done.

Dr. Michael D. Miles, Sr.
Senior Pastor, Azle, Texas

Who Killed My Church? is a delightful read that every pastor or church member will love. The author writes from his experience as a pastor, but what makes the book stand out is his storytelling ability and character development. Whether a pastor or church member, you'll recognize the unique personalities as if Shupp attended your church. The difficulties and frustrations of the pastor are real and relevant to almost every church. The honest and oftentimes humorous ways the story unfolds keeps you turning the pages.

Few authors can get across messages that inform and teach while entertaining also, but Shupp is able to do this, addressing problems in the church in a compelling but not heavy-handed way. I'd recommend *Who Killed My Church?* for anyone that enjoys a great story, but especially for church leaders who deal with difficult people and issues.

Who Killed My Church?

John Walters, Director

The Missional Association.

James has done a masterful job writing his book in story form. I found the pages educational, encouraging, and entertaining all at the same time. Many pastors will believe James is writing about their church. If you are a pastor or lay leader of a declining church, I believe this book will help you discern where your church is in its lifecycle. It will stir your imagination for what could be for your congregation and community, and help you design and develop a course of action to reverse the decline of your church. As a ministry coach, I highly recommend every pastor read this book from cover to cover. The ideas contained within will energize the future of your ministry.

Marshall Shannon,

Ministry Coach

Who Killed My Church? is an exceptional novel that I expect will have tremendous impact on churches, not only in America, but worldwide. Author and Pastor James Shupp does a masterful job of developing characters and storyline, interspersing humor between the characters that caused me to occasionally laugh out loud. This book is a thoroughly enjoyable read, all while presenting a brilliant way to evaluate and restructure "the way we do church." *Who Killed My Church?* has the potential of revitalizing dying churches everywhere and rescuing the younger generation. Entertaining, engaging, and highly informative, *Who Killed My Church?* should be required reading for the laity, giving them insight to the burdens and toll that church leaders experience, while mapping a way for laity and leadership to join in new efforts to make church relevant. If your church isn't growing, by definition it's dying. James Shupp offers wisdom and insight, complete with application questions. This book will reinvigorate you, your leaders, and church members to reach the lost for Christ.

Pamela Christian,

Radio and TV Host, Author, Speaker

James Shupp had me with those four words: *movement, monument, museum,* and *morgue*! His description of the actions taken in the various seasons of the life of a church clearly demonstrates his familiarity with church health issues. From being missional communities marked by vision, sacrifice, flexibility, and catalytic multiplication, to the cold hard Winter marked by contempt, decay, and frozenness, and everything in between, Shupp captures the challenges faced by pastors and church leaders of declining churches who desire to see their congregations revitalized and useful in the Kingdom.

With all the material being published today on "Church Revitalization," I urge you to consider adding *Who Killed My Church?* to the list.

Dr. Lonnie Wascom, Director of Missions and Ministries

Northshore Baptist Association, Hammond, LA

Who Killed My Church? by James Shupp entranced me. I was privileged to help edit the book, and as I did, I fell in love with Pete, Monica, and Marcus. I empathized with their care and concern for Green Street Baptist Church and was fascinated by the actions taken to turn the church around. Having been in churches that have reached the morgue stage in my past, I was also interested to see the techniques used. Shupp has written, very well, I might add, a wonderfully educational and entertaining book. The book should be read by all pastors—and by the laity as well. Five stars!

Deb Haggerty,

Author, Blogger, Freelance Editor, and Speaker

Revelation Series

Book 1

"To the angel of the church in Sardis write: These are the words of him
who holds the seven spirits of God and the seven stars.
I know your deeds;
you have a reputation of being alive, but you are dead"
(Revelation 3:1, NIV).

Part 1

Chapter 1

"…the night cometh, when no man can work" (John 9:4, KJV).

Monica lay on the bed, sobbing. Pete stood motionless in the open doorway of their bedroom. He wanted to comfort her somehow, but he was uncertain about what to do next. Years ago he believed he could fix any problem given a decent opportunity and enough time. Things had changed of late, so he hesitated.

She lifted her head and broke the silence. "What are we going to do? Why do you keep tolerating this situation?"

"Things are improving."

"These people are *not* following you, Pete. They're not acting like men who believe in your leadership anymore. It's not your fault, but how much longer do we have to live like this?"

Pete listened. Not that he was a good listener. He thought about a response, but they'd discussed this too many times over the last year.

There were no answers. Every attempt to move the needle out of the red zone failed. Their condition was quickly overheating.

There was one rationale, however, that made sense to Pete when the problems first manifested. On a walk through the park one Saturday afternoon, Pete stated his plan with confidence.

"You know me, Monica. I'm a competitor by nature. I hate to lose. I never quit or admit defeat. God won't let us fail!"

Monica loved his passion and sense of fight, but she was unconvinced. She knew he was drawn to hopeless situations. He was tenacious and driven, and she liked that about him most of the time. But this was not one of those times. When they met in the cafeteria of Baylor University, his self-confidence and optimism were among the magnetic qualities that attracted her to him in the first place.

"Things will get better."

She found his eyes. Her cheeks glistened as she spoke. "What makes you so certain?"

"Do you remember that day when we first moved here?" he said softly. "All I ever wanted to do was make a difference and leave a mark. All of this was for us. This church was supposed to be my one chance; my best opportunity to—"

"Stop, Pete. Please stop. I'm not buying these arguments anymore. That day is gone." She buried her head in the pillow and continued to cry. For her, sleep came quickly. It always did.

Pete spent the next several hours surfing the web. Every ad posted for a new senior pastor looked like the previous. *I wonder why the last guy left. What was his story?*

He closed his eyes to reflect on the day. Sleep overcame him like a gentle tide. The chair groaned throughout the night.

Chapter 2

You will not fear the terror of night,
nor the arrow that flies by day (Psalm 91:5, NIV).

The next day started out like any other. Pete made the three-mile journey to the office. Green Street Baptist Church in Ft. Worth was known as one of the flagship churches of the denomination. Green Street still had the reputation of being an extraordinary place where exciting things happened. Although those events occurred decades ago, lives were changed and people remembered. A few old stalwarts still attended from those days, but funerals had culled their numbers significantly over the last five years.

Five years. Pete sighed. *How things have changed—but not the kind of change I dreamed about.*

As Pete's Camry turned the corner for the last mile, he could already see the hill leading up to the church. The property was prime real estate back in the day. A massive steeple touched the sky, a testament to the financial strength of those early years. *Or was that strength merely the eager lenders who stood in line to loan the church money?*

The thought reminded Pete that today was the day he was to meet with the finance committee. Lately they were not a happy group of people. And who could blame them? Offerings were down, which necessitated pleading for money from the pulpit more frequently. However, asking for money seemed to have the opposite effect. The more frequently he issued the plea, the more often people quietly slipped away. They left for other churches where things were going well financially, numerically, and, of course, spiritually, unlike Green Street.

As Pete drove into the parking lot, he thought about the other places he'd served as the senior pastor. Those churches grew.

Why not this one? What am I doing wrong here? I thought I was chosen by God, selected by Him to restore a great church back to its spiritual heyday.

He thought of Monica back home. She was still asleep when he left. There had been no words since the last words that still rang in his ears. She wanted him to admit defeat and move on. *What keeps me here?*

Pete was so lost in his thoughts that he failed to notice two things. For one, his reserved parking spot was occupied by a young mother dropping her child off for preschool. He grew agitated, not because she took his space but because almost no one who attended the preschool came on Sunday morning—a bitter pill to swallow. *Can I really blame them? Green Street wouldn't be my first choice either, and I'm the pastor. We're an old church that doesn't appeal to young families.*

Pete's thoughts shifted when he noticed the second thing. Frank Sanders was standing in the parking lot waiting for him to arrive. *That's odd.* Frank wasn't wearing a jacket on this cold November morning. *Why didn't he wait inside?*

Pete hated surprises, and this one didn't bode well. He turned off the ignition as a knot began forming in his stomach. The sense of apprehension was palpable. He barely had one foot on the asphalt when Frank delivered the news.

Who Killed My Church?

"Brother Pete, I wanted to warn you that the meeting began an hour ago."

Pete managed his trademark stoic posture. *Never let them see you sweat.* He adopted this motto long ago as his mantra for ministry. The saying seemed to help even though it wasn't biblical.

"They're mad at me for letting you know, but I thought it was only fair. There's been a lot of discussion about your job performance. They want a drastic change, Pete. What are you going to do?"

Pete felt a surge of adrenalin rush though his body. The same thing happened before he stood in the pulpit to preach each Sunday. Lately, the intensity of these episodes bordered on panic attacks. And this meeting was to start in five minutes, hardly enough time to gather his composure.

The truth was that Pete could hardly bear arriving at Green Street any earlier than necessary these days. Every day drained more from him than he was able to replenish. Long gone were the days of high energy, limitless enthusiasm, and unbridled courage. He felt like a mere shadow of the man he was five years ago, but he needed to think quickly. He felt like kicking himself for not arriving earlier.

Pete swallowed hard and cleared his throat before responding to Frank. "I'll meet you there." He bolted toward the private entrance of his office. During the course of the last year, Pete began using this secluded entry point more frequently, simply to avoid going through the main entrance of the church. Not that he was antisocial. He just felt that everyone glared at him like he was the main problem.

Maybe I am....

Then Pete remembered something. A little over two years ago he attended a church growth conference. There was one speaker who seemed to describe Pete's church as though he'd given it birth and then watched it die. *What was his name? Where did I put his business card?*

He rifled through the top drawer of his desk. Within was an odd assortment of pens, paper clips, Post-it notes with brilliant but unused ideas, quaint mementoes church members had given him, and rolls of antacid tablets.

The card. Where's that damn card?

Pete never cussed out loud—just in his head. He stopped swearing aloud when God called him into the ministry. *Sheep shock,* he called it. Sheep wanted a shepherd without flaws, a man they could believe, a man better than themselves. Monica didn't count, however. Lately she'd heard him spice up his speech more often.

Found it! The card was stuck to the back of a Post-it note. *Marcus Cunningham,* he read. *Church Consultant, Author, Speaker, Founder of Movement Strategies.*

Pete grabbed his Bible and stuck the card inside. Not that he had plans to give a devotional or share anything special during the meeting. He just wanted the Bible to appear a part of him, a part of his calling, and the reason he was there today. *Maybe looking the part will help.*

He exited his office, rushed down a long hallway, and then ran up the stairs to Conference Room 212b. He was short of breath when he opened the door.

All eyes were on him.

Chapter 3

"Have I not commanded you? Be strong and courageous.
Do not be terrified; do not be discouraged, for the LORD your
God will be with you wherever you go" (Joshua 1:9, NIV).

"This is awkward for us, Pastor, but we needed an opportunity to discuss some things without you being present."

Pete sat in silence, eyes focused intently on Gary Lovejoy, chairman of the finance committee, past deacon chairman, a member of the pulpit committee that invited Pete and Monica to Green Street Baptist Church—and the one who'd spoken aloud when he entered the room. Gary was one of the original twenty charter members who'd founded the church over sixty years ago. Back then he was a young man in his early twenties. The other nineteen founders were either walking on streets of gold or had disappeared over the years. As the only remaining charter member, Gary enjoyed the status, and, despite his humble objections, the attention as well. Every church member could repeat his story verbatim of how the church began in a house two blocks down the street. "The house is gone," he'd solemnly say, "but the church still stands."

"We've not conspired against you, Pete." Gary paused for effect.

Pete's ears were throbbing. He could feel his blood pressure rising. A year ago Pete and Monica had gone for counseling in the Ozark Mountains. The psychologist told Pete he needed to listen more as a leader. He could hear the counselor's words echoing even now: "The CEOs of Fortune 500 companies listen more than they talk. Be a good listener, Pete, and then you will be a great leader."

Pete snapped back to attention as Gary continued in sober tones, "All great leaders know when to take responsibility for failure and admit defeat. We've arrived at such an occasion. The church won't last much longer under your leadership. We don't have a plan for turning this ship around. You know we love you personally. Brother Pete, you're a good man with a good heart, but we need more than that right now. Do you have anything to say in response to our evaluation of your job performance?"

Time stood still. Pete had been a pastor for twenty-five years. He never dreamed he'd be in such a position. These situations happened to other people, not Pete Blackman. He thought of all the hopes he'd had when they arrived five years earlier. "Green Street will be a great church for us, Monica," he'd said. He remembered her sense of caution and concern that he was being overly optimistic. She always saw things he didn't, but he never admitted she was right until he got blindsided.

He wished she were here right now. She could make this better. He tried to imagine that she was in the room sitting next to him. Despite the fact that he couldn't comfort her last night, she always knew what to say to keep him going. How he wished he had her gift, like in this moment.

"Well, Pete, do you have anything to say?"

Pete sat motionlessly without responding. His head started swimming as the conference room began rotating around his chair. The knot that had formed in his stomach earlier released a wave of nausea. Pete closed his eyes and lowered his head. Stabs of humiliation and fear pricked his insides like blistering specks of lava. He wanted to disappear from the room like Jesus did after the crowds sought to lay their hands on Him, or even run away as the disciples had from the Garden of Gethsemane.

For the briefest of moments, Pete's imagination carried him away to another time and place. An old childhood memory of a beach on the island of Haiti emerged from the rubble of the past. He watched the waves as they rolled over the white sand and listened to the bubbling sounds as they fell back into the ocean. He remembered jumping over funny miniature crabs that scurried beneath his feet. He heard the laughter of his missionary parents as they chased him down the shoreline. *Those were happier times, but they ended badly too. We were forced out of the country.*

Pete opened his eyes and concentrated on the options before him. The clearest and most obvious choice was the path of least resistance. *Should I hand my resignation over to Gary and end this nightmare? And what about the hard road—the path of courage? Should I fight?* He glanced at the card extending from the corner of his Bible. *Markus Cunningham.* Something about the name and card felt strangely familiar, like the road less travelled or a distant memory trying to find its way back home.

A strange peace descended upon Pete. Not too long ago he'd watched a show on the Nature Channel. The cameraman captured the precise moment that an African lion attacked a wildebeest. Just before the poor creature was eaten alive, it grew very calm. Pete felt like a wildebeest sitting in Room 212b. Or was this peace coming from somewhere else? Was God giving him an unusual calm and presence of mind to speak into this crisis?

"I need Your help," Pete prayed beneath his breath. No sooner than the words had taken flight, another set of memories came rushing back like an incoming tide. Pete hadn't thought much about Marcus Cunningham's speech over the last two years. But that day now seemed as clear to him as yesterday. He recalled how inspiring Marcus had been. His style of speaking wasn't what grabbed Pete during the conference. No. What stimulated his imagination that day was the content, the ideas, the brilliance with which it all came together logically, even practically.

"Pete, do you need more time to process this? Would you like to go home and discuss our comments with Monica?"

"Gentlemen," Pete began, "let me tell you a story."

Chapter 4

Look to the rock from which you were hewn
And to the quarry from which you were dug
(Isaiah 51:1, NASB).

Green Street Baptist Church was founded in the heart of what used to be one of the most affluent sections of Ft. Worth. Like so many churches built after World War II, Green Street filled up with young families giving birth to the baby-boom generation. Young men who lived through the horrors of combat found they needed stability and sanity. Churches sprang up all across America to capture this generation for Christ. Many of the strongest ministries of the last century were built upon their sense of duty, honor, and commitment.

Green Street was an innovative church in the early days. They pioneered effective strategies for growing their congregation. They were among the first to utilize radio to broadcast their services. When radio gave way to television, their Sunday morning services were shown all over the state of Texas. Ultimately, satellites allowed them to reach an even wider audience.

The satellite broadcast of the church services was first-class. Green

Street's reputation grew to the point where people drove for miles to experience firsthand the thrill of what took place on an average Sunday morning. Solo performances by some of the best vocal artists in the region inspired the members to deepen their love of God and firm up their walk with Christ.

Musicals and cantatas were presented to standing-room-only crowds during the holidays. As the choir sang "O Little Town of Bethlehem," live animals casually moved in and out of the nativity scene. Easters were all about the passion of the Christ. Authentic costumes transported audiences back on a journey to the foot of the cross. After an ironclad centurion cried out, "Truly this was the Son of God," he then asked the congregation a question in baritone: "Were You There When They Crucified My Lord?"

The services were all pretty amazing, but the most important part of all was the preaching of the Word of God. Early on, Green Street was blessed to have a leader whose growing success was celebrated throughout many Christian circles. His name was Jim Jake. Brother Jim founded most of the ministries and became a catalyst for spiritual renewal. He wrote popular books about practical Christianity that enabled people to understand Scripture in ways they never dreamed were possible.

Pastor Jake had a larger-than-life personality in the pulpit and a reputation that spread like wildfire across the Baptist denomination. Everyone seemed to want him to speak at their conferences, camps, and revivals. The church loved their popular pastor and benefited greatly from his reputation.

Most people would describe what happened at Green Street Baptist Church as a rare movement of God. The church was always crowded, always building new facilities, always growing, always adding first-class ministries that were envied by other churches. Everything the church touched turned to gold—that is, until it didn't.

When the slide began was hard to say. The change didn't happen all at once; it was a slow process. For starters, the city grew in a different direction. Old members moved to new locations to fight the urban creep. They found churches closer to their homes and invited their friends to join them. The neighborhood around Green Street began to decline slightly, but most importantly, economically.

The celebrity pastor grew older and probably stayed too long before stepping down. The world moved on, markedly faster than Green Street was willing to adapt. Churches with guitars and casual environments were attracting young families who once would have gone to Green Street. The seasoned saints didn't see this change coming, and they were soon caught in an awful dilemma. "Shall we change who we are for what we don't like to reach people who are not here?" they asked each other. The question was honest, but the answer was a resounding "No!"

Some of the more persnickety saints were overheard saying things like, "Those Seven-Eleven songs are driving us crazy. We stare at a screen and repeat the same seven words, eleven times." "The people who come here want to dress their best for God and sing out of the hymn book." "We shouldn't have to compromise our principles."

So they fortified their position and refused to yield. The only problem was that their time-honored traditions failed to inspire the generation that followed. The newer generations voted with their feet, and the church suffered as a result. The attendance drop wasn't that large from one Sunday to the next, but enough people slipped away during the year that budget planning was something of a challenge. Every year there were cutbacks and reductions to ministries that once had plenty of funding. Green Street was forced to swallow a bitter pill.

Pete understood one thing for certain. When a church comes to recognize that the world is passing them by, they can respond in one of two ways. They can choose to catch up, change, and modify their methods. Or they can dig in their heels and rail against the culture that left them behind. Sadly, Green Street chose to do the later.

Unfortunately for Pete, he had a tough assignment ahead of him when the search committee invited him to become their next senior pastor. Dr. Pat Sheets, the president of the Baptist Seminary in Ft. Worth, recommended him over all the other candidates. During one private conversation with Pete, however, he was less than optimistic.

"Pete," he said, "prepare yourself for the most difficult challenge of your life."

Pete wasn't afraid, but he was naïve. He was enamored by Green Street's reputation and dreamed of recreating the former days of glory. In his mind, the church merely needed a fresh approach to ministry that was more culturally relevant for the times. He believed he could convince people to accept the things they didn't like and become something with which they really didn't agree. He'd helped churches change before. Perhaps he could succeed again.

But culture and relevance don't mix when culture refuses to adapt. Pete had a hard time coming to grips with the reality of the church, and now he seemed to be losing the battle. The resistance to change was stronger than his ability to endure the pain the resistors could inflict upon him.

So Pete and Monica died a little each day. And now he was stuck in this room with the gatekeepers of the legacy. The scales were most definitely leaning in their favor. Perhaps they'd achieve what they really wanted most—Pete's quiet and humble resignation, something not all that uncommon in situations like these. But what if there happened to be a different path to take—a road less travelled?

Chapter 5

I care very little if I am judged by you or by any human court; indeed, I do not even judge myself. My conscience is clear, but that does not make me innocent. It is the Lord who judges me
(1 Corinthians 4:3-4, NIV).

Sitting in Room 212b on the second floor of the three-story education building, Pete took a deep breath. He reached for his Bible and opened to where he'd placed the consultant's card. A single verse of Scripture that he'd highlighted years ago leapt off the page. He seized the moment to reflect on Joshua 1:6: "Be strong and courageous, because you will lead these people to inherit the land I swore to their forefathers to give them."

Perhaps this is a sign.

"Well," Gary Lovejoy said in a condescending tone, "you want to tell us a story?"

Frank Sanders' eyes shot across the table. "Gary, I'm sorry, but you need to let the man speak. He's been our pastor for five years, and he deserves an opportunity to respond without your intimidating ways."

Pete was surprised by this. During his tenure at Green Street, no one had ever challenged Gary Lovejoy. Gary winced a little at the remark and conjured up a more positive tone as he continued. "Yes, of course. As I said earlier, we love you, Pete. You're a good man of God. Take all the time you need with your story. We could use some levity about now."

Pete no longer hesitated. "A few years ago I went to a church-growth conference in Nashville. There was one man there who talked about the natural lifecycle of churches as they trend from breaking ground to being broke."

A chuckle erupted from one of the other members of the finance team. Christian Marsh had a sense of humor but rarely said anything in these meetings. Like the others, he always agreed with Gary.

Pete acknowledged Marsh with a grin, his confidence returning. He put more enthusiasm in his next words. "His name is Markus Cunningham."

"Are you serious?" Chad Boswell's eyes widened. He was another member of the finance committee who hardly ever said anything. Pete couldn't figure out if this latest interruption was positive or not.

"I met Markus." Chad beamed enthusiastically. "He was the pastor of my sister's church down in Birmingham many years ago. He was a young man back then, fresh out of seminary with a bunch of little ones running around in diapers, but the congregation loved him. That church turned around. My sister still talks about him."

Everyone noticed Gary Lovejoy shifting in his chair rather uncomfortably.

"We live in a shrinking world," Pete affirmed. "The words Marcus used to describe the various stages of a church weighed on me for a long time after he spoke. He said that churches start out as movements. Then they become monuments, next museums, and finally morgues. He says that whenever a church stops being a movement, the morgue phase is inevitable. I'll have to admit that over the last few years, I've felt more like the curator of a museum than the pastor of a church."

Pete thought there should have been a little mirth or some verbal response to his last statement, but there was none. Instead, to his surprise, the words seemed to sink in deeply. He could see the men processing what he'd just spoken. Everyone sitting in Room 212b was already convinced that the church was dying, but they really didn't understand why. They just knew death was coming. Since Pete was the leader, he must be responsible or somehow to blame for their condition.

Monica often told Pete he was responsible as a leader. "All leaders are responsible for what they lead," he remembered her saying once. "But you are *not* to blame for this. Never blame yourself for this, Pete. Blame is a more complicated issue than responsibility. There's always enough blame to go around."

Gary broke the silence, and Pete's thoughts moved away from Monica and back into 212b. "So what are you saying, Pete? Are we to sit idly by and become Green Street Baptist Morgue, exchange our buses for hearses, and hope the rapture comes before the bank takes our property? We need a plan. We need—"

Pete cut Gary off, another first for the record books. "I have a plan. And yes, that is what I'm saying. I have Marcus' card. He asked me to call him if we ever needed anything. He's heard about our church. For that matter, everyone who's ever been a Baptist has heard about our church. I believe an outside expert is what we need to help us reverse the trends. Let's bring him in and fix our problems together."

"So you're not going to resign," Gary said.

"Not today."

"You want us to spend money we don't have to hire someone we can't afford to tell us what we already know?"

Gary's words had a chilling effect. Pete's eyes drifted to the window.

He didn't know how to respond to such a forceful objection. The thing he hated about this situation was that Gary made sense most of the time, probably more so even now.

As Pete looked through the window, his mind went elsewhere. He saw Monica in their bedroom once again, himself standing in the open doorway. Her image looked so different than the previous night. No longer weeping or in anguish, her eyes glowed with confidence. He heard those same words, only now spoken softly. This time they unlocked something hidden away deep within. *"These people aren't following you, Pete. They're not acting like men who believe in your leadership. It's not your fault.... It's not your fault.... It's not your fault...."*

"Stop doubting me and start following me." Pete's eyes snapped away from the window so suddenly to make contact with Gary that even he was startled. In fact, everyone in the room cringed momentarily.

"This is at the heart of our problem. I can't do my job as a leader if you won't respect my calling. You've been here longer than I have, but our hearts both desire the same thing in equal measure. This is really not about my job or your reputation as a church. This is about us being the body and the bride of Christ in good times and in bad, in sickness and in health, for rich or for poor, till death do us part. There is more at stake here than my livelihood or whether or not we'll be able to pay the mortgage next month. There was a day when these halls were filled with visionaries and dreamers. Let's figure out what's happened, start over, and be that church again."

Immediately Frank Sanders stood up from his chair, visibly shaken. He fought back tears as he tried to speak. His voice was wavering so much that no one could understand him at first. He tried again, but his voice cracked. The third time he was successful.

"I'll pay for Marcus Cunningham to come here out of my own pocket. The church won't have to spend a dime from the budget. I love this place. I was saved here. I believe my pastor has spoken truth. This is the best plan I've heard in over a decade. I make the motion that we follow our pastor."

Chapter 6

Oil and incense bring joy to the heart, and the sweetness
of a friend is better than self-counsel (Proverbs 27:9, HCSB).

The day Marcus Cunningham arrived at Love Field in Dallas, Pete
and Monica had been standing in the baggage claim area for over an hour.
Some of Pete's old ways were creeping back into his natural rhythms.
Truth be told, he never liked showing up only a few minutes early and
punished himself whenever he was behind schedule. He always wanted
to arrive first. Perhaps that feeling was a carryover from the days he ran
track at Baylor. He wanted to win, and winning always meant that you
got there before everyone else.

Monica, however, preferred to be "socially late," as she often
expressed it. She felt there was no reason to show up early most of the
time. The more people who gathered for an event, the easier she was
able to maneuver through the crowd and avoid awkward conversations.
Pete and Monica were exact opposites in so many ways, but the tension
their differences created kept them excited about each other.

Monica heard a new shuffling of feet coming from the corridor
around the corner. Another group had disembarked their plane and now

passed behind the TSA security checkpoint. "Do you think you'll still recognize him?"

"I showed you his picture on the card."

"Most men put their baby pictures on their business cards." She locked eyes with Pete and flaunted her most alluring smile. "They're as vain as women."

"Don't give our secret away. We have so few advantages over your sex."

Monica noticed Pete was happier over the last few weeks, even playful. She was in a better place too, but she always felt she mirrored Pete's emotions. Not that he was as expressive as she was, but she was a reflection and the voice of how he felt most of the time. He always relied on her in this strange way. She was the window into his soul.

Just then Marcus appeared.

She was right. That *was* his baby picture!

Marcus sat in the passenger seat as Pete drove to the hotel. Monica gladly sat behind them, but not because a lady's place was in the backseat. She despised that reason and would have objected quite loudly. Her generation was so unlike most of the women who made up the congregation of Green Street. Sometimes feeling comfortable around them was hard for her. She liked laughter and telling funny stories about things that happened during her childhood. She felt that most of the older women just stared at her like she was some kind of marble statue. "Pastor's wife," they called her—a title that came with awkward baggage. Everyone was so guarded around her.

One day I'll figure that out.

In any case, Monica enjoyed the animated conversation Pete was having with Marcus. She was reminded of fond memories from long ago, when as a newlywed couple, they lived in seminary housing. Those were happier times when they were just students surrounded by their friends. No one had a church to lead or a job that paid them enough to afford tuition. What they did have was more fun than money: dreams that stretched to the horizon and an unwritten future. She felt a glimmer of hope as Marcus explained what was occurring across the landscape of American Christianity.

"Changes are happening everywhere, Pete. I travel from church to church across the country, and the issues are remarkably similar. For every new church that opens, four close their doors. In the past decade alone, church attendance has declined nearly twenty percent. Eighty-five percent of all churches in America are either plateaued or declining. It's not your fault, Pete...."

Monica listened intently as Marcus painted a statistical portrait of Christianity in America. But what she loved most was hearing Marcus say the same words to Pete that she'd spoken over him earlier. For too long she'd watched helplessly as Pete punished himself over these same trends in their own church. Having someone say they weren't alone was refreshing. Even if being in the same situation meant that everyone was suffering, suffering in tandem was far better than the hopelessness of free-falling alone.

"So what can be done about this problem?" Pete questioned. "Sometimes I feel like the CEO of Kodak must have felt when he saw the first digital camera. When your business model is threatened by a revolutionary technology, it looks and feels like the grim reaper has arrived."

"That's not a bad analogy, Pete. But I believe changing a church culture is more difficult than changing a corporate culture like Kodak's. The vast majority of people in a church are volunteers, not employees. Volunteers pay. They don't get paid. They have a tendency to become entitled and wed themselves to the status quo. An employee, however, will fight the natural urge to avoid change in order to keep his or her job secure. That's the incentive. There's more leverage in a corporate culture."

Monica held her tongue. Over the last several years, she'd thought many times about firing some of the volunteers at Green Street. She'd start with the finance committee and work her way through the rest of the committee structure, one by one until the house was clean. *Good thing I'm not the pastor. The church would already be gone. Pete's the kinder soul.*

"So, Marcus, what's our first step?" Pete asked.

"That's a good question. We'll meet together with all the staff and leaders of the church and drop the bomb."

"A bomb? What's the bomb?"

Marcus gave Pete a devious grin. "If I told you, Pete, I'd have to kill you."

Chapter 7

When you are about to go into battle, the priest shall come
forward and address the army (Deuteronomy 20:2, NIV).

Bob and Georgette Freeman sat dutifully in Green Street Baptist
church on Thursday night. Several of their fellow church members
and friends had received the same cryptic communication from the
church office about "The Meeting." Not only were the details sketchy,
but having a gathering of leaders scheduled on such a short notice was
highly unusual.

Rumors were flying.

Suzie Whitmore, who sat behind the Freemans, was certain the
meeting was about removing the word Baptist from the outdoor sign.
She'd previously vowed, if it ever happened—*God forbid*—to leave
Green Street BAPTIST Church. She made this clear long ago when the
pattern was set by other churches in the area. The reality was that she
didn't like any of the other churches in town. Most everyone knew that.
She was all so much bravado.

Buck Simpson, who sat on the same pew with the Freemans, was
a widower. His wife, Becky, had passed away nearly five years earlier

from a sudden heart attack. Hers was the first funeral service Brother Pete officiated as the new pastor. Buck had a special place in his heart for Pete, but he was also conflicted. The church had been losing members, money, and its reputation as a vibrant house of worship in the community. As much as he loved his pastor, something had to be done. He just didn't know what.

Kate Shoemaker was something of a permanent fixture on the front row of the sanctuary. She always sat there out of habit and necessity. After serving as the church organist for the last thirty-six years, she found climbing the steps leading to the platform increasingly difficult. Nevertheless, Kate had a sneaking suspicion that tonight's meeting had something to do with the "new music," where organs were notoriously mothballed, never to be heard from again. She once claimed there'd been a conspiracy to auction the pipe organ on eBay on account of the failing budget. Nearly everyone heard about the special meeting Kate scheduled with Pastor Pete. She sought his absolute assurance that the church would never sell the pipe organ. No one knew where the rumor began, but Pete suspected Kate initiated it herself.

Representatives from every standing committee of the church were present: Deacons, building and grounds, personnel, sports, benevolence, the committee on committees, and even the smelling committee, whose critical mission was to eradicate unseemly odors. Of course, every member of the finance committee was there, and they were feeling a little insecure about being the only ones who knew what this meeting was all about. Even the ministry staff, which roamed through the audience patting backs and shaking hands, was oblivious. There were many others, and those present noted that such a meeting of church leadership hadn't been assembled in many years.

Noticeably absent was Monica. She never came to these meetings anymore, and the other ladies in the room always seemed to care.

"Honey, we missed you at the meeting last night" would be the first words she'd hear the next time she set foot on campus. She wanted to be there for Pete, but the ever-present possibility that the meeting might become a public lynching of her husband was a strong deterrent. She wouldn't be able to hold her tongue. And besides, Pete felt more comfortable when she stayed at home and prayed for peace.

All across the room people were buzzing about this and that. Strangely enough, the atmosphere reminded many that night of the early years. People remembered the era as one where you could feel the excitement and the electricity in the room. "You never knew what might happen back in those days, but it was always good" was a common refrain.

Pete Blackman and Markus Cunningham sat in the choir rehearsal room. Pete was pale. His eyes were fixed on the door leading directly to the stage in the auditorium. An inner voice reminded him of the proper term he should use to refer to the room—not an auditorium, but "the sanctuary." There had been many discussions between church members as to why Pete called the place where they met "the auditorium."

"Brother Jim Jake always called this place a sanctuary," they commented, usually with a hint of sadness. "Wasn't the sanctuary the place in the Bible were God met His people?" they'd point out. "Why would you call it anything else?"

Pete capitulated on this and many other nuances of speech that seemed to drive people crazy. He decided to choose his battles more wisely. Battles about things that mattered. Like tonight.

"Pete, are we good to go? If you're having doubts, we can back off of what we discussed."

"You're hilarious, Markus. I'm already up to my eyeballs in this.

What do you want me to do, go out there and tell them to pray for rain?"

"You could use some rain. Texas is in a drought. Elijah prayed for rain, and he was known as a great prophet. You might reach a meteorologist or two for Jesus."

"That's good." Pete smiled, using his facial muscles for the first time all night. "I think the phrase 'drop the bomb' is appropriate here. Where did you dream up this plan?"

"Sometimes you need to shock the system. Churches are like computer-operating systems. Over the years, people keep adding programs, and eventually the whole system crashes. There's too much stuff happening here and not enough focus on the right things. You're busy but not effective. We need to convince the people to erase the hard drive and start over with a new operating system."

"Will they buy into it?"

"Pete, if they don't, you can leave knowing that you gave it your best shot. You're doing a courageous thing. Think about Moses going to Pharaoh, David staring down Goliath, or Yoda battling Count Dooku."

"I can hear the theme song of *Star Wars* playing in my head right now. I think you finally inspired me. Just one thing, though," Pete added. "If this blows up like bombs are known to do on occasion, will you hire me to be one of your consultants?"

"No. You are a pastor, Pete. I'm a solo act. I blow in, blow up, and blow out. Now get out there and introduce me. Make the intro good, or I'll haunt you in my next life."

Chapter 8

Again, if the trumpet does not sound a clear call,
who will get ready for battle? (1 Corinthians 14:8, NIV)

Despite Markus Cunningham's whimsical personality, he was a man of deep spiritual convictions. He was bothered to see good men like Pete wrecked by the hardship of ministry. He knew churches seldom recovered from the type of crisis now brewing in the hallways of Green Street Baptist Church.

He understood the bitter reality all too well. He'd once lived through a similar situation. As a survivor, he now travelled from one crisis situation to the next. He had a reputation of fighting for each church and every pastor who called for help. And he did so like a dying man with nothing left to lose.

"This is not my job," he often claimed. "It's my mission. This matters to the heart of God. The bride of Christ is worth our best efforts."

While he understood that no two churches were alike, each troubled congregation had one common problem. Tonight he planned to shine a brilliant spotlight on what was wreaking havoc in the pews. After Pete introduced him, Markus said a quick prayer for strength and presence of mind.

Bob and Georgette Freeman looked around the room as Markus walked to the pulpit. They didn't know what to think about him. Other than the glowing introduction from Pastor Pete, this was the first time they'd heard anything about an outsider addressing the leaders of their church. Many that evening had similar thoughts: "How could this man possibly know anything about us?" "We've never seen him here before." "What does he plan to say?"

Suzie Whitmore, Buck Simpson, and Kate Shoemaker did what everyone else did. They grew very still and very quiet. The silence could be felt, like the calm before the storm.

"Let me get to the point quickly," Markus began. "I was invited here tonight to help you through some very challenging times. I'm excited about spending the next few weeks here at Green Street Baptist Church. I want to get acquainted with you and paint a picture of what's happening today in the vast majority of churches I visit in America.

"Here's what I know to be true. Your problem isn't unique. The same problem has crept through the backdoor of every church I've had the opportunity to work with. Your story and their stories run on parallel tracks.

"The first task before you is to give a name to your problem. Not just any name, but the right name assigned to the real problem. Imagine yourself showing up at a party filled with strangers. Your name is Bob, but the host sticks a nametag on you that says 'Sally.' Now you're in for some real misery. You're not going to enjoy any of those conversations. Trust me. For you, that party will be lame."

Laughter spilled across the room.

"A stranger—and, mind you, I'm not that stranger…" Markus paused for the ripple of laughter then continued. "…a stranger has entered this fellowship with a nametag that reads 'Friend.' No one had him on the guest list tonight. I'm pretty certain of that because I checked. Though he appears warm and sociable, he's merely a man in disguise. Beware of this outsider. We must understand that he's a fierce enemy. If he's allowed to roam freely, he'll crash this party and end our celebration.

"Few people recognize what he's doing, but I can assure you he's stirring up problems and causing a pretty big stink. Do not extend the right hand of fellowship to this stranger. I suggest we bless him with the left foot of censorship instead. Since his arrival, this so-called friend has already spiked the punch bowl, and the saints are growing more confused by the hour.

"When good church members get tangled up in problems that are difficult to understand, they run the risk of pointing their fingers at the wrong cause or the wrong person. Let me be clear. The real enemy here tonight is not your pastor, your circumstances, or anyone else in this room. Ephesians, Chapter 5, says that we do *not* wrestle against flesh and blood."

He paused for effect before continuing. "The enemy we're up against is called death."

All across the room there was one harmonious, resounding, "Amen!"

Pete breathed a little easier. So far, the crowd was receptive. *This might work.*

"On many occasions and throughout many seasons of our lives, we've faced this enemy on the field of battle. Death is the most powerful weapon the devil has ever held in his hand. Death has been used to steal God's best from us, to kill us inch by inch, and to destroy our future. But don't be afraid. The Good News tonight is that death has already been defeated. Just moments after the stone was rolled away from the grave,

Jesus grabbed death by the tail, snatched the stinger away, and smashed him beneath His feet.

"Now I can hardly wait for that 'one glorious day.' In the twinkling of an eye when time is no more, death will be swallowed up in hell itself, never to crash our party again. As believers in Jesus Christ, we know this to be true."

Pete could feel the crowd getting fired up. They definitely enjoyed this type of preaching. Speaking in this manner wasn't necessarily his style, but he was taking notes. He wondered how Markus planned to steer the message toward the big idea. At some point, there was a bomb to drop. Pete redirected his attention to Markus after the applause died down.

"But until that day arrives, death will pursue us with evil intent. He'll nip at our heels. He'll mock our efforts and attempt to steal our dreams. He's a relentless foe.

"The failure to recognize how death is manifesting himself in your church is the quickest way to lose this battle. There's grumbling and frustration in this church. Make no mistake; this is death. There are many clinging to yesterday in this church. This is also death. There are political agendas, critical spirits, and even blatant gossip in this church. Call this death too. There's a lack of spiritual vitality and joy in this church. All of this is the direct evidence that death is working feverishly to destroy your hope and end your future.

"What do you say to death when you see him rear that ugly head? You say, 'Death, you have no place in the house of God or among the people of God. We bind you in the name of Jesus. His blood seals your defeat and guarantees our victory.'

"Church! You never hide death. You expose him. You call him by name and take authority over him.

"So what happened here?"

Who Killed My Church?

Markus stopped and scanned the room carefully. The lengthy pause felt awkward to Pete. No one was clapping or shouting anymore. All this preaching about death, and now the room was deathly silent. Markus didn't appear to be bothered in the least. No, he seemed to be searching, perhaps trying to connect with some distant memory from his own past. Then Pete noticed his countenance suddenly change. Markus had indeed connected with that familiar emotion buried long ago, and his audience was about to taste the intensity.

"This place was once aflame for the glory of God. You took insane risks to reach the lost. You grew in Christ like a tall weed after a summer rain. Everything was new to you. Each and every day was fresh and bright. You shined with the radiance of heaven's gates. People flocked to this place just to fill a thimble of what you possessed.

"At some point, and I don't know when, you got busy 'doing church' instead of being the church. You let your relationship with Jesus Christ grow stale, and then you replaced that personal relationship with the emptiness of religion. You did the right things, but you lost heart. You thought you could rekindle the flame if you stayed busy, but the fire wasn't real anymore. Painted fire doesn't burn. Imitations never do and never will.

"Death, the great opportunist, saw your vulnerability. Death plotted and schemed and entered your camp as an enemy under the cover of darkness. On the field of battle, death captured your victory banner and your promised birthright.

"That's when you panicked and lost your focus. You added more ministries than any church could ever do well in a failed attempt to turn the ship around. That strategy might have worked, but God won't bless what He doesn't start. When I saw the list of things that Pastor Pete is attempting to oversee as your leader, I wondered how his marriage survived. Many good men would have fallen apart long ago."

That statement caught Pete off guard and hit him hard as hot tears stung his eyelids. Reflexively he tried to restrain the emotions building up inside. In his mind, he saw Monica sobbing on the bed again. "How much longer do we have to live like this?" Those words threatened him on that night. They should have broken his heart instead.

He missed her now more than ever. He wanted to run out of the room and drive home as quickly as possible. He needed to hold her like he should have held her that evening. He wanted to break the grip of death on their marriage. He needed to ask forgiveness for all the times he neglected her for what he thought was the greater work of God. Suddenly he realized his marriage was God's best work in his life, unequaled by everything except his salvation. Finally, he lost control. His shoulders shook as he did his best to sob quietly.

As he preached, Markus could see there were many emotions drifting through the room. He discerned that some were hanging on every word, affirming that he should keep going. Others appeared angry at being critiqued by an outsider. Many were weeping like Pete, trying to gather their composure.

He could feel the emotion, though, unmistakably. There was an anointing in the room, empowered by the Spirit of God. He knew the change in atmosphere was more than the words he spoke. The power of truth was piercing the hearts of men. He could sense this happening and decided to draw in the net on his listeners.

"There are only three things you need to do over these next few weeks: stop, wait, and listen. In order for this to happen, we need to shut down everything that prevents us from being silent and still before the Lord."

Pete wiped the tears from his eyes as he looked around. He couldn't see very well at all. That being the case, he simply made a mental note of the moment. *There it is. He just dropped the bomb.*

Who Killed My Church?

"Let's close the church office and shutter the ministries for a season. We need to take every event off the church calendar. We'll gather on Sunday mornings and at other times throughout the week to pray and listen to God. Sunday morning will not be business as usual. And I assure you, we won't restart the business, ministries, or programs of the church until we've heard the voice of God clearly and in unison. He'll tell us which things to begin anew and when to start.

"This is the time for courage. Now is the season of faith. Let's start over with a blank slate and ask ourselves this simple question: If we were to establish Green Street today as it started in the home two blocks down the road, what would we do differently to reach the people who aren't here?

"You were once a movement in the City of Ft. Worth. But that season died years ago. Tragically, you didn't discern the day, the month, or even the decade you stopped being relevant. You kept doing the same things the same way you had always done them before. Death saw an opportunity, and tonight we must take responsibility for allowing this to happen.

"All churches that began as a movement have a way of getting stuck in a moment. When they get stuck, they transform into monuments that do little more than honor the past. Nostalgia can roll through a house of worship like a heat wave on a summer day. A church that collects too many of these monuments ultimately becomes a museum. There are pastors and staff all across America who feel more like curators of a museum than men and women of God with fire in their bones. If churches don't reverse this trend, they eventually become morgues. The frozen chosen are always the last ones to turn out the lights. Don't let this happen to you.

"Please, I'm asking you to follow Pastor Pete and me on a new journey. I'll walk with you and show you how to become a mighty movement of God once again. I've seen God work in churches that were in the same place you are tonight. They made the tough decisions. You can too.

"I know this to be true because 'greater is He that is in you than he that is in the world.' You 'can do all things through Christ, who gives you strength.' 'No weapon formed against you will prosper.' You will succeed because of 'Christ in you, the hope of glory.'"

Markus stepped away from the pulpit and sat down.

Pete was still weeping. He didn't know what to do next because he hadn't talked to Markus about how to end this meeting.

Members of the finance committee who met with Pete a few weeks earlier were looking nervously around the room. They were, after all, the ones who gave the green light for Markus to come.

The leaders sat in stunned silence. Some were weeping, a few looked angry, but no one moved. A hush hovered above them like some spiritual mist.

At that moment, the doors at the back of the church opened wide. A gray-haired man came walking slowly down the aisle. Nearly every member present dropped their jaw and gasped.

Jim Jake had entered the room.

Chapter 9

The one who enters by the gate is the shepherd of the sheep
(John 10:2 NIV).

Six years had come and gone since beloved Pastor Jim Jake and his wife, Frances, retired from their ministry at Green Street Baptist Church. Though separated by many years and even more miles, he never stopped loving the church where he experienced the best years of his life. "Whether or not to step down," he often claimed, "was the most difficult decision I ever faced."

Pastor Jim saw clearly during the later years of his ministry that he and Green Street were aging. As he looked over the audience most Sundays, there was more gray hair and almost no young families. Visitors arrived in fewer numbers and joined even less frequently. He knew the time had come to resign and give another man the opportunities he'd been given.

He and Frances always wanted to be closer to their children and grandchildren, and lately, great-grandchildren, who settled in Florida. Because of the demands on his schedule when he pastored Green Street and weekends spent behind the pulpit, family reunions were rare occasions.

Jim discovered that he loved retirement. His health was declining considerably, but he still had the opportunity to preach on many weekends around the Ft. Lauderdale area where they settled. One of those churches was having issues and hired a consultant by the name of Markus Cunningham.

Jim and Markus became an easy match for friendship. They shared many common interests—a passion for helping struggling churches through rough times was among the greatest. Consulting with each other over the challenges they faced soon became a pleasure for both.

A few weeks earlier, Markus called Jim and asked him to purchase a plane ticket. He also asked him to keep this a secret, even from Pete Blackman.

Pete was stunned. His tears dried up as he joined the others in the audience in their disbelief. He turned his head toward Markus who sat on the platform next to him.

"Remember what I said, Pete: 'If I told you, I'd have to kill you.'"

Bob and Georgette Freeman were the first to rise to their feet. Others followed as former Pastor Jake sauntered down the aisle. Spontaneous applause erupted all over the room. Those who were lucky enough to have seats in the aisle patted Jim on the back as he walked toward the front. Shouts of "hallelujah" rang from the crowd. Those who weren't already weeping from the message just delivered were overcome with emotion now. Tears flowed. Smiles emerged. Joy filled the room.

As Jim walked up to the platform, he winked at Markus. He came first to Pete, however, and stood before him wearing his trademark smile. Pete had never met Jim in person. There was a full year in between Jim's leaving and Pete's arrival. They'd discussed many things on the phone before Pete accepted the invitation to become the next pastor of Green

Street. But as the church began to decline shortly thereafter, Pete was simply too embarrassed to pick up the phone and call Jim for advice.

"Pete, don't you worry about a thing." Pastor Jake's words were perfectly chosen and exactly what Pete needed to hear. "I've come to help you. Sit back, relax, and let the Spirit of God do His thing."

The applause grew louder as Jim stepped toward the pulpit. Every committee member, deacon, and member of the staff grinned from ear to ear. It had been a long time since the room was filled with this much emotion.

"If you don't stop clapping, I'll keep you here all night," Jim announced.

Laughter replaced the clapping. Someone shouted, "We love you, Jim." Then all at once people spoke their hearts:

"Welcome home."

"We missed you."

"Haven't changed one bit, Jim."

"Where's Frances?"

Jim slowly leaned into the microphone on his old wooden pulpit. Decades ago it had been tailor-made just for him. As he touched it, the wood felt like a piece of home. "Oh, I've missed you, too. Frances wanted to be here, but she's at home watching soap operas."

"Be nice, Jim!" someone called out as people snickered.

"This reminds me of the good old days. How you bring back the memories! Fantastic. Let me tell you what I think about what you've just heard tonight."

He glanced at Pete and pointed a finger in his direction. "I have the greatest respect for Pastor Pete. He's a good man. He's a better man than you'll ever find again. If you can't see that, you're hopeless."

Jim smiled, and everyone laughed as if on cue.

"I also have great admiration for Markus Cunningham. The man knows his stuff. We've been friends over the last several years since Frances and I moved to Florida. You do know we moved to Florida, don't you?"

He paused intentionally and waited for the response.

"Please come back!" someone shouted.

"Now that's your problem. If you'd been listening to Markus and believed anything he just said, you wouldn't desire that in the least. You're good people, but you're not thinking straight. You have some work to do over the next few weeks, and I'm here tonight to challenge you to get the job done.

"But first, I'm going to tell you your problem. When we were at our peak as a church, you were flexible and open to whatever God had in store for the future. You didn't know what that was, but you didn't fight change. You embraced it. You made my job easy, and I grew into the man I became because you let me be Jim Jake. I didn't need to be anybody but me. You loved me for who I was. You followed me and trusted me without questioning my motives or casting doubt on my integrity. The only reason I was successful is because you followed me.

"And we did some amazing things together. We established innovative ministries that reached far beyond Ft. Worth. We saw people saved. The kingdom grew. The devil got scared. Marriages were saved. Addictions were broken. God was glorified."

Spontaneous applause filled the room.

"But by the time I left, all these things were happening less and less frequently. The trends were down. I sensed it. I could see it. That's why I resigned and retired. Those rose-colored glasses through which you look at yesterday have blinded you to the truth. The truth is that you did church well back in the day. But you haven't grown much over the last few years, either as a church or in your walk with Christ. You stopped feeling the heartbeat of God for the new generation. You felt

His heart beating for your own. Can't you feel God's love for the next? Just because you're older and wiser now doesn't mean your work is finished. You should still be giving the devil heartburn.

"Church, consider who you are in Christ. You're His bride and His body. You'll go to heaven when you die. Your salvation is secure. No one can take that away from you.

"Read Romans, Chapter 8. It's in the Book!

"If you stopped attending church tonight, heaven forbid, you're still bound for glory. Yes! You could all leave this room and hand your property over to the bank. Even this wouldn't keep you from spending all eternity with Jesus. When your time comes, you'll enter through those gates of pearl, walk down those streets of gold, live in a city whose walls are made of jasper, fish in the crystal sea, and cast your eyes upon the very throne of God.

"So why has God left us here for such a time as this? Are we here for ourselves? If we are, then we're here for the wrong reason. Let me state that again. If we've come merely to get out of this ministry only that which pleases and satisfies us, we will kill this church. This church was built on this hill by people who believed in greater things. They understood that one of the most important words in the Bible, and in every human tongue, is the word 'others.' God forbid we should ever live for ourselves alone!

"Christ didn't live for himself. He gave everything away. My life is no longer about me, and yours is no longer about you. Your very existence is about a God who loves you. Never forget these next words. He loves the people who aren't here as much as He loves Bob and Georgette and even old Buck Simpson.

"Christ died for the ungodly. Romans, Chapter 5. It's in the Book.

"Unfortunately—and I say this with a heavy heart—the people who don't attend this church on Sunday can't feel the love of God through us anymore, and it may not be our fault alone. Strange things are happening in the world today. Our eyes aren't closed to this reality. But if we refuse to figure this out while living under the power and wisdom of God, it *will* be our fault. We don't want the blood of the next generation on our hands.

"I ask you this question: How many of your children and grandchildren want to come to church with you? You've invited, and they've declined. They've either left this place for worldliness and paganism or for other churches down the road.

"This church needs to reinvent itself or it will *not* survive. If you fight change, you'll kill Green Street. Everyone in this room knows we will stand before God one day. When that day comes, we want to hear Him say, "Well done, thou good and faithful servant." You don't want to hear God say, "What were you thinking?"

"If you can't figure out a way to reach the people who aren't here, then give this church to the people who can. You know I've never minced words or held back from giving you my opinion. If I were here today, I don't believe I could get the job done. I'm old, and my days are numbered.

"But I know a man who can. His name is Pete Blackman. Get behind him. Markus is a good man too. Together they'll lead you into the next new thing God wants to do. Are you ready? Don't be shy. I want to hear what you plan to do. Will you follow these men as you followed me?"

One by one people stood to their feet and shouted, "Yes."

"All right then!" Pastor Jim smiled. "I have a plane to catch back to Florida."

Chapter 10

The grass withers and the flowers fall,
but the word of our God stands forever
(Isaiah 40:8, NIV).

Pete focused on the flashing taillights up ahead. "Markus, have you ever thought about writing movie scripts?" Jim and Markus were in Pete's Camry driving down Airport Freeway toward Dallas Love Field. Traffic was moving more slowly than usual, but they had plenty of time before Jim's return flight was scheduled to depart.

"The best dramas are the ones you get to live right now. Hollywood could never do them justice. I don't imagine there's much of an audience among the movie-going public for what we just experienced."

"You could have warned me that Jim planned to descend from heaven riding a white horse. I would have appreciated the advance notice. Surprises make me tense."

"You're going to have to get over that, Pete," Jim stated firmly. "You can't control the Spirit. He blows like the wind, and no one knows where He comes from or where He's going. John, Chapter 3. It's in the Book."

"That's what I like about you, Jim," Markus stated. "Scripture interprets reality. But Pete's right. I thought I saw heavens open above Green Street when you rode down that center aisle. The only thing that could have made the evening better is if Kate Shoemaker had been able to run up to the organ. Something like the intro to the *Phantom of the Opera* would have been outstanding." He grinned. "I'll save that one for the movie script."

"My son," Jim said, "you have a singular wit and are slightly irreverent, I might add. I fear Kate's running days are over. But God has set the stage for something grand to happen. I can feel it, and it feels good. We can lift up our eyes to the hills, men. We know whence our help comes. God is on the horizon, and better days are ahead. Psalms, Chapter 121. It's in the Book."

Pete noticed flashing red and white lights on the horizon. Planes were lined up in the traffic pattern. He loved to fly. In fact, he possessed a private pilot's license. He didn't golf, fish, or hunt. Flying had been his one great indulgence. In the past, this was how he managed stress and escaped. His crazy schedule at Green Street had kept him away from aviation lately, and his skills had grown rusty. *The rust has spread to other areas too.*

His thoughts made a hard landing when Jim asked, "How's Monica, Pete? Is she hurting?"

Pete never knew how to answer this question. He didn't even know whether he had permission, either from Monica or God. He was well aware of the myths people maintained about a pastor's family, especially the one about everyone living in some kind of happiness bubble. *It's more like a fishbowl. Pretend or pay dearly.* Sometimes he wanted to answer such questions by saying, "She feels like crap! Can you blame her?"

So he said what he felt. "She feels like crap!"—another first in the changing landscape.

"Good! You're being honest. If you'd told me otherwise, I would have called you a liar. She wasn't there tonight. She doesn't feel safe. You're the spiritual leader of the home, Pete. God expects you to make her a priority."

"Where do I begin? She takes everything more personally than I do and tolerates things even less. I haven't told her half the stuff I deal with on a daily basis. That would only make matters worse."

"What you say isn't what keeps her from feeling safe," Jim countered. "What she can sense that you haven't told her is what bothers her. A woman's intuition is more powerful than your ability to keep things hidden. It's in the Book."

"Okay, where is that in the Bible? You just made that up."

"He tests me, Markus." Jim laughed confidently. "Read the story of David and Abigail. She prevented him from doing something stupid. After King David realized this, he cried out, 'Praise be to the Lord, the God of Israel, who has sent you today to meet me. May you be blessed for your good judgment....' When a man isn't listening to God, He often sends a woman with good judgment to get his attention. First Samuel, Chapter 25. It's in the Book."

Pete didn't respond immediately. He just sat there, driving, processing, and then regretting. *If I'd taken her seriously, listened more carefully to what she was trying to say, maybe I wouldn't have been so blind. She felt things I should have affirmed. Instead... How could I have missed this?*

Markus broke the silence. "Don't be so hard on yourself, Pete. God loves you so much that He's selected you for a first-class, fast-track season of growth. You'll look back on these days with gratitude. They'll make you a stronger leader and less whiny."

"Whiny?"

"It's a joke. Don't be a baby. Besides, we're here."

The Camry came to a stop at the entrance of the main terminal.

"I can take it from here, gentlemen. Frances will be waiting for me. We've had a good day. Thank you, Pete, Markus. One more thing, what are you planning to do this Sunday? It's only a few days away."

Markus conjured up another one of those devious grins. "We're going to light a bonfire during the morning service."

"Would that be a metaphorical bonfire or the real thing?" Pete looked a little nervous.

"You still don't know me very well, Pete."

Chapter 11

To everything there is a season, and a time to every
purpose under heaven…a time to keep silence, and a time to speak
(Ecclesiastes 3:1, 7b KJV).

"You want us to do what?"

The same question was asked repeatedly as Markus and Pete met with the chairmen of the standing committees and the ministry staff. They'd never considered doing anything like this in church before, especially at Green Street Baptist Church. Not only that, but they'd never heard about any church doing anything remotely similar to what they were being asked to do.

To Pete, the congregation appeared to have reached the summit of the spiritual mountaintop when Pastor Jake walked into the room. *Can't they see there are other peaks to climb?* The thrill of Thursday night had faded like the morning dew. Pete had experienced this all too often at Green Street. They raised the same objections whenever his ideas were shot down in flames. *Now they're doing it to Markus. He's about to get a taste of what I've been battling.*

Pete listened quietly as they presented their objections one by one.

"It sounds crazy and risky."

"What if it splits the church?"

"What if it doesn't work?"

"Prove to me that this is biblical."

"Shouldn't we pray about this first?"

"Markus, will you refund your fee if this creates a financial crisis?"

"Pastor Pete, do you trust this man's leadership?"

And on and on it went. Pete studied Markus and observed how the questions, even the absurd ones, didn't seem to faze him in the least. The consultant sat patiently waiting for what appeared to be "the critical moment." After all the chattering had ceased and the silence began, perhaps the moment would arrive. But Markus extended the silence even longer and allowed the tension in the room to run out of steam. Timing was definitely his art.

"Have you ever heard about the Cheyenne Dog Warriors?"

In unison, their faces grew inquisitive. "Who?" Buck Simpson was usually very quiet in meetings. He became less talkative and more sullen after his wife passed away. Pete was glad he spoke first—a good sign.

"The Cheyenne Dog Warriors were fierce soldiers. Whenever they went to battle, they wore long sashes and pinned themselves to the ground with sacred arrows. They stayed fixed on that small piece of land until they achieved victory or died fighting. When one went down, another Dog Warrior took his place. Their enemies feared facing them in battle because they knew a Dog Warrior would never retreat. He lived by a code of sacred honor. He didn't let his personal fears control him. He was willing to risk and sacrifice his own life for the future safety of the tribe."

Marcus paused for a moment. "Do you get my point?"

"I'd be willing to do that." Buck didn't even allow the group time to ponder the meaning of the story before he embraced the challenge. "My wife's in heaven. She loved this church, and she was a better saint than I'll ever be. She served and worked her fingers to the bone anytime there was a need. Give me one of those sacred arrows you're talking about. I want to pin my sash to the ground somewhere in my church and hold the line. About time we got a backbone and started fighting alongside our pastor."

"Kind of a nice ring," Bob Freeman added. "Dog Warriors for Jesus. I like the sound. That's what we'll be on Sunday morning when we do this bonfire thing Markus has been talking about. Count me in."

Pete caught a glimpse of Josh Duncan. Josh was on staff at Green Street—had just reached his tenth anniversary a few months back. In many ways, he'd become like Pete—burned out, frustrated, and waiting for something to happen. He did his job as the education minister well, as well as any man could do in a downward trending church. Most importantly, his opinion carried weight and could tip the scales at a moment like this. Pete intensified his gaze.

"Give me a whole quiver full of arrows," Josh boomed.

Word spread quickly from Thursday to Sunday that something was happening at Green Street Baptist Church. While most church members were not in attendance when Markus and Pastor Jake spoke to the leaders of the church, various versions of what transpired circulated through the grapevine. Sunday school had the largest attendance in over three years. Before the worship service began, cars continued to roll into the parking lot. The auditorium, or "sanctuary," was as full as the day Gary Lovejoy introduced the Blackman family and Pete delivered his inaugural message.

The music portion of the worship service wasn't much different than on an average Sunday. However, worship was lively. People sang with gusto. The offering plates even looked more full as the ushers passed them up and down the aisles.

Markus sat on the stage with Pete. Just before Pete was to get up and speak, Markus said, "Check your fly." Pete had a horrified look on his face until he noticed everything was decent and proper.

"I believe I'm starting to figure you out, Markus," he whispered. "You haven't been saved yet."

Markus laughed a little louder than he intended, and his laugh was heard throughout the sanctuary. Smiles from the audience intensified over the rapport these two men apparently shared. The fact that their pastor was having a good time was a refreshing change.

"This will go well," Markus said. "Remember what we discussed. And by the way, I turned off the sprinkler system."

Chapter 12

A time to tear down and a time to build…
(Ecclesiastes 3:3b, NIV).

Monica sat on the front row. Over the last few years, she'd been sitting close to one of the exits strategically located on the right side, just near the rear of the auditorium. Her reasons were pretty obvious, at least to her.

She tried to avoid as many conversations as she could. She was accustomed to being cornered by church members who wanted her to deliver a message to her husband. Invariably, they had some problem the pastor needed to address. Sometimes the message was for her, however.

"You should be teaching," they claimed. "Attend more events. Support your husband better. Be more visible, less sad, more vocal, and less aloof."

She got an earful most Sundays until she reached a saturation point. Then the walls went up.

Pete had a hard time adjusting to her withdrawal. Until recently, he was concerned about how her actions made him look in the eyes of the congregation. But last night he had a long conversation with her starting with the words, "Please forgive me." Then he continued with, "I didn't see you."

Those words had a healing effect. She needed Pete to see one of the many yokes she wore for him. Yes, the ministry had been difficult on him over the last few years, but he'd had a hard time seeing beyond his job and what his problems were doing to her. They were serving together in a large prestigious church, but the church in their hearts was shriveled up and tiny by comparison. She began to have hope now that all of this was about to change.

She watched as her husband walked up to the pulpit. Something was stirring inside of her as he stood there. This was the man she fell in love with so long ago. He was a good man—honorable and pure. Emotions that had been ebbing low were now rushing over her. Her tears began flowing before he even said a word.

"There's a story in the Old Testament that I want to share with you this morning about a snake. He even had a name. It's in the Book."

That brought a few snickers from the audience. Apparently Pastor Jake had rubbed off on Pete during his whirlwind visit.

"Anytime someone mentions a snake in the Bible, our minds take flight to the third chapter of Genesis. We know this snake to be the great tempter in the Garden of Eden, 'that serpent of old who is called the devil and Satan.' He was the one who deceived Adam and Eve into eating the forbidden fruit. Everyone knows this story, but that's not the only snake in the Bible with a name."

Monica's curiosity was aroused. This wasn't some sermon Pete had pulled out of the filing cabinet. Over the last twenty-five years, she'd heard every sermon Pete had preached. *This one must be new.*

"Allow me to state this for you in the form of a riddle. At first the snake was a good snake. Then the snake was an old snake. In fact, the snake was hundreds of years old. Then the snake became a bad snake. Are you intrigued?"

Someone shouted, "Yes!"

Pete smiled at the audience, something he noticed his predecessor did frequently when he was there a few nights ago, but the smile was genuine nonetheless. Many smiled back with slightly puzzled looks on their faces.

"My message is entitled, 'What Do You Do with a Good Ol' Snake when that Good Ol' Snake Turns Bad?'"

Monica looked out over the auditorium as people chuckled. The church members looked like eager statues frozen in a pose. Most had Bibles on their knees ready to open, just waiting for the chapter and verse to be announced.

"Numbers, Chapter 21, tells the story of God's people, wandering in the wilderness as a result of their disobedience to God. They failed to enter the Promised Land, and now they're drifting about aimlessly. They're miserable people who dream of a day when they can go back home and be happy slaves in Egypt. How quickly they'd forgotten the heavy hand of Pharaoh!

"Centuries have come and gone, but people haven't changed much. Our Creator hardwired each of us to dream God-sized dreams and make something special out of our lives. Anyone wandering about with no clear purpose will tell you it's a miserable way to live. Not only is it a frustrating way, but draining, more so than running hard and fast after a goal.

"When I was a teenager, I remember my father telling me once, 'Son, if you keep spinning your wheels in life, you'll soon grow impatient with the lack of traction.' That's exactly what happened to the children of Israel. Verse 4 tells us they became impatient in their journey. Their minds were agitated. Tensions ran high. They began a whispering campaign against Moses and against God. Their conversations turned into poison. They accused God of bringing them into the wilderness without bread and without water simply to perish. And God was not pleased.

"He responded by unleashing an army of venomous snakes. Picture how terrifying this must have been. I imagine the snakes slithering between people's legs, into their tents, hissing, coiling, striking, and creating quite the panic. In my mind I can picture women running hysterically from one snake only to encounter another one just a few feet away. The children of Israel should have thought twice before grumbling in the face of God's goodness.

"I wonder how many of us make this same mistake in our own lives. Let me remind you of how easily you can miss the fact that you're blessed by God. We're rich by comparison to the rest of the world. We sit in a free church in a free land and have plenty while most of the world suffers."

Pete spoke the next words very slowly and with great force. "We've been given so much. What right do any of us have to complain all the time? We should be counting our blessings, not our miseries."

Monica joined the rest of the crowd in voicing her approval. She was proud of her husband for bringing up the subject of complaining. As levels on the complaint meter redlined at Green Street, Pete backed away from talking about the problems. She understood how difficult airing dirty laundry on a Sunday morning could be. She was frustrated, however, that he didn't confront the issue from the Word of God. But something was stirring inside him now. She could see it clearly. She also noticed that others in the audience were still engaged and listening intently.

"Tragically, many lost their lives that day. Anytime there's a decision to be made between trusting God or destroying one's life, choosing shouldn't be all that difficult. They should have placed their confidence in the One who carried them on 'eagles' wings' to a place of freedom. The list of things God had already done for them is breathtaking. He was their great I AM, who split the Red Sea and drowned the armies of Pharaoh. When they were hungry, bread fell from the sky and quail flew into their camp. He even quenched their thirst from a stream that flowed from a desert rock. God showed them His glory; they gave Him their defiance. We need to be reminded of the high price to pay for cheap faith.

"As many lay dying with poison in their veins, they wept over the error of their ways. They raised their eyes and confessed their sins beneath the desert sky. And as you could only hope He would, God responded with mercy.

"Moses received a priority message from God. At His command, Moses crafted a snake, affixed the snake to a pole, and raised the pole up for all the Israelites to see. Those who were bitten by the vipers survived when they looked upon this curious image. God had shown them another miracle.

"Now that's what I call a good snake, and it's the only snake I'm aware of in the Bible that ever did anybody any good. There's a powerful truth here. We serve a God who's able 'to work everything together for good, for those who love him and are called according to his purpose.'

"Romans, Chapter 8. As Pastor Jim would say, 'It's in the Book.'"

Several shouts of "amen" punctured the silence in the room.

"But the story doesn't end there. Hundreds of years later, there appeared a courageous king in the land of Judah. His name was Hezekiah. He was only twenty-five years old when he began to reign. That's the age when most men are still trying to figure out what life is all about, but these things were no mystery to Hezekiah. He already knew.

R. James Shupp

"Listen to what the Bible has to say about his character. 'Hezekiah trusted in the LORD, the God of Israel. There was no one like him among all the kings of Judah, either before him or after him. He held fast to the LORD and did not cease to follow Him; he kept the commands that the LORD had given Moses. And the LORD was with him; and he was successful in whatever he undertook.'

"Second Kings, Chapter 18 tells the story of what Hezekiah did shortly after ascending to the throne. One day he took a short walk from the king's palace to the Temple of God. What he came across shocked him to the core. He saw the very same snake Moses made in the wilderness nearly eight hundred years earlier. Only now things were very different. The people had given a strange name, Nehushtan, to the snake, which means 'a bronze thing.' They worshiped the snake and burned incense to the idol like Nehushtan was some kind of God. This is how the good snake became a very bad snake.

"The king was filled with righteous indignation. He seized the bronze snake and smashed the idol before their eyes. I imagine those who were on their knees praying to Nehushtan a few moments earlier were stunned as the statue crumbled before their eyes. The Bible doesn't leave any question as to how he handled this situation. Scripture says of Hezekiah that 'he did what was right in the eyes of the Lord.'

"In the final analysis, this is the story of a mighty movement of God. God moved in the wilderness to save the lives of a sinful nation. He did this repeatedly. But over time, the original significance of the movement was twisted into something that broke the very heart of God. Instead of focusing on Him, they fixed their eyes on a monument that He left behind. As they worshiped Nehushtan, the statue was transformed into a worthless idol, a very bad snake.

"Great movements of God don't lose their significance because of something He does or fails to do. The power of a movement begins to wane whenever God's people take their eyes off Him and fix them to a monument that takes His place. Brother Jim never minced words. I'm going to shoot straight with you as well. Over the years, we've become a museum filled with monuments to the past. This has drained the very life out of Green Street Baptist Church.

"Until recently, I was unaware of the part I played in this drama. When I first came here five years ago, I was mesmerized by our church's history and the reputation of the man I followed. But I didn't lead you toward the Promised Land just across the river. Now, get ready. That's all about to change.

"God raised up Hezekiah to show us how to handle all the bad snakes, those menacing serpents that wrap their coils around our legs and prevent us from moving forward. Let's have the courage to do what he did. I challenge you to stand with me as we smash the 'bronze things.' Let's shut down everything and seek God for the new thing He wants to do. The old ways have become nothing more than monuments of a bygone era. They were good while they lasted, but now they're failing us.

"God never wants His people to get stuck in a moment. This will be a new season in the life of our church. Today we're restoring our focus on what God has for us on the horizon. The days of maintaining a rearview mirror approach to life and ministry are over."

At that moment, Monica saw a stirring in the crowd. A few dozen people who were seated all over the auditorium stood to their feet and began walking down the center aisle.. Each held something in their hands, including notebooks, a few sheets of paper stapled together, a metal trashcan, a small table, and what looked to be a fire extinguisher. As they approached, Pete continued.

"The challenge before us today is to give our church a fresh start. During the early years, we benefited greatly from the structure set in place by our church constitution and bylaws. The personnel handbook, along with the job descriptions, kept the staff focused on what was considered most important. Over the years, volunteers and leaders worked together to produce an effective committee structure. We have notebooks filled with organizational charts, minimum requirements documentation, long-range, mid-range, and short-range plans sitting on shelves all across this church. All these plans, as well as most of the ministries we operate, were designed decades ago. Hear me when I say that we can no longer afford to be trapped by our traditions.

"What served us well back in the day no longer works today. These were once good snakes, but they've wrapped their coils around us and squeezed the air from our lungs. They've kept us from dreaming about new opportunities and revolutionizing our culture for Christ. We're so busy serving the structure put into place years ago that we're missing the new thing God wants to do now.

"Today we do what Hezekiah did: we smash the snakes. And we do what our founders did long ago in a house two blocks down the road: we start fresh. We start new. We trust God to show us the way forward."

Bob and Georgette Freeman set the table in place. Buck Simpson placed the trashcan on top of the table. Josh Duncan was the first to toss his job description inside. Others filed by, one by one, leaving behind what could be considered the complete administrative and ministry documentation of Green Street Baptist Church.

Then Gary Lovejoy, chairman of the finance committee and one of the original twenty charter members who founded the church over sixty years before, started the blaze.

The smoke rose and filled the rafters of the sanctuary, just as the smoke had in Old Testament days.

Who Killed My Church?

Monica rushed to the platform where Pete stood. She gave him the kind of kiss he'd given her on their wedding day, right there in front of the whole church and for everyone to see. She was hiding no more.

Kate Shoemaker, sitting at the organ and caught up in the moment, cranked out Mendelssohn's Wedding March from memory. The crowd cheered.

And just as Markus promised, the sprinklers did not activate.

Part 2

Chapter 13

He leads me beside the still waters.
He restores my soul... (Psalm 23:2-3a, NKJV).

Early Monday morning, Pete sat on the living room sofa with his Bible open. The light from the fireplace flickered across the pages of Exodus. Moses was on the mountain of God, preparing, listening, and getting ready to lead the former slaves to the Land of Promise.

Pete meditated on the events of the previous days. Markus had given him a few parting words last night. "Pete, you're not finished yet. The real work begins now. But the work must first begin in you!"

The intensity in his voice caused Pete to shudder. Over the years he'd observed how Christians cycled through different phases. First comes the emotional high on the spiritual mountaintop—peaks like yesterday. Then they descend back into the familiar—those valleys of indifference that could last for years. Pete wanted what happened yesterday to ignite a lasting movement of the Spirit of God, one that never evolved into something less. He didn't want to go back… No, he couldn't go back to business as usual. Of that much, he was certain.

But the change must begin in me first. If Markus could see my need clearly enough, then others were able to see this in me too. Oh, God, start a fresh work in me. Like Moses, I want to learn how to rest with You on the mountaintop.

The log in the fireplace crackled and hissed. Pete looked at the clock—time to head for the office.

Pete wished his office had been set up outdoors. Nature freed his mind and allowed him to process the most important things happening around him. There was something about sitting behind a desk underneath fluorescent lights in a building that smelled like old clothes that shut down his vital brain functions.

The truth was he seldom left the office. His desk was cluttered. He rarely had enough time to complete his work. Most days he left the church realizing the next day was already full.

And he was exhausted. The stress had taken its toll. Every day he woke up, ate breakfast, went to work, did his job, came home, kissed Monica, and went to sleep. On the next day, he hit repeat and did the same things all over again.

But not today.

This morning he drove right past Green Street Baptist Church. He hadn't intended to do this when he left the house. But somewhere along the way, the need to stop was overpowered by the impulse to bear down on the accelerator. He called to inform his secretary—"administrative assistant," as she preferred to be called—as his Camry whizzed past the church.

Fanny Mae Cook had been Pastor Jake's secretary for nearly twenty years when Pete inherited her. All the information she gathered about the church over the last quarter century was overshadowed by what she didn't comprehend about computers. Most days Pete felt as though he worked for her, instead of the other way around.

Fanny Mae expressed her concern over the abrupt change in their routine. "Do you want me to place you on the prayer chain? I'll call the captains right now. Just let me know what to tell them."

"No, but thanks anyway, Fanny Mae." Pete's tone was positive. "I'll just be in a bit later than usual."

He wasn't sure what to think about the prayer chain. The chain functioned like an outdated social network, more adept at circulating gossip than eliciting power from on high. *You need to stop that. There's no reason to be cynical.*

Twenty minutes later, Pete found himself sitting on a fallen tree overlooking Lake Worth. The day was beautiful and the overcast sky reminded Pete of his great love for flying. Years ago, days like today would have provided him with an excuse to drive to the airport and climb into the cockpit of a Cessna. Soon Pete imagined himself on the departure end of some runway. He savored the thrill of pushing the throttle to the firewall and feeling the acceleration in his bones. He loved to slip the surly bonds of earth and soar among the floating cathedrals shaped by clouds.

The lake offered a different set of pleasures this morning. Pete drew strength from the friendly breeze that caressed his face. The air currents gliding past him also brushed the waves, pushing them gently to the shoreline. *This is not an auditorium. This is a sanctuary. Today this is my house of worship.*

Deep within the void fashioned by years of frustration, something awakened in Pete. A summons from his Master appeared in his mind like a bolt from the blue. He felt a quickening of emotions.

Recently Pete had been reading from *The Message*. He loved Eugene

Peterson's artistic translation of Scripture. He opened the Bible, which fell to a familiar place. His eyes recognized the highlighted section of Matthew 11:28-30. Long ago, he'd carefully circled each word with black ink. He intended to revisit the passage and reflect upon the words more deeply.

The moment finally arrived. He read to himself silently at first. Then he whispered with lips barely moving. Halfway through the passage, he read out loud, almost shouting.

Are you tired? Worn out? Burned out on religion? Come to me.
Get away with me and you'll recover your life. I'll show you how
to take a real rest. Walk with me and work with me—
watch how I do it.
Learn the unforced rhythms of grace. I won't lay anything heavy or
ill-fitting on you. Keep company with me and
you'll learn to live freely and lightly.

Pete jumped off the fallen tree and rushed toward the water, his heart stirring, beating faster. He threw his shoes aside, rolled up his pants knee-high, and stepped to the edge. Waves of emotion crashed over him as the waves of water glided past his feet. Before he realized what happened, Pastor Pete was waist-deep in water without a soul to baptize.

And he spoke, loud enough that any passersby would have heard him clearly. As far as Pete knew, his only audience consisted of waves, the birds of the air, and the tiny little fish tickling his skin. He lifted up his eyes and stretched his hands toward the heavens. A flurry of words now resonated across the open water.

"If this isn't true, then nothing else is. I accept your invitation. Only You can restore the years the locusts have eaten. Please bring back what the enemy has stolen. I reclaim my birthright and my calling for your service. Restore my soul. Mighty God, come take my hand.

"Oh, Jesus, if You can see me, I'm so sorry for what I let my life become. If You came once again in human flesh, I don't believe You'd discover anyone more used-up or burned-out than Pete Blackman. I want to enter this rest. Show me how to lead Your people there too. Let these 'unforced rhythms of grace' flow from my life. Fill up the hearts of those I lead. Together we will make a beautiful noise for your glory.

"This day I renounce everything heavy and ill-fitting. I choose to keep company with you. I make my stand here. From this day forward, I will 'live freely and lightly' beneath the umbrella of Your grace."

His confession ended. The silence returned. As he lowered his arms, he wiped the tears from his eyes. Up above, one of those floating cathedrals fashioned by clouds opened a door—just enough for the sun's rays to shine upon Pete. Some might call the timing a coincidence. Pete never believed that for a moment.

He rushed home to Monica, as quickly as the law allowed.

Chapter 14

I will fear no evil; For You are with me...
(Psalm 23:4a, NKJV)

On the other side of town, Monica sat alone in her living room. Her Bible, opened to Galatians 5:22-23, rested on her knees. The night before she'd heard Markus say to her husband, "The work must begin in you!" Though the words were intended for Pete alone, they caught her off-guard.

Her thoughts drifted to their children, actually men now, both away at college. She glanced over to their pictures resting on the fireplace mantel. She remembered helping them memorize this same passage of Scripture now opened before her. Sadly, they weren't attending church anywhere and didn't seem to feel guilty in the least.

But Monica felt guilty. *No. I feel angry.* After years of growing up as PKs, "preacher's kids," both her sons had become cynical about organized religion. Zane and Dustin complained that a pastor's house was more like a fishbowl than a normal home. Prying eyes followed them throughout their childhood. They never had a chance to be normal.

Everyone expected them to be different, even special. They rebelled against the pressure and the hypocrisy like so many PKs do.

Monica wanted the church to minister to her sons, not stalk them and cast judgment upon her family. She tried, ever so hard, not to hold Green Street Baptist Church responsible for the loss she felt in her mother's heart. She was only bothered when she thought about the injury caused to her family, which was most of the time. *This needs to end.*

Perhaps the Bible verses she planned to study this morning could offer her some kind of assurance that the healing process had already begun. Looking down, she silently read a familiar passage: *But the fruit of the spirit is love, joy, peace, patience, kindness, goodness, faithfulness, gentleness, and self-control.* Years ago Pete preached a message on "The Nine Characteristics of the Spirit-Filled Life." She loved that sermon—one of her favorites. She remembered him saying the first three fruit have one syllable: love, joy, peace. The next three have two syllables: patience, kindness, goodness. The final three have three syllables: faithfulness, gentleness, and self-control. Ever since that sermon, recalling the fruit of the Spirit became as effortless as saying her own name or remembering how to brew coffee.

Love, she thought. *I haven't loved as I should. Joy. Why do I feel so deflated all the time? Peace. My problem is that I'm unsettled. I never know when the sword is going to fall. I have run and run and even hidden—all to avoid the pain.*

Monica began praying softly. "Lord, how can I be filled with your Spirit when there's no evidence of the fruit of the Spirit?"

In the stillness of her meditation, she heard a whisper in her heart: *Do not get drunk with wine…instead be filled with the Holy Spirit.* Monica knew Ephesians 5:18 from memory. *But I don't drink wine,* she argued silently. *I'm a Baptist. I'm a preacher's wife. I don't because Pete would pay dearly.*

Who Killed My Church?

Deep within the void fashioned by years of frustration, something awakened in Monica. She, too, received a summons from the Master and felt a quickening of emotions.

Ever since she'd been a little girl, Monica had believed God spoke to her directly. This was another one of those moments. *My child,* she heard in her heart and mind, *you're not drunk with wine, but you are drunk. You're intoxicated by your anger. You're inebriated with fear and frustration. You're under the influence of depression. You're mad at all the people who are mad, depressed over all the people who are depressed, and frustrated by all the people who are frustrated. You believe if I change them, then you'll heal, too.*

I don't work that way. Monica, come to the cross with Me. Your freedom will come when you die to the things that are killing you.

Monica left the living room and went into Pete's study. She opened the top drawer and pulled out a pen, along with a pad of sticky notes. Then she went into the living room and pondered a wooden cross hanging on the wall—an old family heirloom shaped by her father's hands when she was just a little girl. He'd given this cross to her as a special gift not long before he passed away. She believed the unadorned and rustic cross to be the most beautiful piece of art in her house. Very quickly she wrote four words on four separate pieces of paper: anger, fear, frustration, and depression. Then she stuck those to the cross.

The piece of paper that contained the word "anger" fell to the floor. *I know what that sign means.* She went to the garage and found Pete's hammer. Then she opened the tool box and discovered some nails.

As she went back to the living room, Pete came rushing through the door.

"Help me," she announced.

Right then in the living room, Pete assisted Monica as she nailed the little pieces of paper to her father's cross. The sound of the hammer hitting the nails made a beautiful noise for the glory of God.

In the coming years, Monica would have many opportunities to share this story. She'd always end by saying, "At that moment my heart was set free. The Son broke through the clouds of frustration, the mists of fear, the fog of depression, and the storms of anger. He restored the years the locust had eaten. He gave me beauty when I gave Him my ashes."

But there in the living room that day, Monica looked into her husband's eyes and said, "The work must begin in me too."

Then she finally noticed her husband's appearance. "Pete, what happened to your clothes?"

Chapter 15

"Deep Waters"

The purposes of a man's heart are deep waters,
but a man of understanding draws them out (Proverbs 20:5, NIV).

"Pete, have you ever heard of the philosopher, Frederick Nietzsche?"

"The atheist? Sure."

"His most famous quote is, 'When you look into an abyss, the abyss also looks into you.'"

Pete nodded. "I remember that appearing on a test in a Philosophy of Religion class during seminary."

"I skipped that class." Markus laughed. "I remember the quote from the James Cameron movie, *The Abyss*."

"That's funny. The next thing we need to tell the church is that our consultant spent his seminary days at the movie theater. That'll go over like a lead balloon," Pete jibed.

"Dr. Pat Sheets handed me the same degree here in Ft. Worth that he gave you. And one more thing, Mr. 'four-point-oh' Pete," Markus teased. "I had hoped God had loosened you up a bit at the lake."

"He did, but the change came after reading the Bible, not from some pagan philosopher's words."

Markus raised his eyebrows. "Ah, touché. But seriously, Pete, Green Street needs to look into the abyss and let the abyss stare back."

"Okay, so where do we find the abyss? Are they selling that now at the Christian bookstore, or did you happen to bring some of the abyss with you?"

"I tried, but they seized it at the airport security checkpoint."

Markus and Pete both chuckled. That Tuesday morning they sat in Pete's office planning out the next phase of revitalizing Green Street Baptist Church. Actually, Markus had all the plans. Pete was open to whatever Markus suggested that could solve problems and create momentum.

"Perhaps we should come up with a comedy routine and hit the road," Pete added.

"Most comedy is born of pain. After you've endured all the pain I'm about to send your way, I'll take you up on that offer."

"Bring it! I was baptized by fire in the lake yesterday. Who's afraid of a little abyss?"

Frank Sanders took his eyes off the road momentarily. He looked over at Buck Simpson sitting in the passenger seat and said, "What did he mean when he said, 'It's time to look into an abyss?' I find that a little disturbing, don't you?"

"I don't know. He's pretty intense, but I think he knows what he's doing. You're not experiencing a little buyer's remorse are you?"

"Who told you I'm paying for the consultant? That was supposed to be anonymous."

"Frank, you're in a Baptist church. Nothing's anonymous. Everybody knows that if it weren't for you, Gary Lovejoy would have forced Pete to resign."

"That wasn't me. I heard God shouting at me to do something."

"Thank you for listening."

Frank paused before voicing the next question. "Buck, what do you think about what's happening in our church?"

"Do you mean over the last several years or the last few days?"

"Both, really."

Buck adjusted his focus to look out beyond the front windshield. As he reflected on the question, he noticed the line of cars up ahead. An eastbound convoy from Green Street Baptist Church stretched out across I-30. Their destination was the Jan-Kay Ranch in Detroit, Texas.

Markus and Pete had enlisted several church leaders to attend a two-day retreat there. He described Jan-Kay as "the place where Africa meets Texas." The ranch was the only Christian camp the consultant knew about that featured monkeys, tigers, camels, and even a rhinoceros. They'd be staying at the Buffalo Hotel and Conference Center to hear Markus explain the abyss, whatever that was supposed to be.

Buck glanced over to Frank. "I believe the world changed and we made a business of resisting the change. In the early days, we were more in touch with what was happening in our community. Most of us lived within a stone's throw from the front door of the church. But we sold our houses, moved to different areas, and lost touch with the people we were called to serve."

"Do you think we're getting too old, Buck?"

"I thought so when my wife passed away. Now, I don't know what the consultant has in mind, but I've already seen the abyss. I took a long hard look at Becky before they closed the casket. I was numb for days… no, years."

"Buck, I don't even know what to say. I prayed for you often during that time."

Buck nodded. "Those prayers were what got me through. Strangely, if you don't look into the abyss and choose to walk in the other direction, you'll fall in there yourself. I finally realized that. God gave me the strength to move on."

"Maybe that's our problem in the church. We didn't move on well."

"I never heard Pastor Jake say anything about 'shaking hands with the devil,'" Fanny Mae Cook stated bluntly.

Suzie Whitmore and Kate Shoemaker locked eyes momentarily in the front seat of the Suburban. Neither was sure how to respond to the statement. They were in the same meeting with Fanny Mae and hadn't heard anything about shaking hands with their archenemy.

Suzie concentrated on the slow-moving truck up ahead. The Green Street convoy was changing lanes to avoid any delay. "I don't think you heard him properly, dear. He specifically said we need to 'look into an abyss.'"

"The devil lives in the abyss. It's in the Book."

"Well, you know, dear, Jesus took His disciples to a graveyard one day to stare into an abyss," Kate said confidently. "That's in the Book too. He delivered that poor demon-possessed creature who called himself Legion. Sometimes you have to confront evil and death if you want to change the world."

Fanny Mae tried to think of some kind of response to that. When she couldn't, she changed the subject. "I wish Pastor Jake had stayed a little longer. He should have brought Frances with him, though. She used to sit beside my desk and tell me all the funny things her husband said over the years. Monica never comes to see me."

"I think that poor girl has been compared to Frances so much that she feels intimidated," Suzie responded. "Do you remember what Pastor Jake said the other night? 'I didn't need to be anybody but me. You loved me for who I was.' He was right about that."

Kate didn't verbalize her thoughts, but she wondered, *Could the abyss be how we've treated each other over the years?*

All up and down the convoy headed to Jan-Kay Ranch, people discussed the abyss.

"Why did Markus choose such a strange word?"

"What does it mean?"

"Our church isn't an abyss, is it?"

"What are they teaching in the seminary these days?"

By the time two dozen vehicles rolled through the front gate, a collective sense of curiosity had taken hold of the travelers. And they weren't disappointed by what they saw as they entered the property. All manner of animals stopped what they were doing to concentrate on the procession of cars headed toward the Buffalo Hotel.

Christian Marsh, one of the members of the finance team, noticed a massive rhinoceros behind a flimsy fence. "I hope his name isn't Abyss."

Looking through the sizable foyer windows of the Buffalo Hotel, Markus and Pete surveyed the scene unfolding before them. Markus glanced at Pete and called attention to the irony at hand. "Curious animals inspecting curious humans."

From the back of the room, a man walked quietly across the foyer and positioned himself directly behind Markus. Pete noticed first and turned his head rather abruptly. The newcomer rested an oversized hand on Markus' shoulder.

"Old friend," Markus exclaimed after wheeling around suddenly. "Still sneaking up on people I see."

"Only those with a guilty conscience. You wouldn't be plotting another one of those crazy schemes, would you?"

"Pete, I'd like you to meet John Dewayne, the owner of Jan-Kay Ranch. He's the only person I know who may be more insane than I am."

"Pastor Blackman," John bellowed, "Markus tells me you have some real moxie. I like that in a man of God."

"Thank you," Pete responded feeling a little self-conscious.

John extended a calloused hand and placed it on Pete's shoulder. "This week, my ranch is your ranch. Whatever you or your church needs, my staff will accommodate. Make yourself at home."

"We'll try not to frighten your animals," Pete chuckled.

"Unlikely," John replied. "Markus, let the church members walk the ranch for the rest of the day and get a good night's rest. As for tomorrow, the stage is set."

Pete immediately zeroed in on the last statement. The curious way John inflected his voice caused him to wonder if the two men were up to something. So he asked a simple question.

"What stage?"

"All the world's a stage," Markus replied. "Brush up on your Shakespeare, Pastor."

John and Markus exchanged knowing smiles.

Chapter 16

Look at the behemoth, which I made along with you
and which feeds on grass like an ox (Job 40:15, NIV)

The next morning was a delight for one and all. Early risers strolled around the camp. Christian Marsh learned from an attendant feeding the rhino that his name was not Abyss. No, his name was far worse. They called him Ripper. Christian was also informed that several rhinos on the run were called a "crash."

"You don't want to get in the way of a crash of rhinos," the attendant said, "unless you're ready to walk on streets of gold."

Others noticed that Markus had given only a partial list of the exotic wildlife at the Jan-Kay Ranch. They were unprepared to step into a menagerie of lemurs, macaques, kangaroos, bears, peacocks, deer, and of course, buffalo. Suzie and Kate drank a cup of coffee as they watched several Sulcata tortoises lumber across a field. Tigger and Lilly, two massive Bengal tigers, eyed Buck and Frank as they wandered past their cage.

"I get the feeling they believe we're food," Frank said warily.

Buck chuckled.

After a gluttonous breakfast of scrambled eggs, bacon, sausage, biscuits, gravy, and gallons of coffee, Pete gathered his flock for a short devotion in the conference area of the Buffalo Hotel. He read from Psalm 104:24, which seemed appropriate for the occasion. "How many are your works, O Lord! In wisdom you made them all; the earth is full of your creatures." Pete then spoke on the topic of "God, the Creator of Variety."

"God is never boring," he stated. "His world is full of surprises. At this ranch, we've seen the diversity of His handiwork. Every creature here bears testimony to His glory.

"We know our God never changes. He's the same yesterday, today, and forever. On the other hand, He's a creative God whose mercies are new every morning. 'Unchanging' should never be equated with 'unexciting.' This is true of His Word as well. The words I just read from the Bible will never change or fade away. But they should also inspire us fresh and new every morning—especially on mornings like this one. When I heard the tiger growl and the bear roar, I gave thanks. I praised God for His wisdom and the wonders on display at this ranch.

"We have a clear mission this week. Our unchanging God has given us an unchanging task. We call this 'ministry.' The challenge to reach our community should never fail to excite our imagination. This is why we're here today. We should seek new ways to inspire those living in darkness to step into the light. I dream of the day when our church brings a variety of ministries to our lonely city. Our God has called us. Our world needs us. 'His works are many.' Ours should never be few. It's in the Book!"

Pete stepped away as Markus rose from his chair. Applause broke out across the room as they reflected on their pastor's brief devotional—

first, because it was good, and second, because it was short. Even Markus would admit he'd never heard a bad short sermon. "For a sermon to be bad it only needs to be long," was one of his mottos.

Pete sat back down in his chair. After five years, the leaders of Green Street were warming up to the man who followed Jim Jake. Pete's devotional reminded many in the room of their former pastor. Pastor Jake was known for his short and sometimes spontaneous messages. They had a way grabbing the emotions and placing feet into motion.

Markus replaced Pete on deck. Warm smiles transformed into curious expressions. "So you're wondering about looking into an abyss. I'm glad that you're up for it this morning. Let me shoot straight with you. You're already staring into the abyss."

Gary Lovejoy perked up as did many others. On account of Gary's age, he was a slow mover but still a quick thinker. When Markus and Pete went to his home with the "big ask," Gary was reluctant to be the man to light the bonfire. Pete looked him straight in the eyes that day. "Gary, there's not another man on the planet who can get this job done." He perked up then too, thought for a moment, and the rest of the story was quickly becoming the local rave.

"I agree." Gary's affirmation rippled through the room. His voice was raspy, perhaps from being a little too close to nature. The bed he slept in was not his own. He looked a little paler than usual. The change in routine didn't suit him well. But he'd become a believer nonetheless, and something of a bonfire advocate. There were still more blazes to set.

"Thank you, Gary," Markus affirmed quickly. "Now let's get everything on the table this morning."

Pete handed out several papers Markus had asked him to copy before they left Ft. Worth. The first graph showed the decline in average attendance over a ten-year period. The second illustrated the decline in giving during that same timeframe. Both charts looked remarkably similar to the backside of a mountain.

"Great if you ski, not so good if you're a church," Markus commented. "Each chart illustrates a trend that hasn't been reversed, and there's no evidence that it will be, at least not yet. Extend the chart along the same trend line into the future, and you'll discover the date you disappear. By my estimation, you have two years remaining to exist as a church."

"Ladies and gentlemen, *that* is the abyss. And I do hope looking at it makes you uncomfortable as it stares back at you."

Everyone's eyes were so fixed on the ski-slope charts they failed to notice what was happening outside the Buffalo Hotel. The door swung open abruptly, making such a startling noise that all eyes shifted immediately in that direction. There were several gasps, as the air was sucked out of the room.

Standing before them was an attendant holding the reins to a harness. Ripper entered the building.

Chapter 17

Its bones are tubes of bronze, its limbs like rods of iron.
It ranks first among the works of God (Job 40:18-19, NIV).

Markus had met John Dewayne five years earlier during a marriage and family retreat hosted by the Jan-Kay Ranch. Markus led a weekend clinic for about thirty couples in the throes of one crisis or another. When he wasn't busy saving marriages, he spent hours with John learning about the camp, the animals, and their mutual passion for helping churches. A few weeks ago, Markus had called John on the phone with an unusual request.

"That old white rhino is thirty years old," John stated. "His crashing days are over. Ripper will be less of a danger to them than your church group will be to each other."

Before the Green Street group arrived, John simulated a trial run with the camp staff to make certain Ripper didn't fall through the floor or tear the place down. The test went so well—with the air conditioning and all—that Ripper didn't want to go back outside. A bucket of oats finally got the job done. Markus measured the risks involved after hearing the results of the experiment. He was confident Ripper wouldn't move until he could be properly coaxed.

Pete shouldn't have been as shocked as everyone else. *Why didn't I see this one coming? Another movie script from the guy who skipped seminary classes.* A nervous laugh escaped his throat. Others didn't find the event so amusing.

Fanny Mae Cook let out a sharp squeal. She hadn't done that in years, probably since she was a little girl. Buck had made the mistake of leaning back in his chair while he viewed the ski-slope graphs. The abrupt commotion sent him back in the wrong direction. His head came to rest on a rather plush bear rug, nothing injured but sweet old pride. Several came to his aid, one stumbling over a large briefcase Buck had brought to the meeting.

The sudden movement caused a snort from Ripper. More gasps followed. The wooden floor of the Buffalo Hotel creaked beneath Ripper's three tons of flesh.

"If you were to meet Ripper in the wild, you would have a very bad day." Markus lifted a finger and pointed at the massive beast. He spoke the next words with his eyes fixed on Ripper. Everyone else in the room did the same. No one blinked.

"I love the words your pastor read earlier: "Lord, the earth is full of your creatures!" This one weighs fifteen times more than any of you and runs three times as fast. He has poor eyesight and probably can't see to the other side of this room. So when he's running at thirty miles an hour, he doesn't have time to react or change directions quickly enough to avoid most obstacles. But because of his size, obstacles don't matter much. That's why a herd of rhinos is called a crash.

"Churches are a lot like Ripper here. Over the years, they may get very big and extremely bulky. Many churches are a 'crash' waiting to happen. As church facilities age, the upkeep becomes more expensive.

Debt that you thought you could pay off when the loan was secured becomes a severe burden. The ministry budget suffers and attendance declines. People who said they were committed to the bitter end leave and take their friends with them. Those who remain are left holding the bag, prone to anger and in peril of bitterness. The sweet spirit is replaced by attitudes that put a stranglehold on outreach and growth.

"Let me paint a picture of what's happening in churches just like yours all across America. For every new church that's planted, four close their doors. *Crash.* Church attendance has declined nearly twenty percent in the last decade alone. *Crash.* Sixty-five percent of all Americans have no vital church connection. *Crash.* In the U.S., fifteen thousand people per month are converting to Islam. *Crash.* Only twenty-eight percent of people between the ages twenty-three and thirty-seven attend a church. *Crash!*

"The good news is you still have time. You have two years to turn this ship around. The Titanic only had two minutes. *Crash.* Don't waste a day, a month, or a year on business as usual. Don't spend your time dragging your feet or debating. Spend your time *doing.* Make tough decisions on the hard choices. You've done this much so far.

Hang in there with me to the bitter end, and you'll become an example of church renewal across this land. You don't have to...*crash!*"

As Markus finished, the door opened again, and a bucket of oats arrived. Ripper happily left the building. From that day forward, church members no longer talked about the animals that appeared onstage during Green Street's live nativity performances. That was so last decade. Ripper was the new rave.

Pete thought back to his devotion earlier and smiled. *God is never boring. His world is full of surprises.*

Chapter 18

Be wise in the way you act toward outsiders;
make the most of every opportunity (Colossians 4:5, NIV).

After a brief but necessary bathroom break for the group, Markus stepped to the front of the conference room again. Pete passed out more documents he'd copied before leaving Ft. Worth. There was an air of vigilance in the room now. Everyone scanned their surroundings more carefully. Those gathered listened with an ironclad focus. In their minds, Ripper may have only been the first act.

Markus wrote three words on a dry erase board: Attractional, Invitational, and Missional. "Every growing church displays these three characteristics and executes them with excellence," Markus began. "First, they know how to attract people. This never happens by accident. Growing churches are intentional about being attractional.

"Read through the four gospels. Jesus was magnetic. His personality was charismatic. His teaching was captivating, and the multitudes followed Him. They came for food. Some came for salvation and healing. Others were attracted by the spectacle of His miracles, or merely because they felt threatened by His popularity. But they came anyway.

"Was there one common attraction that drew them? Yes! They had high hopes that a new day was dawning, one in which the kingdom of Jesus would collide with the underlying problems creating their misery. Many wanted front-row seats to watch Him crash into the corruption and emptiness holding them hostage. Had our friend Ripper been there, he'd have led the charge alongside Jesus."

Pete snorted at the same time he took a sip of coffee. Others laughed more freely as they gazed through the window to the open field beyond. Ripper was behaving quite stubbornly. John couldn't seem to get him on the other side of the flimsy fence. *Give a rhino oats and air-conditioning, and he's spoiled for life.* Pete laughed.

"My mistake," Markus said. "Lend me your eyes and ears once again." Compliance came quickly.

"The disciples Jesus attracted were a band of misfits and troublemakers, definitely not the *crème de la crème*. A few were outright rebels and zealots. They didn't see in Jesus a man who was fond of the rules of men. They followed Him against the tides of the status quo. And although many people disagreed with Him, they couldn't ignore Him. His teaching changed things. And 'the common people heard him gladly.'

"Mark, Chapter 12. It's in the Book.

"According to what Jesus said in the Sermon on the Mount, an attractional lifestyle takes on the characteristics of salt and light. First, I want you to think about the importance of salt in your life. Most of you would agree that it makes everything you eat much more interesting. Salt intensifies the flavor of whatever you place on your tongue. Have you ever had popcorn without any salt? It tastes like cardboard."

Markus grimaced when he said the word "cardboard." A few people laughed. He was glad because what he had to say next was much more intense.

"Eating food without any salt is like working without getting paid—frustrating and unsatisfying. What happens at Green Street either satisfies a deep hunger in your community, or they avoid you like a restaurant with a bad reputation. Let me be clear. I wouldn't be here if your church had been satisfying the needs of your community. You're not doing what Jesus asked you to do."

Markus paused as he reviewed his notes. Not that he needed to. He just wanted the words to find a tender spot in the hearts of his listeners. What grieved him most was the tasteless behavior so often tolerated in the house of God. A pastor in a troubled church recently asked, "Why do we attack our own witness with a wrecking ball?" He had no response then, only sympathy. But the emotions he felt on that day surfaced once again and added an air of intensity to what he said next.

"Jesus said, 'You are the salt of the earth.' Turn your shaker upside down and shake yourself from the inside out. Shake until your hands are numb. Then shake up your community. Sprinkle ministries throughout your neighborhood. Yes, sprinkle some love. Be a salty saint! Then people will hear you when you claim, 'Taste and see that the LORD is good.'

"Psalms, Chapter 34. It's in the Book."

He smiled. "Let's take a fifteen-minute break here." The abrupt nature of the announcement surprised a few people. Markus spoke softly to Pete. "Can I see you outside for a moment?"

As the pastor and Markus exited the hotel, Kate noticed Fanny Mae had a curious expression on her face. "What's the matter, dear?"

"We just took a break. Are they going to fetch another critter?"

"Oh loosen up, dear. That might do us some good."

"Good?"

"Yes. There are tigers here too. One is named Lilly. Wouldn't you like to hear her purr, dear? Or maybe they should bring in a grouchy old bear."

Fanny Mae's eyes suddenly grew very large as curiosity turned to panic. "I'm going to the lady's room. Come get me after we're finished with all this abyss nonsense."

"You're not going anywhere." Kate smiled. "You're going to sit right here, or I'll tie you down, sprinkle some salt on you, and let Ripper use you for a great big salt lick."

"That's not funny."

Kate didn't respond.

"I said, 'That's not funny!'

More silence. Then Kate finally said, "I grew up on a farm, dear. I know a salt lick when I see one."

"Why, I never… What's come over you, Kate?"

"Sweetheart, before this is all over, you're going to be a new woman. You're my new mission in life."

Fanny Mae didn't say another word.

Once outside, Markus had a riled look in his eyes, "Pete, I need your permission for something."

"That's a first."

"Yes, and probably the last. But seriously, two things need to happen here for this retreat to be a success."

"Only two? That's manageable."

Markus grinned. "Yes, it is. When we lit the bonfire last Sunday, the blaze was only symbolic. First, churches never really change until the negative culture is replaced by a sweet spirit. I want to crash into this head-on when we go back inside. And second, we need to enlist a volunteer from the laity to embrace this as his or her ongoing crusade."

"Who do you have in mind?"

"God knows. Start praying now."

Pete led the way back into the conference center. He noticed a strange look on Fanny Mae's face that he'd never seen before, very surprising after working with her over the last five years.

"Fanny Mae."

"Yes, Pastor."

"When we get back to the office, I want to talk with you about how to turn our old prayer chain into a brand new ministry. Let's call it 'The Salt Shaker.'"

Flabbergasted, she didn't have an immediate response, so Kate jumped in for her. "You're not going to believe this, Pastor. Fanny Mae was just telling me how she wanted to be a more 'salty saint.' Isn't that right, dear?"

Kate flashed a penetrating gaze into Fanny Mae's eyes. Then she narrowed the whites of her own to indicate just how serious she was, hoping to illicit some kind of positive response.

"Salt was all we talked about—that's for certain."

Kate detected the obvious sarcasm in Fanny Mae's answer and narrowed her eyes even more at the woman. Then, in a most stunning transformation, she looked up and offered Pete her most generous southern smile. "I plan to help her. Thank you for asking, Pastor."

Pete nodded. "And thank you, ladies." Pete turned and headed for his chair, certain he'd missed something in the exchange. Then he heard a merry shriek coming from Kate Shoemaker's direction. He sat down grinning over the over the mental image racing through his mind. *Fanny Mae must have poked her in the ribs.*

Others were still looking around for the source of the shriek when

Markus walked back to the front of the room. Everyone quickly shifted their attention to Markus, full-well knowing they'd hear the story about the shriek later. The nature of church life was no mystery to them.

"Thank you for sticking around," Markus continued. "There's just one more characteristic of an attractional lifestyle that we need to talk about. To His first disciples Jesus said, 'You are the light of the world.'

"Though they may not understand why, the people you want to reach for the Gospel are seeking the source of your light. That's why Jesus commanded us not to hide our light under a bushel. 'Put it on a stand,' He said. 'Let your light shine before others, that they may see your good deeds and glorify your Father in heaven.' There's no need to tell any of you in this room that this is in the Book. Before many of you knew how to read or tie your own shoelaces, some Sunday school teacher in some church somewhere taught you how to sing 'This Little Light of Mine.'"

Gary Lovejoy cleared his throat and slowly articulated each syllable, "Amen, Brother! Amen!"

"That man knows what I'm talking about," Markus responded. "Now imagine a ship filled with sailors. Tonight they're adrift on some dark and lonely sea. They've been lost for months. There's no more food or water aboard their ship. Some won't see another sunrise. How can they fight to survive? There's only one hope now. They must search for a lighthouse.

"When a man truly realizes he's lost, he desperately hopes to be found. Shine for him. Increase the candle power in your hearts. These people matter to God, and He doesn't want them to perish. This is the reason He blessed you in the building of your church so many years ago. That same light is what will keep it alive.

"Green Street Baptist Church…" Markus stopped mid-sentence and moved to the center of the room, his audience now surrounding him on all sides. "Let me encourage you. You're not finished yet. The real work of being salt and light begins now. But first the work must begin in you!"

Pete cried out, "Amen," rather unexpectedly. Those last words reminded him of the lake and the old wooden cross in their living room. An image of Monica appeared in his mind from memories of long ago. He was back at Baylor. Monica stood in the bleachers near the finish line. He was running. She was cheering, shouting his name, encouraging him to press onward. He always ran to her in the bleachers after winning a race. When he lost, she came to him. They married the day after graduation. She made life more interesting and the days less dull. She was his salt and light, and the attraction still held.

The memories faded as Markus continued.

"Thank you, Pete. Every preacher loves a hearty 'amen' from another preacher. I hope you agree with what I say next." He smiled at Pete, an indication that the plan they'd discussed outside was about to unfold.

"In order to be an attractional church, you must rid yourselves of all the ugly things that repel. This is hard work, but it must *not* be avoided. Politics must cease. Anything poisoning the fruit of the Spirit must go. Whatever quenches or grieves the Spirit of God must end. Sin must be dealt with, and yes, you need to exercise church discipline when someone violates the sacred trust. If anyone sullies the bride of Christ, you must rise up and defend her honor. Her reputation is worth protecting."

Markus paused for a moment and scanned the audience. Then he drove the point home. "The least attractive thing about the modern Church is that she looks so unlike the bride Christ envisioned. Fix this problem, and you won't have many others."

Pete considered the awkward silence now descending on the room.

The only noise was the sound of Frank Sander's pen scratching out a flurry of words on a rather large yellow notepad. But even this stopped abruptly.

Pete watched Frank with growing curiosity as he raised his pen high in the air. He loved this man like a brother. He recalled Frank standing in the cold in the parking lot waiting to meet him, and then offering to foot the bill for a crazy consultant to invade their church. *What's on his mind?*

"You're Frank, I believe," Markus said.

"You have a good memory."

"This is a good point to ask a question. What's on your mind? I'm sure others may be thinking the same thing."

"I don't know if it's a question or a comment," Frank said, "but here it is anyway. When our church started declining, people were so confused. We started pointing fingers and blaming each other. We became very critical. Suddenly everyone was an expert on what the problem was and how to fix it. The biggest problem was that no one agreed. I don't know how we could ever attract people to that kind of environment. Visitors might come one or two Sundays, but then they'd overhear something in the hallways and we'd never see them again."

"Thank you, Frank," Markus said. "That's about as honest as I've ever heard anyone analyze a situation. Let me state three things in response to your observation. First, you are correct. Second, you are correct. Third, you are correct.

"It's obvious you have the passion, Frank. But what do you plan to do about this personally? As I stated earlier, if you don't rid yourselves of all the ugly things that repel, nothing else matters. The game is over before you flip the coin.

"Every survey shows there are good reasons people stay away from church. Pardon me for being blunt, but the people who don't come don't want to be like the people who attend. There's nothing attractive or magnetic about the environment. We can rant about this all day long, but the reality that pews across America are becoming emptier by the year won't change.

"We could blame the devil, and I'm certain he has something to do with our problems. Perhaps we need to search our own house for the underlying cause. Take a look within from the eyes of someone who's on the outside. Invite some people to give you feedback on their first impressions when attending your church. If you discover negative trends in the feedback, deal with them."

He paused briefly before continuing. "Don't bury your heads in the sand and pray the problems go away on their own. Sometimes we use prayer as an excuse to avoid action. As I stated when I began, growing churches are intentional about being attractional."

Frank raised his hand again.

"Frank, you don't need to raise your hand."

"Sorry. I just didn't want to take over your meeting."

"I understand. Shoot!"

"Would putting someone like me in charge of this attractional thing you're talking about be appropriate? I'm no expert, but I'd like to be given the responsibility to help fix this problem."

Pete's mouth fell open. *God knows.* Markus' words, spoken just moments ago, now rang in his ears.

Seeing the stunned look on his friend's face, Markus asked, "Pete, how would you like a volunteer staff member?"

He had to clear his throat before managing an answer. "I can use all the help I can get."

"Frank, come up here, please," Markus said.

Frank made his way to the front of the room, somewhat uncertain about what would happen next. "Do you want me to face you or the crowd?"

"Why don't you just look up into the heavens?"

"What? We're in a building."

"That doesn't matter." Markus beamed as he placed a friendly hand on Frank's shoulder. "Just look up and imagine God looking down. Now repeat after me.

"I, Frank..."

"I, Frank..."

"Commit myself..."

"Commit myself..."

"To be..."

"To be..."

"The Guardian of Salt and Light..."

"The Guardian of Salt and Light..."

"And when I discover a problem..."

"And when I discover a problem..."

"Crash..."

"Crash!"

"Like a herd of rhinos..."

"*Viva la* Ripper," Frank cried.

As the story was told in the coming days, the ending was always, "You just had to be there to really get it."

Chapter 19

And whatever house you enter, first say, "Peace be to this house."
And if a man of peace is there, your peace will rest on him;
but if not, it will return to you Luke 10:5-6, (NASB).

After things had settled down, Markus gathered everyone's attention. "We're off to a good start. My prayer for you today is a simple one. May you learn something new that shakes up the way you think about church and ministry. May you embrace these ideas with your heart and let them guide your hands and feet as you enter the harvest. And may there be others in this room like Frank who will answer the call to serve."

Several affirmed the prayer with hardy shouts of "amen!" Markus smiled back as he walked over to the dry-erase board. He underlined the two words he'd written side by side earlier: Invitational and Missional. Then he drew several circles around each for emphasis. Pete noticed all eyes moved in sync with the casual, nearly hypnotic motion of Markus' hand. But when Markus turned around to face the audience, his countenance took on an air of intensity.

"Revolutions begin with words, simple words like the two you see behind me. We've already discussed the importance of cultivating an attractional environment in your church. No…" Markus looked over to where Frank was seated and pointed in his direction. "No. We've done more than have a discussion. We've acted. Not only are actions louder than words, they're much more powerful.

"I'm convinced, if you act to build an invitational and missional culture at Green Street Baptist Church, you'll start a revolution. So let me define these two words for you and then demonstrate how Jesus modeled them in His own ministry.

"An invitational church thrives on inviting people to begin a relationship with Jesus Christ. This isn't the same thing as inviting people to church on Sunday morning. In case you haven't figured this out yet, most lost people don't want to attend church, not yours or anyone else's."

Pete was glad to hear Markus say this. He was growing ever so weary of fighting against the "if you build it they will come" philosophy occupying center stage in American Christianity. What he loved most was simply talking to strangers about Jesus, especially if they were in some kind of crisis. But he didn't have much time to do that anymore. He was too busy trying to spin all the plates in the air, hoping to prevent his church from sinking into the ground.

Monica said to him once that she loved his "harvest eyes." *My eyes are blue, not hazel,* he remembered saying. *Pete, you're in seminary,* she'd teased. *Go read what Jesus said about lifting up your eyes and praying to the Lord of the harvest.* So he did and then realized how great a compliment she'd given him. The surprise set of earrings she received in return increased the size of their family from two to three. Pete didn't even realize he was grinning as Markus continued.

"Invitational is so closely related to missional that defining one without the other is nearly impossible." Markus stopped when he caught a passing glimpse of Pete. "Did I say something funny?"

Pete realized he'd just been busted. "No. I was just thinking about…" His mind drew a blank. "…Jesus!" he blurted out. "Jesus had harvest eyes, you know."

"Harvest eyes," Markus repeated. "I like the way that sounds. Your phrase fits right in with what I'm about to say next. Would you mind explaining the term for us? My vocal cords could use a little rest."

"Sure." Pete tried to hide his reluctance. He stood to his feet as Markus scanned for the spot where he'd last left his water bottle.

"I get really excited when I think about harvest eyes." With that statement, curious expressions sprouted on several people's faces, and Pete grew a little nervous. He hated speaking extemporaneously. Preparation was critical to his confidence, which presently was running a little on the short side.

"When I say harvest eyes, I don't mean hazel. That would be a mistake." *This is not going well.* "What I'm trying to say is that Jesus was a very passionate man. We should all be passionate like He was." *God, if you don't help me right now, I'll become an atheist. Not really, but please!*

"Ever since I was first called to preach the gospel and lead a church, I've had only one desire. I just want to join God in what He's doing. This is what I call 'missional living.' Jesus said it best: 'As long as it is day, we must do the works of him who sent me. Night is coming, when no one can work.' I believe that's in John, Chapter 9."

"It's in the Book," the crowd called back.

Thank you, Jesus!

"In John, Chapter 5, Jesus explained that His Father was always at work. Furthermore, He stated that the Son did only what He saw His Father doing. These two statements from our Lord form the basis of a missional lifestyle. Our job is to stop, look around, discover what God is doing, then get involved. The task is really very simple when you do what Jesus did.

"The most important part is our personal willingness to get involved after we know where God is moving. In John, Chapter 4, Jesus said, 'I tell you, open your eyes and look at the fields! They are ripe for harvest.' Someone who has harvest eyes sees people the way Jesus saw them— as ripe and ready for the work God wants to do in their lives. They're waiting for someone to enter their domain and invite them to the banquet table in God's kingdom. If you believe the neighborhoods around Green Street Baptist Church are harvestable, then you too have harvest eyes, whether they're blue like mine, brown like my wife's, or as hazel as the autumn leaves. They're the eyes that see what Jesus saw. And they're the most beautiful eyes you'll ever behold in all of God's creation."

He turned to Markus and nodded, giving the floor back to him.

Spontaneous applause erupted as Pete sat down and Markus strolled back to center stage. "Poetic, my friend. Dang, you stole my thunder!"

More laughter spilled across the room.

"I want to touch on one thing Pete said, and then we're done. Just do things the way Jesus did them. Okay, so we're not perfect like He was. I get that too, and so do most of the people who know me. However, modeling Jesus gives us a solid place to begin. What He did was both simple and reproducible—simple enough that someone like Simon Peter, an unlearned fishermen, could understand His strategy and then teach the method to others.

"So what was that strategy? He taught His disciples how to find the man of peace. The man-of-peace strategy is outlined in two passages of Scripture that are often neglected and even less understood by the average Christian. In Matthew, Chapter 10, Jesus commissioned His twelve disciples to find a man of peace. He did the same thing in Luke, Chapter 10, when He commissioned the seventy-two to find a man of peace. Can you see the progression here? The twelve reached enough people to increase their number to seventy-two, and the seventy-two reached the multitudes, all of which began with discovering the man of peace.

"So who is this man of peace? Simply stated, he is someone who's receptive to the gospel and will influence others to follow Jesus. Jesus was so intent on finding these people that He was willing to send his followers into the harvest as 'sheep among wolves.'

"Fact: Matthew was a man of peace. When Jesus issued the invitation for this man to follow Him, Matthew's new mission in life became reaching other tax collectors. He threw a party in his home and invited Jesus to meet his coworkers.

"Fact: the woman at the well was a woman of peace. Sorry, guys, but this isn't an exclusive men's club."

The ladies laughed, even Fanny Mae, who was now loosening up a bit after her tussle with Kate.

"Jesus invited this woman with a checkered past to enjoy a drink of living water. Afterwards, her mission was to go back into town and tell everyone about the Man who seemed to know everything about her. The Bible says: 'Many of the Samaritans from that town believed in him because of the woman's testimony.'

"Fact: the demon-possessed man who called himself Legion was a man of peace. Jesus invited him to a new life free of the six thousand demons raging within. After being delivered by the power of Jesus, his mission was to go back home and tell people 'all the wonderful things that the Lord had done' for him.

"Jesus modeled the man-of-peace strategy, but what about the early apostles? Did they do the same? Absolutely! Even after Jesus ascended into heaven, the apostles kept doing exactly what they'd been taught by their Lord. They went searching for a man of peace.

"Fact: the centurion named Cornelius was a man of peace. Peter was invited to his house to share the good news of Jesus Christ. Cornelius' new mission was to reach his family.

"Fact: Lydia, a seller of purple garments, was a woman of peace. Paul invited her into a relationship with Jesus Christ. Then Lydia invited Paul to start a church in her home. Together they launched a mission to reach Philippi with the gospel of Jesus Christ.

"Find the man of peace. Invite him into a relationship with Jesus Christ. Then give him the mission to reach his friends and family for Jesus. The strategy was simple and reproducible. This is how Jesus changed the world. This is how the neighborhoods surrounding Green Street Baptist Church will be captured for the glory of God. This is what I mean by invitational and missional."

Kate Shoemaker was undone. Words couldn't express the emotions running through her mind. She'd never heard anything like this before. All she knew was that she had to act. What that looked like, she didn't know. But she remembered what Frank did. So she raised her hand high in the air.

"Kate," Markus said.

"Oh my, you've brought things together in my mind that have been at loose ends for years."

"Thank you. So what is God saying to you right now?"

"You have a way of getting to the point, young man. Could God use an old organist to lead our church to find these men of peace? The task sounds like simple southern hospitality to me, but I want to devote the rest of my life to this quest. And I'm pretty sure Fanny Mae will help me."

Fanny Mae was flummoxed, but stayed silent nonetheless. Her prayer chain was being dismantled, first for Salt Shakers and now for these men of peace, whoever they might be. "Signs of the times," she murmured. "Signs of the times."

"Now that's what I call heart," Markus said. "Come on up here, Kate."

"Would you like me to do what Frank did?"

"Yes, please."

"Shall I look up to the heavens like he did?"

"Reach as far as you can, my dear, and repeat after me."

"I, Kate..." Markus began for the second time.

"I Kate..."

"Devote my life..."

"Devote my life..."

"To find..."

"To find..."

"What Jesus found..."

"What Jesus found..."

"A man of peace."

"A handsome man of peace."

The crowd roared. Everyone knew Kate was widowed. But she wasn't quite finished yet.

"And may he have the most beautiful Georgian harvest eyes."

Chapter 20

Do not say, "Why were the old days better than these?"
For it is not wise to ask such questions (Ecclesiastes 7:10, NIV).

The leaders of Green Street enjoyed a feast of burgers and fries for lunch. They were informed that the hamburger meat came from the ranch, but sadly enough the potatoes were from Idaho.

"What animal are we eating?" Fannie Mae asked, eyeing her burger before taking a bite. When no one answered her question, she spoke again, but with much greater volume.

"I hope this is a cow."

Everyone stopped eating momentarily.

"We're in a civilized country, Fanny Mae." Susie Whitmore's tone was intentionally sharp. "Of course you're eating a cow. What else would it be?"

"Well, you never know what they might try to slip past your gullet in a place like this," Fanny Mae argued. "With all these strange animals on the loose and running amuck, suppose one got hit by a car and made it to the dinner table."

Kate smiled back at Fanny Mae just before she took another bite of her delicious burger. "Then here's to road kill."

After the main course, several magnificent pies were brought in and displayed on the desert table. Ironically enough, the chef called them "peace pies"—a special recipe he discovered online.

Pete asked Markus whether or not this was intentional in keeping with the man-of-peace theme.

"What do you think?" Markus asked.

"I think men who answer questions with another question need help."

Markus grinned. "So the man who needs help has been asked to help the helpless. I hope the irony isn't lost on you, Pete. Didn't Jesus say something about the blind leading the blind?"

"I see the irony, but I might get a little unhinged if you don't answer the question."

Markus smiled. "My plans are so thorough that every detail, including how you'll spend the next several weeks, is already mapped out."

"That sounds thrilling and scary all at the same time."

"Yes, I agree, 'Mister Harvest Eyes.' What had you grinning from ear to ear back in the conference room?"

Pete frowned. "What do you mean?"

"You know good and well what I mean. I know of only one thing that puts a smile like that on a man's face."

"Markus, you dirty-minded little consultant."

"I'm not being dirty-minded. Adam knew Eve, right? Isn't that in the Book?"

"Yeah, but..." Pete couldn't come up with a quick response.

"Lighten up. Just confess you were thinking about Monica and ignoring me."

"Okay, I was ignoring you."

"And thinking about Monica, right?"

"Don't you ever think about your wife?"

"Not only that, I dream about her."

"Then fly her over. I'd like to meet the woman who has the ability to tame your wild ways."

"Tame me? That woman made me the crazy man I am today!"

For the afternoon session at the Buffalo Hotel, Markus suspended a large banner from the second-floor walkway. Pete estimated the size to be about twelve feet long and three feet wide. The banner stood in sharp contrast to the wild game trophies hanging on the walls up above. Stuffed moose, deer, feral hogs, and wild cats gazed down on the assembly below. The members of Green Street looked up as they attempted to decipher the meaning of the banner.

"Take a moment to reflect on what you see before you," Markus said.

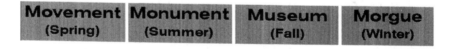

Movement	Monument	Museum	Morgue
(Spring)	(Summer)	(Fall)	(Winter)

Pete remembered seeing this same banner on another occasion when he'd attended a church-growth conference in Nashville a few years ago. Pete wasn't a fan of conferences, but he went to this one out of a growing sense of desperation. Sitting in the audience with several hundred ministers from churches all across America, he listened to a keynote address on "The Four Seasons in the Lifecycle of a Church." After the speaker had finished, Pete made a mad dash to the platform and introduced himself to Markus Cunningham.

"I'm headed for the morgue."

"Do you want me to call an ambulance?"

Pete was taken by surprise. He was about to explain himself, but stopped when Markus placed a hand on his shoulder and grinned.

"I've kissed that buzz-saw. Here's my card. I can help you."

Pete took the card and noticed a long line of eager pastors forming behind him. Undoubtedly there were others seeking out Markus' expertise. Pete awkwardly stepped out of line and placed the business card in his shirt pocket.

After returning to their home in Ft. Worth, he remembered describing the conference to Monica enthusiastically. "I heard a man describe the condition of our church like he's been here all along."

"We *have* been here all along, Pete. Where's the joy in that?"

Those words stung more now than they did back then. *Why didn't I call him earlier?* Somehow the card had made the journey to his private study and for years rested in the top drawer of his desk beneath the piles of various and sundry things.

Pete leaned to one side of his chair and pulled out his billfold. He searched through the small leather pockets and removed Markus' card. The edges were worn, more so than usual, but most likely from being shifted back and forth in the drawer as he searched for an antacid tablet. The texture felt very common as he rubbed the card between his fingers. *This may have saved my ministry.* "No," he imagined Monica saying. "The card has saved your life."

"Let's dive deeper," Markus began.

Pete's excitement blossomed as he began to realize what the leadership of Green Street was about to hear—the power of words in their finest hour. For one brief moment he locked eyes with Markus. Pete's lips moved though he didn't make a sound. Markus understood the meaning clearly enough: *Thank you.*

Markus' voice cracked slightly as he continued. "In the previous sessions, I introduced the three things that every growing church does well. These qualities were attractional, invitational, and missional. Over these next few moments, I'll explain the relationship of these qualities to the four seasons in the lifecycle of a church.

"Shall we begin?"

"Yes!" Buck Simpson shouted back.

Markus chuckled. "Thank you, Buck. Maintain that enthusiasm. And while you're listening, please make sure I don't trip over your briefcase. A broken neck would put me out of commission—far worse than anything Ripper might have done."

Buck turned red, perhaps from the embarrassment that others had already stumbled over his large piece of luggage.

Frank looked up from his big yellow notepad long enough to enjoy Buck's chagrin.

"Just teasing, my friend," Markus said. "I believe God has something special for you today. The best is yet to come."

He turned his attention back to the entire congregation. "When you learned the names of colors, the letters in the alphabet, and how to count to ten, you probably memorized the four seasons as well. I understand that in Texas you don't have the same four seasons everyone else has. I've been told the four seasons in this neck of the woods are hot, windy, drought, and tornado."

The observation generated several shouts of "amen"! Nods of approval followed.

"The first season is spring. I believe you call this tornado season around here. In other parts of the world, spring is a wonderful time of the year—my personal favorite. Life takes root and flourishes during this season. Flowers bloom. Trees produce new leaves. Nature emerges from hibernation. Spring is a time of rebirth and new beginnings.

"When a humble pastor or a small group of people want to plant a new church, they sow gospel seeds in an empty field. If the timing is right and the soil is receptive, a new church will spring into existence. Sometimes that church is planted in a home just down the road like Green Street Baptist Church, other times in a school cafeteria or some local restaurant.

"Though the church is just a tiny little baby, there's an extraordinary amount of life running through her veins. Her heart, though much smaller than yours, is strong and will beat for many years. Her mind, although containing less information than yours, is like a sponge ready to soak up every drop of knowledge. Like all babies, baby churches are fun to raise. This is the season of rapid growth, high energy, and great expectations. Life thrives in this environment.

"People who view movements from the outside often wonder how they become so successful. The reason shouldn't be a mystery to any of us. When God is on the move and people are moving with Him, together they form an unstoppable force.

"Don't attribute the success of a movement to some killer strategy or a secret sauce in the recipe. That would be a mistake. While these things may exist to some degree, they don't fuel movements. If you want to understand what does, look to her children.

"The sons and daughters of a movement have heart and soul. They live for Christ and would die for a Christ-like cause. Protecting and honoring their shared values is second nature to them. Their convictions are not mere words but actions, clearly seen by the way they worship together, work together, and play together.

"If you visit one of these fledgling movements, expect a little culture shock. That you may feel a foreigner in an unfamiliar land is highly probable. Take some words of advice from those who train new missionaries: Be slow to judge and quick to adapt. And who knows but that you were born for such a movement as this.

"Unfortunately, spring is not eternal, and most movements drift into the next phase of their growth cycle. The second season is summer. Summer is hot. This is the season where you wish spring had never ended. In a similar fashion, movements transform into monuments like spring gives way to summer. Church growth slows significantly. Everything bakes beneath the rays of a hot sun. Members of the movement grow weary and begin to lose heart. Passion wanes. On average, a movement becomes a monument within the first ten years of its inception.

"If you're like me, you might wonder, Why does this happen?

"The reason is simple. Nostalgia, one of the greatest threats to the vitality of any church, casually enters through the back door on a hot summer day. What a monument needs most at this stage is a fresh supply of living water. It's the only thing that will prevent it from entering a state of total spiritual dehydration.

"Nostalgia is a powerful force that quenches the natural urge to drill new wells. People come to believe the temperature is too hot and the ground too hard once summer has arrived. Searching the old wells for yesterday's living water seems like a good decision at first. Members of a monument-class church often remain confident that the wells from a bygone era will never fail. But the water table drops—inevitably, ever so slowly at first—and the reservoir runs dry.

"Consider the contrast between movements and monuments. A movement-class church looks forward. A monument-class church looks back. Dreams build movements. Hands build monuments. Movements are about vision. Monuments transform vision into sacred cows and worn-out strategies.

"As things slowly grind to a halt, the next season draws nigh. The third season is fall. Autumn has an unmatched beauty all its own. A new color palette emerges with rich hues and stunning colors. This season is a feast for the eyes. The beauty, however, masks a bitter reality. Everything is slowly dying.

"When a church falls into the museum category, everything and everyone exist in a plateaued state. Life and death hang in a delicate balance. The odds of a new threat or a crisis developing are great. The probability that a church will destabilize during this period is high. The hope that this state will last forever is vain. Fall is a most fragile season.

"In a museum-class church, the movement is no longer alive. It's merely a collection of significant memories and artifacts set upon the high places. Devotion to the past becomes the new form of worship. The lampstand has been removed.

"Now there's one common mistake often made during this season. Members talk about reviving the old revival. The conclusion of Scripture and Christian history, however, is that God never revives a revival. He's not interested in resuscitating old revivals. He only awakens the new.

"The fourth season is winter—a time of death. Unlike the other seasons, winter marches in like a lion. When a church enters this season, it becomes a morgue. The frozen chosen are all that remain. If you listen carefully, you may hear them quoting Shakespeare during this season: 'Now is the winter of our discontent.'

"All across America on every day of the year, ten churches close their doors for the very last time. Some will never open again. The scene is painful. Just imagine, somewhere there's a woman who attended her church faithfully for decades. She considers the facts. Most of the members are gone. All the money is gone. The clergy have either left the ministry or found other places to serve.

"She looks out over the empty pews for the very last time and remembers the days when the house was full. Maybe she sees the children who ran up and down the aisles. She hears echoes of their parents chastising them to walk instead of run. The baptistery where her sons and daughters were baptized hasn't had water in it for years. The pulpit from which the words of life were preached is vacant. As she treasures these memories in her heart, she lifts a quivering finger to the light switch. She flips it and the lights go out.

She locks the door. She sheds a tear. She drives away.

"Something like this will happen ten times today, and I want this to bother you. It bothers me. I'm devoting my whole life to the task of writing a new ending to these sad stories. This is why I came to you when Pete called. We must reverse this trend. Rage against this reality. This matters to the heart of God.

"As the Apostle Paul sat in a Roman jail, he wrote a letter to Timothy. He pleaded with him *to come before winter.* Paul understood that winter would bring an end to his life. He understood the times and seasons. We can do the same. You must accurately discern your particular season in the lifecycle of a church.

"What Paul asked Timothy, I now ask you: Will you come before winter? Some of you might wonder if it's even possible for a dying church to come back to life before the winter arrives. An African-American brother of mine illustrated this point best.

"Son of man, I have a question to ask you. Can these dry bones live?"

"His audience cried back, 'Yes, Lord.'

"Can Nicodemus be born again?"

"Yes, Lord."

"Lazarus, will you come out of the grave?"

"Yes, Lord."

"Did the blind see and the lame walk?"

"Yes, Lord."

"Could the deaf hear and the mute talk?"

"Yes, Lord."

He paused. "If God asks you to become a movement again, how will you respond?"

Everyone shouted in unison: "Yes, Lord."

At this point Markus asked a question. "But what season are you in right now? Is Green Street Baptist Church a movement, a monument, a museum or a morgue? Are you in spring, summer, fall, or winter?"

The room grew suddenly still and very quiet. Despite the obvious answer, no one knew what to say, or if anything should be said at all. The silence was bitter to endure and would have lasted much longer if not for something unexpected that took place.

Monica walked through the door and rescued everyone with a smile.

When Pete first caught sight of her, he remembered a line from Shelley reaching back to their Baylor days: "If Winter comes, can Spring be far behind?"

Chapter 21

She opens her mouth in wisdom, and the teaching
of kindness is on her tongue (Proverbs 31:26, NASB).

Last night the house seemed like such a lonely place. Monica walked through every room. Pete's study was empty. By now he was most likely settling in at the Jan-Kay Ranch. Zane's room was empty. *He took nearly everything but his bed to college. How did he fit it all in that dorm room?* She moved on to Dustin's room. Though it too was unoccupied, most of his things were still neatly in their place. Dustin came home often on the weekends, but even then the house was empty.

Monica left the house and drove to the church, which was as empty as her house. She parked her car in Pete's reserved spot. *Good thing he's not here. He might confuse me for some last-minute mom dropping off a pack of kids.*

She smiled at the thought of Pete circling the parking lot in his Camry. Around and around he'd go just to catch a glimpse of the person who committed the unpardonable sin. He never confronted them when they came back to their car. She knew he wanted to. But he never did.

She left her car and walked across the parking lot toward the main entrance of the church. Each step was a reminder of the first time she'd followed this same path—Pete's fingers wrapped between hers, arms swinging playfully in anticipation of what the future might hold. The congregation was about to appoint her husband as the next senior pastor. He beamed with excitement. *That didn't last long.*

Dustin and Zane were still in high school back then and followed a few steps behind. "Less enthusiastically," she sighed. Monica looked over her shoulder, and for a few fleeting moments, imagined their sweet but disgruntled faces in tow. The memory made her smile. *Those were the days when both houses were full.*

The steeple rose high above her as she peered into the night sky. Her desire to pray emerged, visceral and raw, from a deep place—the same place where she treasured her husband's hopes and wept over her children's struggles. *Father, all these prayers... Have you heard? Do you see us? I think I understand why Martha confronted Jesus outside the tomb of her brother Lazarus. "Lord, if You had only been here my brother would not be dead." Lord, if You would come, this church will live.*

Once again the Lord spoke clearly to Monica.

Back in the conference room of the Buffalo Hotel, Markus grinned first. He loved the perfect timing of a big surprise. Surprise was his art, and this was priceless. Pete jumped from his seat only to pause momentarily after a few steps. He caught a glimpse of Markus from the corner of his eye. Markus shrugged, his body language suggesting this was not part of some script. All across the room faces lit up and glowed in approval. No one was thinking about movements or morgues. They were simply moved.

Monica threw her arms open wide to embrace Pete. "Get my bags,

Runner," she whispered in his ear.

"My Lady, when you sit in the bleachers, I always run to win," he whispered back.

Markus watched the two walk back out through the door of the Buffalo Hotel holding hands. He wondered if anyone else saw what he could see developing. Clearly she'd emerged from the shadows. *A strong woman builds a stronger man,* he thought to himself. *This little girl holds one of the missing keys.*

At the car, Pete reached into the trunk to gather Monica's bags. She touched his forearm, and he stopped momentarily.

"Something on your mind?"

"Pete, may I say something to the group?" She anticipated his hesitation. "Don't worry. If Markus doesn't agree, you'll fire him so I can speak anyway."

He noticed the expression on her face, half jest, half deadly. "When have I ever said no to you?"

"Ten years, six months, and thirteen days ago."

"You just made that up," Pete protested.

"A woman's place is not to fight fair, but only to win."

Throughout their ministry together, Monica never campaigned for the spotlight or the microphone. She was more comfortable serving than leading. She'd had many opportunities to do otherwise, both from Pete and others. Though many years had passed, she was still that same little girl who liked to talk with God. Now He'd spoken to her, and she had something to say.

Monica surveyed the room. It was very still and quiet—and very full. She took comfort in Buck Simpson's approving smile. He had one foot resting comfortably on a large briefcase. She appreciated the way he leaned forward as if he wanted to capture every word.

While driving from Ft. Worth, Monica rehearsed everything she planned to say at this moment. Then she was a bundle of nerves. But not so much now, except that her left foot felt like it needed to twitch. *I can manage a twitch or two.*

"I'd like to thank Markus, my husband, and all of you for allowing me to speak this afternoon. I hope my interruption of your schedule counts for something in eternity. I believe these words will, or I wouldn't be standing here.

"Let me confess that I've not been a model pastor's wife. Last night I had a really long talk with God. Then I had an even longer talk with Frances Jake."

A few eyes in the room shifted to the door. Monica was taken a little by surprise until she figured out what they were thinking.

"No, Frances couldn't be here on such short notice. And I don't have the scheming mind of a Markus Cunningham."

The laughter in the room settled her last frayed nerve. Her anxious foot was now firmly on the ground and fully under her control. Fanny Mae Cook, along with the rest of the ladies, unleashed a generous smile in Monica's direction.

"Ladies, you'll know what I mean when I say this. Frances and I had a really good girl talk. I discovered some things from her about pastors' wives that I never knew. She opened up about her own struggles too. Until our conversation last night, I felt very alone and unprepared in my role.

"While Pete was at the Baptist Seminary in Ft. Worth preparing to be a pastor and building a friendship with President Sheets, I worked a full-time job to help pay the bills. This isn't something I'd change if given the chance. I've never regretted working for a moment. My job was my contribution to the calling of God upon our lives. Pete trained to be a pastor, but no one taught me how to be a pastor's wife.

"One of the things Frances said to me on the phone was: 'Dear, it's been that way for a very long time. We all discovered that being a pastor's wife is the hardest job we'll ever do without the necessary training to do it. There's no job description written. The expectations can smother you. The pressures placed on your family seem to have no end.' She gave her permission for me to share this, as well as what I'm about to say now.

"Frances spoke of nights when Jim came home under such stress and so exhausted that he fell asleep at the dinner table. She pleaded with him to slow down and learn how to rest. She confided in me that those daily pressures ultimately cost him his health.

"Pastor Jake would've never retired from Green Street if not for Frances' pleas, 'Jim, you'll die in that pulpit one day. They've had you long enough. You know you can't keep up with that job anymore. It's my turn to have you for a few years now. And I won't take no for an answer.'"

Many of the ladies were nodding their heads in affirmation while Monica spoke. They knew the story. Frances had either confided in them, or they'd suspected as much. But these details were never spoken of publicly, not until this moment.

"Last night God told me how much I need you," she continued, "especially the ladies here in this room." "I'm ready to be needed, too. Let me tell you what I enjoy and how I'd like for us to become better acquainted. Invite me to pray with you one-on-one. I'll drop whatever I'm doing to pray with a sister in need. If you have any funny stories about what happened to you during childhood, let's grab a cup of coffee and laugh our heads off. If you have a hurt that no one else understands or wants to listen to, I'm the girl that doesn't gossip.

"I'm not ashamed to admit that I'm a much better friend than I am a pastor's wife. How wonderful if no one ever refers to me as 'the pastor's wife' from this day forward—a funny title when you think about it. I'm simply Monica, the girl next door who loves Jesus, loves my husband, and wants to be a good friend.

"Status symbols don't wear well on me. Who I am is more important than any title you could ever give me. I'm able to be one of you far better than I could ever pretend to be different from you. I'm the kind of girl you call for a walk in the park on a beautiful day. Having someone over to help bake a cake would be a pleasure. Cupcakes and cookies are fun too.

"When you want to talk about boring church issues and politics, talk to Pete. God made him to get all excited about that stuff. As for me, take me shopping with you and tell me stories about the families you raised, the dreams you have for your children, your grandchildren, and where you're planning the next vacation.

"God sent Pete to lead you. Thank you for following him. God sent me to bless you. Let me be Monica, and I'll be the best friend you've never had.

She smiled. "Promise!"

The sound of women's voices filled the air. "Promise!"

The Sopranos were now in harmony.

Chapter 22

Then the LORD will appear over them;
his arrow will flash like lightning (Zechariah 9:14, NIV).

Everyone enjoyed the afternoon off.

Already the day had been full of surprises. Both Monica and Ripper crashed the party. Who would generate more conversation in the coming days was a toss-up. Markus placed his bet on the girl who'd cast her shackles to the wind.

Outside the conference room, Monica amused the ladies with stories about Pete from their Baylor days. Their favorite was the one where Pete slept through the first thirty minutes of a history final. Though they weren't dating at the time, both were enrolled in the same class.

Monica recounted, "Pete burst through the door, disrupting the whole class. He had this painful look on his face. His hair was disheveled, and his cheeks were etched with the crease marks of a pillow case.

"'Where have you been?' the professor barked.

"'Sleeping.'

"He heard me laughing the loudest that morning. My laughter unnerved him a little, but he still made a better grade on the final. I had more fun in college, though. And our diplomas don't indicate that he was the better student."

Markus had difficulty gathering everyone back into the conference room of the Buffalo Hotel. Monica was giving him stiff competition as the *entertainer de jour*. The group reluctantly found their seats.

After everyone had settled in, Markus broke the ice with a characteristic twist. "Bravo, Monica! Bravo! You touched our hearts. I'd like to offer you a consultant's job should you ever need one."

Monica chuckled and shook her head. "Pete's already a full-time job. Besides, I don't think you could afford me."

"You should hire Ripper," Pete suggested. "Change your business card to 'Marcus Cunningham and Ripper, Church Consultants, We Crash for Cash.'"

Spontaneous laughter erupted throughout the room.

"Okay, I surrender for now, but I *will* get even." Markus flashed another devious grin in Pete's direction as he continued. "Now let's get started.

"Imagine a church led by John Wayne and James Cameron."

The reaction from the audience was instant. No one said anything immediately, but looks of intrigue were etched on everyone's faces, including Fanny Mae's, whose last visit to the movie theater happened to coincide with the final John Wayne film. She preferred real cowboys over space cowboys any day of the week.

Markus continued to have fun with his listeners, "I'd put John Wayne in the pulpit and have James Cameron placed in charge of programming. Imagine what you might hear on an average Sunday. In a sermon taken from James 1:19, 'Everyone should be quick to listen, slow to speak and slow to become angry,' John Wayne would say, 'You're short on ears and long on mouth.' In a message on wisdom, 'Life's hard. It's even harder when you're stupid.' And discernment: 'A man deserves a second chance… but keep an eye on him.'"

Pete leaned over and whispered in Monica's ear. "I missed the movie critic's class in seminary." While he was still relishing in his sarcastic wit, Monica poked him in the ribs. Markus, and those who were fortunate enough to see Monica's stealthy jab, cracked up over the sight of Pete flinching and then shielding himself from a probable second attack.

Truth be told, Monica never allowed her husband to get away with being a snarky academic. Despite the fact that she called him out, either verbally or to the ribs, he was unfazed by her persistence. She knew he loved the attention, as well as her predictable reaction. "No one prints the GPA on the diploma," she'd reminded him often enough. "They all look the same after you graduate." Very true, but he still teased her about sliding by with an MRS degree.

Markus marched past the disruption with ease. "So what do you get with John Wayne that most professional minsters lack?"

"Masculinity," blurted Kate. Apparently sensing she may have offended her pastor or Markus, or even both, she added a touch of charm to her explanation. "What I mean is that John was America's cowboy and every girl's sweetheart. He wasn't afraid, especially of the truth. Sometimes we spend our energy hiding problems we should have been fixing before they got out of hand. That takes courage. Just like you two gentlemen are displaying now."

"Excellent," Markus exclaimed. "Anyone else?" The other responses were varied.

"He got the job done."

"Authenticity!"

"He was real. Nothing fake at all."

"All your responses are spot-on," affirmed Markus. "We talked about this earlier, but I want to touch on the subject again, especially since Monica's with us now. All of these character traits are attractive to the average person, and many will follow someone who fearlessly lives them out. It's human nature to chase after the people who inspire us.

"Average men and women crave authenticity. John Wayne had it, Jesus even more so. People are searching today for real flesh and blood examples of people they can admire and look upon as role models. If these characteristics are not evident in your own church culture, their search will continue elsewhere.

"The Rock 'n' Roll group U2 captured this reality in a popular song back in the '80s called "I Still Haven't Found What I'm Looking For." Even the Rolling Stones understood that when a man 'can't get no satisfaction,' he'll keep trying to find it. How many times have you watched loved ones persist in a meaningless search until finally they arrived at the edge of a cliff? 'Broad is the road that leads to destruction.'

"Matthew, Chapter 7. It's in the Book!"

Monica glanced at Pete. She knew he appreciated the references to The Stones and Bono's existential lyrics. While he was guarded about revealing such matters, she was less inhibited. *He speaks the truth,* she thought. *So many searching, so few finding.*

The reality sent her to another place. She thought of Zane and Dustin. They grew up in a pastor's home and experienced their fair share of church life. Their problem hadn't been a lack of exposure to the truth or the absence of sound doctrine. They were taught more than most, just like every other PK.

But when they saw little evidence of the truth transforming people, their foundation cracked. "What we got was their criticism," they complained one evening. "What we needed was their love." She remembered Pete's rebuttal. "The truth is not its own evangelist. Truth never operates alone. The truth needs the power of Jesus, who *is* the Truth, before the heart can change." She was thankful for what her husband said next. "You are men now, and you have my blessing. Either learn from criticism or walk away from it, but never walk away from the Truth."

Her attention snapped back when Markus posed a question—perhaps rhetorically, but she didn't care. "Why should we care about authenticity?"

"For the sake of our children," she answered.

Markus paused. "Monica, would you care to elaborate on that?"

She hesitated, uncomfortable about disclosing her sons' struggles with Green Street's leaders. She didn't want to offend or invite scorn. What she wanted now was to bite her tongue. *I'm sure that's what Pete would prefer.* But once again she tossed her fetters to the wind.

"My heart aches for my children. They haven't rejected Jesus, but they struggle with His bride."

Susie Whitmore and Kate Shoemaker were seated next to Monica. They perked up a bit. Kate was the first to speak. "We have the same problem with our grandchildren. They're about the same age as Zane and Dustin."

"We raised our three daughters at Green Street," Susie added. "Two of them still live in Ft. Worth. We invite them to church all the time, and the answer is always the same—'no.' Monica's right. For the sake of our children and our grandchildren, we need to figure this out."

"Good," Markus responded. "Your eyes aren't shut. Seeing is the first step. You might be surprised by what the Millennial Generation has to offer the church. Your children and grandchildren care about the things we've discussed here as much as you do. And as such, they're waiting for you to include them in meetings like these."

He smiled. "Thank you, Monica, Susie, Kate. You've given me the perfect launching pad to continue. Imagine someone with the gifts and talents of a James Cameron in charge of programming at Green Street.

What would it be like to have the director of movies like *Avatar* and *The Terminator* leading the way forward?"

"Highly creative," Buck answered.

"Yes, and imaginative as well," Markus responded.

"People are attracted to environments where creativity and imagination are allowed to flourish. Einstein once said, 'Imagination is more important than knowledge.' I disagree from a theological perspective. In the mind of God, imagination and knowledge are one and the same. He possesses intimate knowledge of whatever He imagines, because He has the power to create from nothing.

"This is why God could say to Jeremiah, 'Before I formed you in the womb, I knew you.' The same is true of you. Before you were conceived, you were first an idea in the mind of your Creator. You represent all the wonder and complexity of His sacred imagination. You are fearfully and wonderfully made.

"All movements, whether secular or Christian, thrive on imagination. Movements are populated by people who refuse to accept that things cannot or should not be changed. The followers believe that present reality will ultimately yield to their dreams. Movements don't operate on the principle that change is simply necessary. They believe change to be mandatory.

"In a Christian movement, the work of the imagination will cause many members to lose sleep. They dream of opportunities to bring Christ to their social networks, schools, businesses, entire cities, and far beyond. Late into the night, they wrestle to crack the code of what's not working. They declare war on obsolete strategies that waste time, energy, and resources. Imagination is a force to be reckoned with. Imagination will refurbish outdated models that have seen their better days. When the imagination drives, movements thrive.

"Moving forward, I challenge you to unleash the spirit of imagination.

Who Killed My Church?

This is how you win great victories. Enlist 'The Imaginators' to forge your battle plan. They know how to regain lost ground. They'll be the first to seize the armor of God and ride into battle. Unleash them, and God will go before you.

"And never forget from this day forward: Imagination is not your enemy. The things that quench imagination are."

Monica sat riveted to her chair. Her eyes darted across the room, and she caught sight of Fanny Mae's puzzled expression. *Perhaps she's trying to determine whether "Imaginator" is in the dictionary.* Monica, however, felt waves of excitement crashing over her. Her right foot twitched nervously. She remembered Pete explaining long ago that the Spirit of God harnesses our 'sanctified imagination' for His sovereign plan. He whispers, sometimes even shouts a word into our hearts during difficult seasons. Like this one...

"Quench not the Spirit," Monica spouted. "First Thessalonians, Chapter 5. It's in the Book."

"What do you mean by that, Monica?"

Her reply was immediate. "Just what you're saying, Markus. When we quench the Imaginators, we quench the work of the Spirit within the church."

Buck Simpson chimed in, stammering somewhat. "The Pastor's wife—I mean, Monica is spot-on." Earlier that morning, he'd measured every word she'd spoken. Calling her by name instead of her title now posed something of a challenge. He fidgeted with his briefcase and gathered his thoughts once again.

"I believe this is where I pin my sash to the ground with a sacred arrow," Buck declared. "I've been trying to figure out what my next role would be in our new day at Green Street, and I've never been more certain about anything as I am this. I volunteer to lead this new tribe of Imaginators."

He stood up then, holding his sizable briefcase in both hands. Several noticed it was the same briefcase that nearly broke their necks when they rushed to rescue Buck from his Ripper-induced tumble. Monica remembered he had one foot propped on the case when she began her speech earlier that morning. Buck opened the briefcase and pulled out a handful of ornamental arrows. Apparently he'd brought them for just such an occasion.

Clutching the arrows in his right hand, Buck thrust them above his head and waved them back and forth in the air. Then he let out a shout, something he imagined a Cheyenne Dog Warrior would do. A manly challenge followed: "Who wants to be an Imaginator? Come get your arrow!"

Brave souls emerged from their chairs.

John Dewayne, the owner of the ranch, stood unobserved on the balcony as the scene unfolded down below. The wild game trophies hanging from the walls all around the conference room appeared to be witnessing the celebration along with him. Both had seen before what began to materialize among the leaders of Green Street Baptist Church. Something deep and visceral, but very necessary was now taking shape. When fundamental changes like these occurred, events as wild as any beast now living on the ranch were soon to follow. John turned and walked back to his room thanking God for this little piece of earth. In his hands was a stack of DVD's—old John Wayne movies that Markus had returned to his office desk. He planned to watch them on the vacation he and his wife would be leaving for the next morning.

Back down below the shockwave had passed, and the celebration had come to an end. In its wake, something new had emerged. Buck Simpson, who some might describe as the Christian version of John Wayne and James Cameron all wrapped up into one man, was riding point at the head of a new society. Membership would soon require all inductees to learn how to open their lungs and belt out the secret ceremonial shout of the Imaginators. Monica noticed that somewhere between twenty to twenty-five arrows had been distributed throughout the room. Even Gary Lovejoy had one resting on his lap.

Markus seized the opportunity to end this day on a high note. "Tomorrow evening you'll depart from this ranch and travel back to the city of Ft. Worth. The people who attend your church won't soon forget the changes awaiting them upon your return. Be ready tomorrow morning. There's just one more thing that needs to be done, and I promise you this: It will be the most significant challenge you've faced leading up to this moment."

Closing with a smile, he said, "I hope you rest well."

Chapter 23

Where, O death, is your victory?
Where, O death, is your sting? (1 Corinthians 15:55, NIV)

That evening Pete left his room after Monica fell asleep. He moved across the walkway on the second floor until he came to Markus' room. He knew the hour was late. Markus was probably asleep by now. He listened for any sounds on the other side of the door. Nothing. He looked for any signs of light escaping from the doorway. Nothing. He felt the door for any vibrations or indications of movement on the other side. Nothing. He decided to knock anyway.

"What took you so long, Pete?"

"You didn't invite me."

"Minor detail. Come in."

Pete sat in a chair, Markus on the bed. There were nearly a dozen pieces of paper spread across the bed. Pete couldn't detect if they were in some logical order. The papers appeared to be scattered haphazardly from end to end.

"Trying to figure something out, Markus?"

"The next step."

An alarm bell went off in Pete's mind. "What? You told everyone at the end of the meeting that we were about to undertake the most significant challenge ever in the entire history of our church's existence. Did I hear you correctly? Please tell me you're not making this up as we go along."

"It's worse than that, Pete."

"I never know when you're serious or just messing with me."

"I was just about to knock on your door. I had an epiphany. You do believe in epiphanies, don't you?"

"Sure. The word comes from a Greek word which means 'shined upon.' Are you saying God shined upon you?"

"Let's hope so. You never know until after it's over. Take Ripper for instance. Do you believe I was convinced that would work? There's always risk involved."

"There's a difference between taking risks and managing risk. Even pilots understand the difference between the two."

"Okay, Pilot Pete, consider that you're low on fuel, losing altitude, and you can see thunderstorms on the horizon. What do you do next?"

"Pray for a suitable place to land and wait things out."

"That's the difference between aviation and church leadership. In aviation, the storms pass. In church life, they just keep coming one after another. Your best plan of action in a church environment is to fly into the heart of the storm and kiss death on the lips. Storms will think twice about gathering over your head the next time around."

Pete was a little flummoxed. Markus wasn't a pilot, yet he took the analogy right out of Pete's hand and hit him over the head with it.

"That's a *non sequitur* argument, Markus—apples to oranges."

"There's no fallacy in my reasoning; you brought up the aviation analogy in the first place."

"What's the point of this conversation? I'm a little lost now."

"Pete, I have this crazy idea, and I think you can pull it off."

"Are you going to tell me what your crazy idea is?"

"What makes you ask that question?"

"I'm having a *d*éjà vu moment here. The last time I asked what was up your sleeve, I clearly remember you saying, 'If I told you, I'd have to kill you.'"

"This time it's different. I need to tell you because it may kill you."

"I hope you're joking. You *are* kidding me, right?"

"A man needs to be told when he's about to face an execution."

"Would this be a metaphorical execution or a literal one?"

"Pete, all this time together and you still don't know me very well. I'd keep my eyes on those sacred arrows. Your leaders are armed now."

Markus gave Pete another one of his devious grins. "Listen carefully. Here's how I want you to kiss death on the lips."

"If death is a woman, Monica won't like it."

Chapter 24

I, even I, have spoken; yes, I have called him. I will bring him,
and he will succeed in his mission (Isaiah 48:15, NIV).

For Pete and Markus, the next morning arrived on the heels of a long
and sleepless night. Now they were back in the conference room of the
Buffalo Hotel. As they'd planned the night before, Pete and not Marcus
now stood before the leaders of Green Street. Pete allowed himself a few
moments to survey the room as people began settling in for the next session.

He noticed Gary Lovejoy sitting in a chair near the back of the room,
which was a strange irony. If Gary hadn't called the infamous finance
committee meeting, this retreat would never have taken place. *Markus
may be right. I kissed death on the lips once before and lived to talk
about it.*

Buck Simpson sat at the front of the room, large briefcase functioning
as a footrest. A man true to his word, and like Nathaniel in John, Chapter 1,
"a man in whom there was no guile." His mission was to gather the sacred
arrows, form a line, and defend the holy ground. Buck had wrapped his
curious mind around every word spoken during the retreat. Now he was
ready for the next wave in the attack. He would never retreat.

Frank Sanders, the new Guardian of Salt and Light, had the look of quiet satisfaction about him. If not for him, Markus would still be in Florida, and Pete would be looking for a job. He didn't know how much money Frank had in the bank or how much Frank gave to the church. But he was thankful to God that he was generous man, especially when funds were needed most.

Kate Shoemaker was to the left of Monica. Pete thought about how she ran her fingers up and down the ivories of the organ that night when Monica kissed him in front of the whole church. Mendelssohn's "Wedding March" was simply outstanding. Her clever spontaneity took everyone's breath away. *Her choice was creative in a traditional sort of way, but I'll never forget that moment. I might even learn to appreciate organ music in the future.*

Fanny Mae Cook, seated on the right, was enjoying Monica's company. She'd been so attached to Frances Jake. Now she'd finally found a way into Monica's company. She just needed a little guidance, and Monica's honesty allowed that to happen.

Monica. There she sat. *What would I do without her? She's the girl that talks to God. She's my girl too.* God spoke to her so clearly that Pete envied her. When she shared the things God revealed to her, it was obvious she was touched by angels.

Pete soaked in the curious looks on everyone's faces. They didn't know what was about to happen next—that much was certain. As far as they understood, Markus, not Pete, was supposed to be leading this morning's session.

Pete switched his thoughts to what he was about to say. *If there was ever a moment I needed You to demonstrate Your favor upon this ministry, this would be it. I need You now.* A song arose from somewhere deep within his memory. The lyrics transported him back to a moment and place from many years ago. He and Monica were leading their first church while he was finishing up seminary. At the end of his sermon, Monica walked down the aisle toward the pulpit where he stood. She held her hand out—a simple gesture to join her in prayer at the altar. The worship leader sang softly at the piano, wrapped up in the words and melody now drifting through the sanctuary.

Oh, I'm so amazed by You,

"Man of God," she'd whispered in his ear, "never stop." Her index finger gently tugged on his chin until their eyes locked in a firm embrace. It seemed as though Monica had timed what she planned to say with each measure.

And all I do is gaze upon You,

"Your words were very encouraging today. They always are."

I find my words to be so few,

"What do you want to name our first child?"

I'll always be in love with You.

"Pete Blackman, you're going to be a father."

As the memory faded, Pete wondered how much time had passed. A flush of embarrassment began rising to the surface. *How long have I been daydreaming?* Yet something about that memory in this moment clung to him and overpowered all sense of fear. *Jesus, I love You. My words will be few. But only You can make them count.*

"So there's been a slight change this morning," Pete said. "I'm not Markus, obviously. We didn't sleep last night, so pardon me if I look a little dazed. We stayed up and talked about what's next for us and what you'll be asked to do when we return to Green Street.

"My words will be few. There's not much left to say. But before I share with you what will happen next Sunday, I need to ask you one simple question—but not the same question Markus asked previously, which was, 'What are you?' Instead I ask, 'Who do you want to be?' Do you want our church to be a movement, a monument, a museum, or a morgue?"

There wasn't a moment's hesitation. The leaders of Green Street answered the question in spades. Two dozen men and women waved their arrows high in the Buffalo Hotel that morning. Then in unison, everyone yelled the secret battle cry of the Imaginators. The scene reminded Pete of something he'd read during his quiet time a few days ago: "...the place where they were meeting was shaken."

Acts, Chapter 4. It's in the Book, he mused.

Like the night before, the celebrating didn't stop. Kate Shoemaker was the only one still seated in her chair. A stream of tears broke from her eyes and rushed down the gentle creases of her aging skin. Monica noticed first. She sat down beside her and smiled, then drew her in for a warm embrace.

"How boring life would be if not for moments like these." Monica smiled. "We have each other now."

Fanny Mae was a hugging force. She hugged Kate, then Monica, then anyone else who came near. "Just like the old days," she kept repeating.

Frank Sanders performed his first duty as the new Guardian of Salt and Light. "No more old days, Fanny Mae. *Crash!*" Waving his big yellow notebook in the air, he redirected her statement. "I can only imagine new days ahead."

A new movement was ready to be born. God willing, the movement would be attractional, invitational, and missional. And if the amount of celebration heard throughout the room was any indication, church life was about to get very exciting.

All Pete had to do next was kiss death on the lips.

Chapter 25

Therefore encourage one another and build each other up,
just as in fact you are doing (1 Thessalonians 5:11, NIV).

During the mid-morning break, Markus took Pete outside.

"Are you ready?"

"You know, dragging Ripper back into the conference room and letting me kiss him on the lips would be easier."

Markus grinned. "I'm surprised I didn't think about that. John Dewayne left early this morning, so that's probably not going to happen. We might be able to manage one of those large snapping turtles for you, though."

The two men shared a moment to laugh together, the idea conjuring up strange images in each of their imaginations. They had grown closer than brothers over the last several days. For Markus, laughter suddenly turned to tears. They spilled over his cheeks and on to his shirt. Pete followed suit, helpless to do otherwise.

"Look at us," Markus said. "We're sissies with soft spots."

"Strangely enough, this is what I needed before I went back in there. I'm ready. Do you think they're ready?"

Wiping away the tears, Markus replied, "Pete, I'm careful about handing out compliments. I only offer them when I really believe in the person and what they're doing. The sheer simplicity of what you did moved me. And you moved them. The mantle of leadership just passed from Pastor Jake to you."

"I'd take a double portion of what that man had every day, Markus."

"You already have it, my friend."

Part 3

Chapter 26

And how can they preach unless they are sent? As it is written,
"How beautiful are the feet of those who bring good news!"
(Romans 10:15, NIV)

Pete walked to the pulpit. He surveyed the crowd and opened his Bible. Attendance looked equal to that of last Sunday. This reality alone contributed to his overall sense of optimism. After watching the burning of Green Street's entire administrative and organizational blueprint the week prior, the members were now more curious than ever.

Markus prayed with Pete before they entered the auditorium. He asked Pete to share the big idea of his message in a few sentences. Pete did, and Markus said, "That's good. Make the idea simple and kiss death on the lips. Your leadership base at the Jan-Kay Ranch has already pledged their support for what you're about to do. Don't forget that the majority are ready to follow you. There may be a few noisy bearings in the axle, but the wheel will keep spinning from here."

Monica was excited, her left foot feeling the urge to twitch again.

She sat on the front row flanked by Kate Shoemaker and Fanny Mae Cook. Last night she listened to Pete rehearse the sermon on their evening walk. In her opinion, he'd written a finely crafted work of art. She desperately wanted everyone in the room to experience his words the way she first heard them. She closed her eyes and reminisced over the conversation that followed.

"Pete," she said, "I've been working on a message too."

"Really! Let me hear it."

"I don't think I've ever said this before. Thank you for the journey."

He looked into her eyes then, searching for the words to respond. She could tell he was deeply moved. The words formed a stark contrast to those from the night she lay on the bed sobbing. She wanted to free him from the grip of that memory.

"I..." He faltered.

"Just listen to me right now," she'd said. "You don't need to say anything. You're everything I prayed to marry when I was a little girl. You're a wonderful man of God, and I respect you for what you've done. Be yourself, Pete Blackman. Don't second guess your heart. Lead with courage, and they will follow."

Today the man she viewed behind the pulpit looked like he was about to summon his second wind. She flashed back to their Baylor years and recalled the many times Pete had sprinted toward the finish line at the end of a fifteen hundred-meter race. When he believed he could win, he rarely lost. Something about this morning felt familiar to those memories from long ago. *Go, Pete, go!*

"I invite you to open your Bibles to Luke, Chapter 10," Pete began. "The setting of this passage is a familiar one to us. You'll remember this as the occasion where Jesus sent out the seventy-two. They were instructed to enter each of the cities He was about to visit. Their mission was to prepare the way of the Lord.

"Let me begin by issuing you a challenge. I want you to view yourself as a character in the story that's about to unfold. So activate your sanctified imagination and come on a voyage with me. I hope to transport you from the pews here at Green Street Baptist Church to the ancient Holy Land.

"Are you ready for the journey?"

"Amen!" Kate and Fanny Mae called out in unison.

Monica glanced at both and smiled warmly. She appreciated these women now more than ever. When Pete told the leaders back at the ranch what he planned to do this Sunday, both women were among the first to stand up and applaud. The hope in her heart now was for the rest of the church to follow suit.

"Many of you have been to Israel. Most likely, you were one of those wide-eyed tourists. Your mission was to snap photos and experience everything there that was connected to the pages of your Bible. Now imagine that you're living in that same land, but..." Pete paused and scanned the room. "...but you're there during the first century.

"Like so many people of that day, you're a typical farmer. You have sandals on your feet and a garment that smells of fresh earth. Ever since you were a little boy following in your father's steps, your job has been to work the land. Year after year you have done this. Now your hands are callused. Your back is strong. Your life is connected to the soil.

"Jesus knew this life as well. In fact, He lives just around the corner next to the carpentry shop His father built years ago. Farmers, fishermen, and builders know Him by name. He's a master craftsman with an unblemished reputation for honesty and hard work. Not only that, but He specializes in fixing broken things.

"While making preparations to plow the fields, you notice the yoke

151

resting in the corner of the barn needs some minor repair. You recall that day long ago when your father taught you how important oxen were to the livelihood of the family.

"'An ill-fitting yoke,' he'd said, pointing to the corral, 'could injure one of those beasts.' You still remember his next words as they echo across the years: 'But a damaged yoke might jeopardize the family's future, perhaps even our lives.'

"Instinctively you decide to take the damaged yoke to Jesus. Because His father and your father were such good friends, the choice is an easy one. Upon your arrival, the Carpenter is quick to greet you at the door. Not only does Jesus remember your name, but He picks up the conversation right where you left off a few months ago. There's just something about this man that never fails to impress you. Not only is He the friendliest person you've ever met, but He's wise—well beyond His years.

"You choose to come here because His work is excellent, maybe even perfect. He understands your predicament and repairs the yoke in short order. Not once has there been an issue in your business dealings with Jesus. As far as you know, no one else has this kind of reputation. You pay Him for the labor and thank Him kindly.

"Just before you leave Jesus says, 'I'd appreciate a good word. Tell the other farmers that my yoke is easy and my burden light.' Then He gives you a firm pat on the back and one final word of encouragement. 'Keep those hands to the plow and don't look back. Cut straight furrows today, and you'll make life easier tomorrow.'

"You leave the Carpenter's shop knowing everything is now ready for the planting season. Over the next several days, you cultivate the fields. Everything happens according to schedule and without incident. As you plow late into the evening, you manage to keep the oxen from falling in a ditch. The furrows are straight, but your work is far from over.

"Next you gather up the medium and large-sized rocks. Piling them in the corners of the field is back-breaking work, but the stone masons will pay you for the effort. A long time ago, your father taught you there's no excuse for wasting good seed on stony ground. 'Feed your family, not the birds,' he instructed.

"Finally, the day of planting arrives. You depart before the sun peeks over the horizon. Your wife and children look upon you expectantly. They understand the importance of this day all too well. You're not just sowing seeds. You're planting the family's future.

"Before entering the field, you step into the barn. Hanging from a rusty spike is an old leather bag filled with kernels of wheat. You reach inside and let them sift across your hand and through your fingers. They feel perfect to the touch. Your farmer's instincts have served you well over the years. That a bumper crop requires hardy seed is common knowledge. You purchased this bag from an Egyptian merchant who passed through your area a few months ago. The seed cost more than usual, but looked husky and full of promise.

"As you step out of the barn and into the dawn, you wonder what the year will bring. Will it rain enough? What about the insects? Will crop disease creep through the land like a silent killer? Your hope is mixed with an equal amount of anxiety and fear.

"Just then you remember the words Jesus spoke over you a few years back. He lifted a finger to the sky one sunny afternoon and said, 'Look at the birds of the air. They neither sow nor reap. God takes care of them. He'll take care of you too.' Those words helped you greatly. Ever since that day, the uncertainty of the future has been a little easier to manage."

Throughout the message, Monica never took her eyes off Pete. She was entranced by the picturesque language he used to craft the story. Today was even better than she remembered from last night. As far as she could tell, he wasn't even using notes. His mind seemed clear and free of the stress of how this sermon would end.

She pictured herself in the story as the simple wife of a humble farmer. She cared for the house and the children while he worked the land. Life may have been harder in terms of survival, but things seemed to move more slowly and much more peacefully back then. *If this doesn't work, Pete and I will move to a farm far away from civilization. If he gets bored, he can preach to the birds like St. Francis of Assisi.* The thought was fun, but she knew he'd never go for farming. She refocused when his words picked up volume and speed.

"This is how you live your life. You're a farmer like your father and his father before him. This land has been passed down for generations. Now you must be a good steward of all that's been given to you.

"Up and down the fields you scatter your seeds. Each one falls to the ground with a hope and a prayer. Some are watered by tears as you remember the year of famine when the crops failed; the faces of friends and family members who lost their lives flash before you. Psalm 126:5 is a verse you think about every day: 'Those who sow in tears will reap with songs of joy.'

"When the bag is empty, you return to your family. Now you wait. The seeds die in the ground. A few days later they resurrect to life and reach for the sun. The soil and rain begin fueling the engine of growth. Each day the promise of plenty grows in your heart.

"You measure the passage of time in seasons rather than seconds. The days drift from spring to summer and into fall. The rains come and go. You watch and you pray.

"In the fullness of time the moment finally arrives. Today the fields are ripe for harvest. As you gaze upon the fields, I want you to wrap all the emotions you now feel into the landscape of Luke 10:2. Hear the words of Jesus to His followers: 'The harvest is plentiful, but the workers are few. Ask the Lord of the harvest, therefore, to send out workers into his harvest field.'

"We know Jesus was referring to people, not merely wheat. He clarified this on another occasion in John 4:35 when He said, 'Do you not say, "Four months more and then the harvest?" I tell you, open your eyes and look at the fields! They are ripe for harvest.'

"Centuries have come and gone since Jesus spoke those words. The times have changed, but the truth of Scripture has not. Today the harvest is larger and riper than ever before. The time for us to connect the dots between first-century Israel and twenty-first-century Ft. Worth has finally arrived. Our city is ready for harvest now.

"Don't you imagine that Jesus felt something deep within His heart when He said, 'but the workers are few'? The question for us this morning and for the ages is simply this. Are you a worker? I know many of you are attenders and listeners, but are you willing to roll up your sleeves and enter the harvest?

"On the day Jesus released His followers to the harvest, He empowered them with supernatural abilities. They travelled 'two by two' and went out as 'sheep among wolves.' They entered every town He prepared to visit and proclaimed that the kingdom of God was near. When the seventy-two went out, Satan fell like lightning from heaven.

"Luke, Chapter 10. It's in the Book!

"That's what I call 'church'—the kind of movement that gathers momentum and becomes an unstoppable force. This is the kind of spiritual reality that your heart yearns to experience. I believe you're fed up with business as usual. You're waiting for someone to lead you on a journey to follow Jesus in the same way the early disciples did.

"You were raised singing the old hymn, 'Wherever He Leads, I'll Go.' Today we need to stop singing about going and just go. Our hymns and preaching don't cause Satan to fall from the sky. Anytime fearless sheep exit the doors of their church to invade the wolves' domain, Satan shudders and enters a tailspin. When we go out, the devil is shot down in flames.

"I'm sure you've seen attack dogs. But I'd wager you've never heard of an attack lamb. A flock of those would be one of the most curious sights on the planet. But that's the genius of Jesus, isn't it? No one expects a lamb to be dangerous. Lambs don't have sharp claws, menacing teeth, or a predator's eyes. They look harmless enough, and the wolves will advance upon them before they sense any personal danger.

"But a kingdom lamb has no rival. He's at the top of the spiritual food chain. You have more power than you could ever imagine. The hour for Green Street Baptist Church to take the battle to the wolves has arrived. For the last several years we've heard them howling, threatening, agitating. I've had enough. Let's go invade their territory.

"How will we do that? I'm glad you asked."

Pete paused for effect, something he picked up subconsciously from Jim Jake. As if on cue, a gentle but nervous laughter drifted across the auditorium.

"As Jesus sent out the seventy-two, so I am sending you out today. For the next month, the doors of our campus will be closed. During this time, we will not conduct worship services here or operate our weekday ministries."

Monica looked around the room. *There it is. He just kissed death on the lips.* The amount of white she noticed in everyone's eyes increased dramatically. Several mouths hung open in disbelief. But no one moved or exited the building. They sat like statues.

"Don't come back until January. All through the month of December, I'm sending you out to discover what God is doing in Ft. Worth. There are nearly one hundred different types of ministries in our city doing some serious damage to the packs of wolves invading our land. I want you to participate in one of these ministries for the next month. Don't come here. Go there.

"I know the idea sounds crazy, but God has spoken to my heart. I'm asking you to follow me on this. Let's go and experience what other ministries are doing to reach the lost people in this city.

"We'll have a great celebration when we come back in January. I believe the party will be like the one Jesus had when the seventy-two returned. We'll share the stories of what we've seen and how we were inspired. We'll talk about changed lives and dream about the future. After this experience, we won't have difficulty figuring out what to do next to reach this city for Christ. God will reveal the plan to us as we go out."

At that moment, the back door of the church swung open with a loud creak. The president of the Baptist Seminary in Ft. Worth entered the building. A large crowd of students followed suit. They soon filled the entire center aisle.

A parade had entered the building.

Chapter 27

Also in Judah the hand of God was on the people to give them
unity of mind to carry out what the king and his officials had ordered,
following the word of the LORD (2 Chronicles 30:12, NIV).

Dr. Pat Sheets had been the president of the Baptist Seminary in Ft. Worth for many decades. He was the one who recommended Pete to the pastoral search committee of Green Street over five years earlier. He was a first-class scholar and a personal advocate for church renewal. He required each seminary student to be involved in a local ministry. In addition, they had to complete at least one international mission trip before they graduated. There wasn't a more respected man among the religious leaders in the city.

Though Dr. Sheets and Pete were mutual friends, Markus was very close to the president. He attended many of the social events sponsored by the alumni. Dr. Sheets and Markus often crossed paths while speaking at church conferences and state conventions. A few nights ago, Markus called him from the Buffalo Hotel with an unusual request.

"I think that's a brilliant idea," Dr. Sheets had said. "I'll bring seventy-two of my students struggling though their first year of Greek and promise them extra credit. They'll jump at the opportunity."

The seminary students made their way into the pews and mixed among the longtime members of Green Street Baptist Church. The stunned look on the frozen statues melted away. Faces lit up all around the auditorium. There were handshakes, hugs, even a few holy kisses.

Dr. Sheets, however, continued walking to the platform. As he passed the pew where his old friend was sitting, the president slapped Markus on the back. Markus stood, and the two men embraced.

"Thank you, Dr. Sheets. How can I ever return the favor?"

"My dear son, you should never ask a man like me that sort of question. I'll give you a list when this is all over."

Monica observed the two men behaving like brothers at a family reunion. All across the room people chatted up a storm. The tension of a few moments earlier had vanished completely. Most forgot they were still in the middle of a church service.

She caught a glimpse of Pete descending from the platform to greet the president. He looked like an overexcited schoolboy about to embark on a daylong field trip. Suddenly the president grabbed Pete's hand and pulled him over to where she was sitting on the front row.

"Monica," Dr. Sheets said, "stand up. I want to bless you both."

All eyes turned to focus on what was happening. The president started praying out loud. There was no microphone to capture the moment, so everyone in attendance compensated by growing very quiet. His prayer could be heard throughout the sanctuary.

"Lord God in heaven, this man and woman were chosen by You for such a time as this. You've called them to lead these people to a land that is fairer than day. Encourage them, Father. Strengthen them. Grant them favor in this house. Allow the hearts of the people who sit in these pews to open up and receive every word that Pete has spoken.

"Bind the work of the enemy in their lives. Tear down the strongholds that have been erected against them. Shield them with the full armor of God. Shelter them under the shadow of your wings. Send your angels to lift them up on high. Stretch out their tent pegs, dear Father. Today the victory belongs to You. Let it count for Your glory. Amen.

"And all God's people said…"

"Amen!" came the reply.

Dr. Sheets reminded Monica of the kind of pastors she knew as a little girl. They seemed to arrive on the scene like ancient prophets emerging from the pages of the Old Testament. She felt a little shy and a lot more reverent when men of such stature were around. As Dr. Sheets walked to the pulpit, she thought of Elijah and Elisha, men who must have radiated a similar air of divine mystery.

"Do you sense the atmosphere in this building?" the president asked.

The students were the first to respond. "Yes!" The members of Green Street followed with a wide range of replies. "Hallelujah!" "Amen!" "Thank you for coming!"

"Oh, you're welcome. Who'd want to miss this? Personally, I feel like I just entered the upper room on the day of Pentecost. I sense a fire from heaven that's ready to fall at any moment. Don't make the mistake of quenching the Spirit. You don't want to stand before God one day and give an account of why you buried your talent in the sand. Those days of producing wood, hay, and stubble are long behind you. Now you're ready to bear kingdom fruit—fruit that lasts.

"Seventy-two of my students came with me today. I believe you've already found that number to be significant this morning. I wanted them to see what's happening here. These next few weeks in the life of your church will be the best education I could ever give them. This experience will form a spiritual marker in their own lives, and even more so when they begin leading churches for themselves.

"So let me say thank you as we get to the heart of the matter. I'm here at the request of your pastor and Markus to help launch a movement. I need you to understand how significant this day really is. The movement we're starting today has the potential of reaching far beyond these walls. In every church where these students may find themselves serving after their graduation, the story of this day will be retold with great enthusiasm. What's happening here will even be shared on the mission field in faraway lands.

"You'll be salt and light for these young students of mine. In return, they'll be your guides as you enter the harvest. They've been serving all across this city in some pretty exciting ministries. They're under my academic commission to study innovative ways to reach every culture for Christ, whether in the neighborhoods of Ft. Worth or the slums of a third-world country. In the coming days, they'll expose you to fresh ideas and cutting-edge strategies that will shape this church's future.

"You'll have the opportunity to bless these students with your sage advice and by the example of your faithful service. They want you to show them what life will look like when they enter vocational ministry for themselves. You need them to help you process how this world is changing.

"Let them introduce you to the latest tools developed by the godliest minds—tools that are effective at penetrating our present darkness. God is doing something new on the outside of these walls here at Green Street. Don't let the light from these stained glass windows blind you to this reality. I challenge you to go and see His activity for yourselves.

"Pastor Pete and Markus have been working tirelessly to build a bridge across the troubled waters. Let me tell you that you can safely cross over. You won't perish. The Hebrew children didn't perish in the Red Sea after they left Egypt. The men who carried the Ark of the

Covenant didn't perish when they stepped into the Jordan River at flood stage. David didn't perish when he entered no-man's-land to fight Goliath. And Peter didn't perish in the Sea of Galilee when he jumped out of the boat to walk with Jesus.

"Those afraid of perishing look dead already. Green Street Baptist Church, I say this under the authority of God, death is not your future. Your inheritance is the abundant life, right here and right now. Lay hold of it. Grab a piece of your inheritance now. It's your holy birthright. And whatever you do, don't be afraid to enter the harvest.

"Be of good cheer. Sometimes the best course of action is to face death toe-to-toe and give him a sloppy wet kiss. The last time I checked, the Bible still maintains that death has been defeated. The grave has been swallowed up in victory. The sting has been removed. The tomb is still empty.

"As your former pastor would say, '1 Corinthians, Chapter 15. It's in the Book!'"

Kate Shoemaker was the first to lead the crowd's response: "Amen."

"Thank you for that, Sister. By the way, Jim Jake and I were students together at Baylor sometime after the lightbulb was invented. I called him up last night in Florida, and he wanted me to tell you how proud he is of what you're about to do. In fact, he shouted 'hallelujah' so loud the dog started barking. I heard Frances in the background saying, 'Settle down.' I couldn't tell if she was talking to Jim or the dog. Whichever it was, both obeyed."

Laughter spilled across the room.

"Let me warn you that if you don't participate in this new endeavor, I'll give your phone number to sweet Frances. If you cause problems, she'll get your address. The church office has your records. You can run, but you can't hide.

"I wish that was in the Book too!"

Monica snickered along with the other ladies. The brief time she spent with Frances on the phone before arriving at the Jan-Kay Ranch was enough to make her appreciate the humor. Frances could be fiercely determined. She didn't always get her way immediately, but she did over time. *I was like that once. Why did I ever start hiding?*

"All joking aside," Dr. Sheets continued, "my students are prepared to gather your contact information. I've placed them strategically all over this room. Listen carefully as they share what God is doing through their ministries. Connect with one or more and become partners for the month of December.

"And now I'm done. Class dismissed. Let me conclude with a prayer. Then link up and get to work."

During the president's prayer, about two dozen people walked forward. Since there wasn't an invitation extended for people to respond, Monica was a little concerned as to what their reason might be for coming down the aisle. Pete left her side and moved swiftly to intervene. Sensing a need to help, she quickly followed.

The men and women who stepped forward didn't know each other for the most part. They'd only recently started attending Green Street Baptist Church, but each expressed the same request.

"May we join your church? This is the most exciting thing we've ever seen happen in a worship service. We want to participate in what God is doing here. Send us out too!"

Chapter 28

This command I entrust to you, Timothy, my son,
in accordance with the prophecies previously made concerning you,
that by them you fight the good fight (1 Timothy 1:18, NASB).

Gary Lovejoy met Ashley Waters and her fiancé, Wesley, at a local coffee shop. When Ashley suggested meeting him there in order to describe her ministry in greater detail, Gary was a little bothered initially. His opinion of these establishments was no secret to his friends. "What sensible man would pay five dollars for a cup of coffee? I remember when coffee cost a dime, and you'd leave the whole quarter for a tip."

Nevertheless, Gary wasn't about to invoke the ire of Dr. Sheets, not to mention Pete and their crazy consultant, Markus. A man had to watch his step around another man, especially when he was connected to seminary presidents and people with dangerous animals.

Gary didn't understand the menu displayed on the wall behind the counter. He thought about ordering black coffee in a mug, but he didn't want Ashley or Wesley to think he was an old stick in the mud. His sweet wife, Gail, who passed away many years earlier, sometimes teased him as such. If she were here, she'd want him to foot the whole bill for the engaged couple. He'd already planned to do that before he saw the prices. With Ashley and Wesley standing behind him, he scanned the menu for something that sounded daring.

The barista interrupted his concentration. "What can I get you, Mr. Lovejoy?"

The look of surprise on Gary's face was immediate. He was about to reply, "I'll have what I always have," then order something at random. Now he was completely flummoxed and didn't know what to say.

Sensing the confusion, the barista rescued him from the moment. "I know you don't recognize me. I was a just a boy when you taught Sunday school for all the little third-graders. You used to sit us down in a circle on the floor and tell us about Moses and about Daniel in the lion's den. The first time I remembered hearing about the plan of salvation was in your class. I made a profession of faith that year."

Gary stood speechless, although grinning from ear to ear.

Ashley said, "It's good to see you today, Bender."

For Gary, another layer of surprise was added to the occasion. "You three know each other?"

Wesley spoke out this time. "We all belong to the same house church network."

"Let me get you something on the house. I'm about to take a break. I'd love to hang out with you, if you don't mind me crashing your party."

"I crash and hang all the time," said Gary.

"I'll take that as a yes." Bender smiled. "What would you like to try?"

Gary cleared his throat and straightened his posture. "Give me your hazelnut macchiato."

"Super! And what can I get for you lovebirds?"

"Just give us two cups of your medium roast. And don't leave any room for cream," Ashley responded.

Who Killed My Church?

Gary began looking for a suitable place to sit near the back of the room. Ashley invited the group to land on the couch near the entryway just as it became available. She moved so quickly there was no time to discuss the options. A soft look of victory beamed from her eyes as she claimed the prize.

Gary spotted a lounge chair positioned catty-corner to the couch that looked comfortable enough. He couldn't imagine a conversation about ministry among four people seated on the same couch—not while each held a cup of coffee in their hands.

"Here you go—three medium-roast coffees and one hazelnut macchiato for the man who told me about Jesus. Break it up, lovebirds." Bender plopped down between Ashley and Wesley, forcing them to move over abruptly. Ashley giggled; Wesley looked annoyed.

Gary was still feeling flattered by Bender's earlier revelation. Then he noticed the cup of coffee, which looked like a work of art. The fact that the masterpiece didn't cost a dime thrilled him even more.

"I gave you the barista's special touch. Try it, and you'll never drink grocery-store coffee again. The beans were handpicked and sorted by our fair-trade partners in Ecuador. Our franchisees run a school for their children. I love selling coffee with a cause. Our house church network sent short-term missionaries to their village last summer. I went too. I sat in a circle with a translator and about thirty kids. Every day I told them stories about Moses and Daniel. Many of the children made professions of faith."

Gary felt his throat tightening with emotions. He took a sip of the Ecuadorian concoction, and his eyes widened. "This is really good. No... That's a wonderful story, I mean. You'll have to pardon me for a moment. I'm a little outside my element this afternoon."

"Bender," Ashley said, "before you go back to work, why don't you tell Mr. Lovejoy about our church's mission?"

"Please call me Gary."

"That won't be easy. We called you Brother Lovejoy when I was a kid." Bender smiled. "Everything was all rather formal back in the day. I used to plead with my father not to make me wear that tie every Sunday morning. 'Stand still, son,' he'd say. 'It's not a noose around your neck. Preacher says we should dress our best for God.'"

Wesley laughed. "Your dad said that too? Mine made me shine my shoes with him every Saturday night."

"Please!" Ashley interjected. "Neither of you had to put on a dress and leggings, then stand for an hour in front of a mirror while your mother fixed your hair."

"Gary…" Bender paused momentarily. "Our generation appreciates all we were given by the traditional church. But as we grew older, we started wondering how to attract our friends to the established churches we were raised in. Churches like Green Street didn't appeal to our lost friends. Excuse me for being so blunt, but they no longer appealed to us either. We prefer casual environments and outside-the-box ministries.

"Our house church network meets all over the city of Ft. Worth. Some groups meet in homes. A few even meet here in the coffee shop throughout the week. We call these small gatherings of Christ-followers 'tribes.' There were twelve tribes in Israel. Jesus had twelve disciples. We patterned ourselves after this model because we believe God created us to be communal. Our vision is to multiply the number of tribes until we penetrate every neighborhood in our city. On the weekend, every tribe gathers in a central location for worship, celebration, vision-casting, and to hear testimonies about what God is doing among us."

Gary finished the remaining bit of coffee. "I've never heard of anything like that before. I've never tasted coffee like this either. How do I join you for the month of December?"

"Wesley and I invite you to visit our tribe that meets tomorrow evening," Ashley responded. "There are over a hundred tribes located all over our city right now. Ours is about to divide into two groups. Once we get over twelve, we start making plans to divide and continue the cycle of multiplication."

"The concept is really simple," Wesley added. "We stick to our strategy and use our resources to reach more people. Because we don't have any debt or expensive buildings to maintain, we're able to maximize our opportunities to be the hands and feet of Jesus. We rent space when we come together on the weekend. We like to say we're portable rather than permanent. We're pilgrims and strangers on a journey with God. Like we were taught when we were little, we're just passing through this world. We want to make a difference wherever we go."

"Gary, I have to get back to work," Bender said. "Do you trust me?"

"You've earned it, son."

"Great. Then let me create my signature drink for you. My treat and for the road. By the way, I respect what your church is doing. I've been reading the blog. I've never heard of anything like that before either. I believe God will honor your willingness to take risks and start something new."

Ashley and Wesley departed as Bender created another specialty coffee for Gary. The lounge chair was starting to grow on him, and he would have fallen asleep had he not had the caffeine in his veins. Instead he began meditating on the conversation. Ashley's spunky nature reminded him so much of his late wife. How he missed that woman! Gail would have loved the coffee shop and a tribe meeting in their living room. Dr. Sheets was right. The world had changed in what seemed like the blink of an eye.

"One for the road, my friend." Bender handed the coffee to Gary. "One last thing. Say hello to Markus for me."

"You know Markus?"

"I'm the leader of this house church network. After I graduated from the seminary here in Ft. Worth, Markus was my coach. He showed me how to start a church in this coffee shop. I own the shop now, but it mostly runs itself. I spend the majority of my time meeting people here and plugging them into one of our tribes."

Bender peered deeply into Gary's eyes. "Amazing what a free cup of coffee can do for the kingdom."

"You're a preacher!" Gary exclaimed.

"Your generation might call me that. I see my vocation a little differently. I'm just a barista by the well, offering living water to thirsty souls. And by the way, thank you for leading me to Christ when I was a little boy. If not for you, I wouldn't be here today."

The emotions of the moment overpowered Gary's ability to respond. He sat for a moment in silence. There were so many kids over the years that had passed through his Sunday school class. He seldom knew where they ended up in life. He was a little embarrassed that he didn't recognize the name Bender.

"Did they call you Bender back then?"

"No. Markus started calling me that. When I first came up with the idea for my church plant, people told me my idea would never work. They said I'd have to bend all the rules of how churches operate. I was rather discouraged one day and decided to relay these comments to Markus."

Bender smiled at Gary. "So I did, and here's what he said in response. 'Jesus changed Simon Bar-Jonah's name to Peter to let him know he'd be a rock. Shawn Davis, I'm changing your name to Bender. You'll bend all the rules of men to follow the heart of God.'

"I was commissioned by Markus that day. The day that followed saw the birth of a new church. I've been Bender ever since."

"That's an amazing story," Gary said.

"Not half as amazing as the one people will tell when Green Street rises from the valley of dry bones. What is it Pastor Jake used to say?"

"Ezekiel, Chapter 37. It's in the Book!"

Chapter 29

To the weak I became weak, to win the weak.
I have become all things to all men
so that by all possible means I might save some
(1 Corinthians 9:22, NIV).

Everyone at Green Street was surprised when their church organist decided to attend a church called Heaven's Angels. Immediately Kate Shoemaker rose to the very top of the Green Street Baptist Church's official prayer chain. The news travelled like lightening.

Fanny Mae, who sent up the red flag to begin with, called her on the phone. "Dear, whatever gave you the crazy notion to join the Hell's Angels?"

"They're not Hell's Angels. I declare, Fanny Mae! They're *Heaven's* Angels!"

"Well, they looked like Hell's Angels to me last Sunday."

Kate smiled, imagining the look on Fanny Mae's face about now. "I felt sorry for them. No one went to hear them talk about their ministry. At first, I was being polite. You know, like Jesus with the lepers and the demon-possessed."

"But He was Jesus," Fanny Mae argued. "You're not supposed to hop on the back of a motorcycle and ride to a pool-hall church with your arms wrapped around some scary man. Have you lost your mind?"

"First of all, they don't call them motorcycles any more. They ride bikes, or 'hogs,' now."

"Well, there you have it. Jesus cast demons into hogs and they ran over a cliff. I don't want to hear about you lying in a ditch somewhere because you fell off the back of a hog. You're not really serious about this, are you?"

"Yes, I am. They invited me to play the keyboard in their band this Sunday. I'm meeting with them tomorrow to get the music. And yes, I guess I have lost my mind. I'd like you to lose yours too, and come with me."

"You're plumb nuts. My daddy would have locked me in a tower if he ever found me in a pool hall."

"Your daddy was trying to keep you from getting pregnant before you got married. I think today you'll remind everyone in the pool hall of their grandmother."

"Grandmother?"

"Yes. One of their members showed me a tattoo of his granny. She led him to Jesus when he was a little boy. 'Every time I see her face,' he said softly, 'I thank God for my salvation.' Maybe they'll want to have us tattooed somewhere."

"Somewhere? Oh, sweet Jesus, she's serious!"

"I'm going, Fanny Mae, and the prayer chain can't stop me. I must obey God rather than men. That's in the Book somewhere."

"If I can't talk you out of it, it's my duty to bear my cross and suffer with you. If we die, we'll die a martyr's death. That's the mercy of it."

"Don't be a martyr, Fanny Mae. That's so boring. Besides, we need to go shopping to fit in."

"Shopping?"

"I asked them where they bought their clothes and leather jackets. It's south of town at a place called The Hog Barn."

"You want me to dress like a pig in a blanket?"

"Girl, where's your sense of adventure? I'll pick you up in five minutes."

Chapter 30

The Word became flesh and made his dwelling among us.
We have seen his glory, the glory of the One and Only,
who came from the Father, full of grace and truth (John 1:14 NIV).

Four bikes showed up at Kate Shoemaker's house the next evening. The sleepy neighborhood shifted into high alert. Several 911 calls were logged with the dispatch operator. The patrol cars simply drove by, took note of the license plates, and departed without a scene. The riders of Heaven's Angels maintained a most-favored-citizen status with the Ft. Worth police department.

Kate was excited. Fanny Mae was excited too, but in a jumpy sort of way. She peaked through the curtains from the first moment she heard the sounds of rumbling in the distance. Then came a knock at the door.

"Oh, sweet Jesus, they're here."

Kate opened the door. A look of pleasant surprise emerged from the four men's eyes. The lady they met at Green Street on Sunday morning had undergone quite a metamorphosis. She sported a pink tee-shirt with a stunning portrait of Marilyn Monroe. An iridescent halo floated mystically over the movie star's head.

"I believe I saw that shirt at The Hog Barn," one of the men observed.

"Nice," said another.

Kate turned on her southern charm. "Oh, my! I haven't enjoyed the company of so many men in years. Do come in and make yourselves at home."

Fanny Mae sniggered nervously. She wore a pair of stonewashed jeans with a black tee-shirt featuring a vivid spider-web pattern that connected from front to back. The outfit represented a major victory for Kate, who offered Fanny Mae a little fashion advice at The Hog Barn.

"Honey, that silver web matches your beautiful hair. Your blue eyes even sparkle."

Earlier, Fanny Mae had complained that all the merchandise looked like "Goodwill rejects." But after Kate's flattering remark, her mood changed abruptly. A shirt with the portrait of a young Elvis Presley went to the register as well.

Everyone found a seat in the living room. Kate surmised that the man referred to as Nails was the alpha male. He started the conversation.

"Ladies, our spirits are fueled to know you'll be joining us over the next several weeks. Let me ask if you have any questions before we get started."

"Oh, yes," Kate bubbled. "Please tell me your names."

Nails said, "Everyone calls me Bob at the office. I'm the president of an IT company during the week. At our church and on the streets, people call me Nails."

"Who gave you that nickname?" Fanny Mae asked.

Something in Fanny Mae's tone didn't set well with Kate. Her eyes beamed with suspicion until she was certain Fanny Mae noticed. Nails answered the question, well aware of the nonverbal sparks flying between the two ladies.

"We're a unique church with a focused vision. Our calling is to reach a particular niche in society that others fear to engage. Most of the riders you see on the road during the week are average men. They blow off steam by cruising on their bikes during the weekend. Most have little interest in the kind of church that doesn't speak their language. That kind of church may have relevance for women and children, but not real men. At least, that's what they believe.

"My job is to debunk their myths about Christianity. Our nicknames are evangelistic tools we use to steer men into spiritual conversations. I became a Christian one evening while reading the story of the crucifixion of Jesus. I realized my sin drove those nails through His perfect hands and feet. On the cross, He took my place. He died my death.

"This reality led me to become a Christ-follower. I was born the first time as Bob. I was reborn as Nails." He stopped temporarily to let the words find their mark. Kate and Fannie Mae were riveted. His testimony often had the same effect whenever he shared it.

"My name reminds me of how much God loves this world," Nails continued. "Each one of us here has a similar testimony. In fact, I'll let them tell their own stories."

"I'm called Bleeder," another one of the men chimed in. "I'm the operations manager at one of the malls here in Ft. Worth. When people ask me where I got my name, I share with them how Jesus shed His blood for me, and how my old nature died with Him. Like Galatians 2:20 says, 'I have been crucified with Christ. I no longer live, but Christ lives in me.' Most people are shocked because they expect to hear something more gruesome, but it's a great launching pad for sharing my faith. By day, I'm simply known as Mike, the manager."

"My name is Rick," the next man said. "I drive a truck for a living. People at the church refer to me as Hater. Jesus said that unless we hate our father and mother, our brother and sister, even our own lives, we can't be one of His disciples. I get a kick out of explaining to people what that means. When you talk to another man who doesn't know Christ and help him understand that following Jesus is the highest priority, he gets shook up a little."

"Your church seems to have a masculine quality," Kate said.

"You're very observant," Nails affirmed. "Most churches have more women who get involved than men. In many houses of worship, everything from the music to the way the ministries are promoted appeals predominantly to women. We don't have a problem with that in other places, but we're driven to reach the hearts of men. When a man sees lilies on church bulletins and hears music that makes God sound like a girlfriend, he checks out. Men want to conquer, be challenged, and change the world.

"We have a fair number of women who drag their husbands to our church. They're fed up with attending churches where their husbands don't get involved. A godly woman desires her man to be the spiritual leader of the home. We teach men how to embrace their masculinity as the design of God and use their gender for God's glory."

"If you can reach the man of the home," Hater added, "you'll reach his wife and children too. It's a fact of life. When men are motivated, things happen that normally don't happen. God created us that way. We embrace this reality unapologetically. We tell men, 'You don't have to turn in your man-card to follow Christ.'"

The last of the four men spoke up then. "I'm called Kittens."

Kittens had the deepest voice among the four and was very large. His size was somewhat intimidating, which was a good thing, because Fanny Mae nearly embarrassed herself by snorting out loud. The way the word "Kittens" resonated in his throat gave him an air of authority. With all the talk of masculinity, the church secretary could hardly wait to hear his story.

"Kittens? Oh my, what a lovely name," Kate teased.

"Originally I wanted to be called cat-o'-nine-tails. When I first read the story of the crucifixion after my wife filed for divorce, I was undone by the scourging Jesus endured. His suffering was much worse than mine. I imagined the devil bearing down on the Son of God full throttle with murder in his eyes. Jesus took a beating for my sins like a shock absorber on a trail bike. By His stripes, I was healed. That's what the prophet Isaiah said.

"Then Bleeder came up with the brilliant idea to use Kittens as an abbreviation for cat-o'-nine-tails. At first I was hacked off when the name stuck, but then I discovered the name was a powerful witnessing tool. After explaining what my name means, I hit men with the hard questions: How brave are you? Would you take forty lashes from a cat-o'-nine-tails for something you believe in?

"Most look at me like I'm crazy," he continued. "And maybe I am. But many of the prophets were pretty crazy too. Ezekiel cooked his food over dung. John the Baptist wore camel hair and ate locusts in the desert. Isaiah walked through the streets naked. Pardon me for referencing that, ladies, but we have a saying that our men live by: 'It's okay to be odd for God.'"

"Yes, I've read those stories in the Bible," Kate commented. "They always made me wonder what God was trying to get across. We never talk about that earthy stuff at Green Street. Topics like that never seem appropriate."

Fanny Mae wanted to say something, but she struggled to find a way to jump into the conversation. Finally she spoke. "You do keep your clothes on in church, don't you?"

Kittens roared with laughter.

The shock on Kate's face appeared instantly. "Fanny! What's gotten into you?"

Fanny Mae looked wounded but defended her question nonetheless.

"I wasn't the one who brought up that incident about Isaiah. You hear all the time about people who bring rattlesnakes to church. Some get bitten and die. I just wanted to know how 'odd for God' they plan to be next Sunday."

"Not that odd," Hater assured her. "Believe us or not, we do have our dignity to maintain."

Kittens' face had turned bright red by the time he stopped laughing. "You're right on, Hater. We want to reach men, not run them off."

"Here's the basic idea behind what we do," Nails added. "We use the word 'incarnational' to describe our ministry philosophy. During the Incarnation, Jesus became flesh. He wore the very skin He created. He became like us so we could be like Him.

"The early disciples did the same thing. Paul became weak to reach the weak. Timothy was circumcised like a Jew to win the Jews. Peter ate things that were previously forbidden under the law just to reach those outside of the law. Christians are called to become all things to all people to reach some for Christ. On the outside, we're like the people we're trying to capture for Christ.

"On the inside, we draw the line in the same place you do. We won't bless sin. Our mission field is buried underneath layers of depravity. Everybody sees it. 'Witness as a dying man to dying men,' we say. Heaven's Angels are intentional about pursuing the lost."

Kate recalled Markus using the word intentional at the Jan-Kay Ranch. "Growing churches are intentional about being attractional," he'd said. Ideas once confusing were now connecting. She felt as though someone had walked into a dark room inside her mind and flipped on the light switch.

"I think that's wonderful," she exclaimed. "Jesus was a friend of sinners."

"Exactly," Nails continued. "If we entered the harvest wearing a suit and tie and hauling a big black-leather Bible, the men we're trying to reach would simply ride away. That's why we're so intentional about embracing an incarnational lifestyle."

"I rarely think about the Incarnation of Christ except at Christmas," Kate confessed. "Becoming like those you're trying to reach makes sense. If Jesus hadn't done that for us, we'd still be traveling to the temple every year to offer a sacrifice for our sins."

Hater sat patiently waiting for an opportunity to turn the conversation. He seized the moment. "I play the drums in our band. We'd be honored to have you fire up the keyboard for us. I brought the music with me. Sometimes Dr. Sheets shows up unannounced and plays the saxophone. Not only is the seminary president a man of God, but he's one fine improvisational musician too."

Fanny Mae's eyes widened. "Dr. Sheets attends your church?"

"On occasion, but he's a busy man. Not only did he recommend Pete to be your pastor, but he also encouraged us to start a church in the pool hall. He may have been trained in the old school ways, but he leads a school that isn't afraid of teaching new methodologies."

"Doesn't that sound exciting, Fanny Mae?" Kate exclaimed. "I'd love to break free from the organ for a few Sundays. Not long ago, I refused to play anything outside the Baptist hymnal. The last several weeks have opened my eyes. Green Street Baptist Church hasn't been very incarnational over the last decade."

"Sister," Hater replied, "with that shirt on your back and a keyboard under your fingers, you'll rock the pool hall for Jesus."

"Like Elvis?" Fanny Mae came to life again.

"That might work in Vegas," Kittens burst out with laughter, "but not Cowtown. As I said earlier, we want to reach men, not run them off."

Chapter 31

It has always been my ambition to preach the gospel where Christ
was not known, so that I would not be building on someone else's
foundation (Romans 15:20, NIV).

Frank Sanders and Buck Simpson sat at a stoplight in a construction
zone waiting to make a left-hand turn. Traffic was brutal, and they were
already late.

"I wish they'd finish working on this intersection," Frank commented.

"They'll just finish here and start working on the one down the road.
Roll with the punches, my friend."

"You're a thoughtful kind of guy, Buck. Or should I call you Mr.
Imaginator now?" Frank took one hand off the steering wheel and
looked at his friend anxiously. "I'm worried that people might leave
Green Street after they participate in some of these new ministries we're
investigating."

"I've thought about that too."

"Care to tell me your thoughts about it?"

Buck watched the light turn green. Frank was still looking his
direction when several cars began honking from the rear. "I think you

should pay attention to the task at hand and drive the car, Frank."

"Sorry." Frank joined the flow of traffic. "But aren't you concerned about what might happen?"

"Many people left when Pastor Jake retired," Buck said. "Others left when Pete tried to fill his shoes. Church members are a strange breed of creature. They're kind of like Ripper. They do what they want."

"That's my point. The church could crash come January if our people don't come back."

Buck hesitated before answering. "They'll come back."

"What makes you so certain?"

"Human nature."

Frank frowned but resisted the temptation to take his eyes off the road to look at his friend. "Okay, you'll have to explain that one to me."

"Curiosity will draw them back. But we'll need more than that to sustain our church over the long term. The only thing that will cause them to stay is ownership. People buy into what they believe. If we figure out how to create that, the majority of our problems will go away."

Frank pulled his car into the driveway. Jessica Sanchez stood on the front porch of a small duplex but moved swiftly to greet them as they exited the car.

"I'm so thrilled you could make it," she said excitedly. "Our lead pastor will join us in a few minutes. This is going to be so much fun!"

Jessica served crumb cakes and hot lattes for her guests. Frank enjoyed the first crumb cake so much that he grabbed a second. Buck envied his friend, but restrained himself from eating another—doctor's orders.

Not long after, Stuart Brown, pastor of Crossroads Mall Church, knocked on the door. Jessica startled her guests by how quickly she jumped to her feet. They were equally amazed, if not a little envious, over how she flew across the room to answer the door. No one and nothing moved that fast at Green Street, and hadn't in a very long time.

"This is so exciting!" The lilt in her voice had a soothing effect on Buck and Frank. "Stuart, these are the men I was telling you about from Green Street Baptist Church. They've been commissioned to explore our ministry for innovative ideas. They want us to help revitalize their church."

"The pleasure is all mine, gentlemen." Stuart gave each a firm handshake. "The word of what you're doing is travelling through the grapevine. The entire ministry community of Ft. Worth is listening in."

"Seriously?" Frank grew a little self-conscious over this latest revelation, causing him to look down momentarily. That's when he caught sight of his shirt. Unfortunately, a few crumbs from Jessica's cake hadn't made the journey to his mouth.

"Yes," Stuart graciously pretended to be unaware of Frank's distress. "If only half of what I'm hearing is true, I can't wait to get involved. Your pastor has some moxie. He should write a book after all this is over. I'll be honored to share this adventure with you two guys."

"Thank you." Frank casually brushed a few crumbs from his shirt. He hoped no one noticed or really cared.

"I have a question," Buck came to the rescue. "I remember the first time I heard that a new church was meeting in the Crossroads Mall. The novelty intrigued me. Do you have difficulty conducting services in a secular environment?"

Jessica jumped at the question before Stuart had a chance to respond. "Not at all. People are using secular sites in cities everywhere." She seemed to catch herself then, and her cheeks flamed. "Sorry, Stuart. I think that question was meant for you."

The pastor smiled. "That's what I like about Jessica. She's the best children's minister on the planet. Her enthusiasm is contagious. She's often the spark that ignites a fire under the feet of our volunteers.

Everyone lights up when she's around."

Jessica blushed again, but not for long.

"The other staff members and I call her 'Sparky Girl,'" Stuart explained. "When we pray about launching a new initiative, someone usually says, 'Let Sparky Girl lead it.' People will participate just for the fun of being around her."

"If you can't get excited about what God promises to do," Jessica added, "why bother? Even the hard things are fun when you mix a little joy into the recipe. Like those crumb cakes, right, Frank?"

Frank was about to take the first bite out of his third crumb cake when Jessica teased him. He immediately turned red over his obvious lack of restraint. Whether to put the cake down or act like he wasn't addled posed something of a mystery.

Buck hooted and poked his friend in the ribs. "My dear Sparky Girl, I think Frank will do anything you ask as long as you feed him first."

Frank swallowed hard. "I'm sorry, but these are delicious."

"The quickest way to a volunteer's heart is through his stomach," Jessica responded playfully.

"Gentlemen," Stuart said with a grin, "let me answer your question. Launching churches in secular environments started long before any of us were born. During the nineteenth century in London, Charles Haddon Spurgeon conducted church services at the Surrey Gardens Music Hall. It was unconventional in his day too, but thousands were saved as a result. Most biographers call Spurgeon 'the prince of preachers.' While his sermons were incredible, the fact that he didn't allow old traditions to stifle innovation and imagination made him more effective. Crossroads is the same."

Buck thought about the Cheyenne Dog Warriors and the sacred arrows. He wanted to add his own story to what Stuart was saying, but something kept him from interrupting. The secret cry of the Imaginators would have to wait for a more appropriate occasion.

"Some people come to Crossroads for the novelty of where we're located," Stuart continued. "Others will come because our church feels like a non-threatening environment. But people stay when they get plugged in and feel connected to one of our ministries."

"And there are a number of those ministries," Jessica added. "We enlist volunteers to set up the band, sound system, lights, and nursery every Sunday. We have greeters, small group leaders, and truck drivers. There are teams of people who develop our social media presence, manage follow-up with visitors, and the list goes on.

"I personally led the team that developed a downloadable app. The app facilitates our volunteer process by allowing members to discover opportunities, sign up, and serve the bride of Christ. It's simple, but it works."

"It really does," Stuart affirmed. "Sparky Girl reduced the complexity of recruiting volunteers and doubled the number of hands and feet in the harvest. Because we don't have a permanent facility, we need three times the number of volunteers just to get Sunday morning off the launching pad.

"The upside is that our members don't think of church in terms of real estate. We don't ask people to come to church. We ask them to come *be* the church. The church isn't a building, a location, or even a time when our people meet. If the theater manager kicked us out of the mall tomorrow, our church would still exist. *We* are the church, whenever and wherever we meet.

"This is a key issue within Christianity. *Being* the church and *going* to church represent two radically different philosophies of ministry. People who go to church have an audience mentality. They want to be served and entertained, and then critique whether the sermon scratched their personal itch. If they're not released before the restaurants get crowded, they murmur like the Old Testament Israelites.

"We're different. We're not looking to build a fan club of Crossroads Mall Church. We want to produce a different kind of Christian—not *fans* but *followers* of Jesus Christ.

"Do you have any questions?" Stuart concluded.

Buck thought for a moment then asked the first and most obvious question that came to mind. "So how do we get involved during the month of December?"

"How would you like to give your testimony this Sunday?"

Buck grew pale. Frank hooted this time. Then he poked his friend in the ribs.

"That's payback," Frank said gleefully. "I'll answer that question for Buck. Sure, he'll do it."

"Great!" Stuart nearly shouted in approval. "I heard from Markus what you did with those sacred arrows."

"You know Markus?" Buck now appeared both pale and surprised.

"Yes, I read his blog. I've been following the amazing things God's doing in your church. Your story inspired me so much that I asked Jessica if I could meet you in person. Not only that, but I stole your idea. After you finish your testimony, I'm going to pass out a few hundred arrows this Sunday morning."

He grinned. "Now, would you please let me hear that secret shout of the Imaginators? I hear it's pretty inspiring."

Buck hesitated for a brief moment and then obliged.

"Nice," Sparky Girl said. "That will inspire people more than my rum crumb cake."

"There's rum in your crumb cake?" Frank asked, feeling his eyes widen.

"No." Jessica chuckled in delight. "I just said that because I know you're a Baptist."

Chapter 32

He who receives a prophet in the name of a prophet shall receive a prophet's reward; and he who receives a righteous man in the name of a righteous man shall receive a righteous man's reward (Matthew 10:41, NASB).

"I made other plans today, Markus. Where do you want to take us?"

Markus grinned at Pete. "It's a surprise. Besides, I just engineered a month-long vacation for you. You owe me."

"He doesn't like surprises," Monica protested. "As for me, serendipity is my middle name."

"Outstanding. Make Pete reschedule and come with us."

"You two are having this discussion like I'm not even in the room."

Markus and Monica exchanged conspiratorial smiles. Both knew Pete didn't have a chance. He realized as much, but kept playing hard to get anyway.

"Sweetie," Monica said, "do you remember our favorite quote from Star Trek?"

"Absolutely: 'To boldly go where no man has gone before.'"

"Nope."

Pete smirked because he knew the answer she was looking for, but he decided to play along with the game. "'The needs of the many outweigh the needs of a few.'"

"Nope."

"'Beam me up?'"

"Pete, you're being evasive."

"'Laugh it up, Hairball.'"

Markus cracked up. "Wrong Universe. That's from Star Wars, and it's Fuzzball, not Hairball."

Pete racked his brain for one last diversion. "'Set phasers to stun.'"

"You're getting closer... almost there."

"Surely you don't mean...'resistance is futile?'"

"Exactly. We're going with Markus."

Pete sighed. "'Warp drive standing by.'"

The three arrived thirty minutes later in the parking lot of a place called Furniture with a Cause. Sam Martin met them at the entrance of the store.

"Come in, stranger! Is this the real Markus Cunningham, famous church consultant, the man too busy to hang out with his old friends? I haven't seen your pretty face in ages."

"In the flesh."

"Seriously, when I heard you accepted my invitation to swing by, you made my day. It's really good to see you, Markus."

After a bear hug that included a few slaps on the back, Markus pulled away and said, "Sam, meet two of the best people in the world—Pete and Monica."

Sam nodded. "You're all over the blogosphere these days. Love it! I heard you thawed out the frozen chosen, pried them loose from the pews, and nailed the doors shut for a month. What a way to take a vacation! You're either going to be out of a job real soon or launching the next Reformation. Which do you want it to be?"

"That's good," Pete said. "What I really want is to join a monastery somewhere and lead a more quiet life."

"Are you sure about that?" Monica struck a melodramatic pose, sighed, and turned her shoulder away. "I'd reconsider if I were you," she teased. "Last time I checked, women still weren't allowed to mix it up with the monks."

"Yikes!" Sam slapped Pete on the back. "No church and no woman. Somebody should have warned you before Markus showed up."

"He's a paying customer, Sam. Don't run him off."

"Save your money, Pastor Pete. Spend your dollars on a massage chair. I've got one that will do the work of ten overpaid consultants. Step into my office and let's make a deal."

Sam guided everyone to the back of the store. For Monica, the surprise of the day was turning out to be a lot of fun. Sam came across as a playful kind of guy, but she could sense there was something much deeper. Her intuition honed in on something mysterious and intense. Whatever she sensed would most likely explain why they were here today.

"Find a place to camp out." Sam pointed to a comfortable leather sofa. "Although Pete, I want you to sit in my deluxe massage chair right over here. I have the remote on my desk. Allow me to set it on number five, just for you. I call that number 'the consultant recovery program.'"

Markus smiled as Pete lunged for the chair like a kid entering a movie theater. Monica laughed at the sight of her husband melding with the furniture. *Now he's glad he came.*

"Let me warn you before I turn the chair on, Pete. Everyone who encounters what you're about to experience ends up buying one of these things from me. So back out now if you need to. This chair is simply magic."

"Bring it on!"

Sam picked up the wireless remote and turned on the chair. He concentrated. Monica watched casually at first. Then in a flash, she discerned an abrupt change in Sam's countenance. Markus didn't seem to detect it. Pete's eyes were closed, his body now enraptured by the massage mechanism churning out spell number five. The intensity she sensed in Sam only moments ago now rushed to the surface. It was palpable.

"Pete, I've been praying about an idea that's been burning in my heart."

"Oh," Pete exclaimed. "You have my attention for the next five hours. I don't have a clue what it is, but I'm all ears. Just don't make me get up."

"Like I said, the chair is magic. Pastor Blackman, I've only shared this with one other person."

"Let me guess. He wouldn't be the one responsible for the fifth program setting on this chair, would he?"

"Yes. But here's the amazing thing. Markus called me up last night to ask how Furniture with a Cause was doing. After I told him, he said I needed to talk with you immediately."

"I could blame this chair, but I think I'm having déjà vu."

"Don't worry, Pete," Markus interjected. "It's not a glitch in the Matrix."

"Thank you, Morpheus. Why, oh why, didn't I take the blue pill?"

"You two, be quiet," Sam quipped. "I'm talking. Don't force me to initiate the self-destruct sequence on the remote."

Monica snickered, but she sensed something coming her way. Whatever it was felt larger than anything Sam was about to say. Her left foot started acting up again.

"Pete, I started this business ten years ago by selling slightly-used furniture. People donate the stuff to us every day. We're a nonprofit organization. All the net profits go back into ministry. But I have a problem, Pastor, and I've been bothered for quite some time.

"The difficulty is that some of the furniture given to us just won't sell. It's good quality stuff, but I can't move all the merchandise. I usually give it away to people in need. I simply have too much in the warehouse and even more that I have to turn down. I decline sofas, chairs, beds, and tables every day of the week.

"So here's what the Lord placed on my heart. The economy is rough for a lot of families. There are many young couples that can't even afford to buy furniture these days. Furniture with a Cause and Green Street are on opposite sides of Ft. Worth. If you have space in your church for some of this furniture, I'll gladly send the stuff to you at no cost. My only expense will be the price of transportation, and I'll freely donate that back to the Lord.

"If you let the word get out that Green Street Baptist Church gives away free furniture to young families in need, they'll beat your doors down just to take a look. It would add favor to your reputation. I can't imagine a better opportunity for outreach."

He paused briefly then said, "What do you think, Pastor Pete?"

"Is that your proposition, Sam? You only took three minutes. I wanted you to keep going for hours. Seriously though, let me pray some and talk with our leadership when we rally next month."

Monica felt a quickening of emotions. Her heart raced. Her left foot began twitching. She knew something was happening again. God spoke very clearly. She remembered nailing the little pieces of paper to the old wooden cross in her living room. The same voice that beckoned her to drive to the Jan-Kay ranch filled her mind with a holy mandate once again, but this time He spoke even louder. She tried to bite her tongue, which never worked.

"Yes," she blurted out. "I want this ministry."

"Monica?" Pete sat up in the chair and stood to his feet. The mechanism inside the chair kept churning out program number five. "We haven't even discussed this, either with our leadership or between ourselves."

"Resistance is futile, Pete. And I don't mean that I'm resisting you. Please, let me lead this. The ladies will follow me. I know they will. We have several old Sunday school rooms filled with cobwebs and VBS material from the 1990s. God wants those rooms for His glory.

"This is the kind of ministry that will reach people who aren't much older than our two sons. Can you imagine Dustin and Zane affording an apartment full of furniture after graduation? Or what if they come across some girl to marry in the near future? They don't have any money.

"Please, honey. God is speaking to me right now. I want to make a difference and leave a mark too. You said that to me in the park once, remember?"

Pete hesitated.

Sam and Markus felt like two flies on the wall. As far as either of them could tell, the pastor and his wife lost all realization that they were still in the room. Markus already knew how this story would end, however. He'd watched Monica cast her shackles to the wind once before. The way he saw things, Pete didn't need to control her. He just needed to unleash her. The rest would take care of itself.

Pete lost himself in Monica's eyes. They were deep wells of conviction. Her cheeks glistened. He lifted a hand and gently brushed the hair from her face. Then he kissed her forehead.

"Monica, I just realized something. For all those years back at Baylor when you stood cheering in the bleachers and for all those Sundays you did the same while I was preaching the gospel, thank you. I never understood how much strength I drew from you until this moment. You've always been my greatest source of inspiration.

"Now it's my turn to cheer for you. No matter what you need, this ministry will launch. Promise!"

Monica tried to say something in response, but her emotions got the best of her. She placed her face in Pete's chest and soaked his shirt with tears. Words would have to come later.

Markus looked at Sam. He was teary-eyed too. "Do you need a man-hug, my friend?"

"I'll be okay. Just give me a moment."

Monica raised her head and gathered what little composure she could. She locked eyes with Sam. "Wrap up one of those massage chairs for my man. I like what it does for him."

On that day, Pastor Pete Blackman learned how to appreciate a good surprise. He would never be the same again. Neither would his marriage or his back.

Chapter 33

Two are better than one, because they have a good return for their
work. If one falls down, his friend can help him up. But pity the man
who falls and has no one to help him up!
(Ecclesiastes 4:9-10, NIV)

Pete reclined in the magic massage chair in his living room. "There
are ten different programs on this remote, Markus."

"Is that all?" Markus grinned.

"But number seven might be my favorite."

"I thought you liked number five the best. What did Sam call that? I
believe it was 'the consultant recovery program.'"

"That one's good," Pete replied "but seven's better. I've given each
numeric setting a name."

"So what do you call number seven?"

"I've decided to call it 'the abyss recovery program.'"

"That sounds familiar. Let me guess. You also have one called 'the
bomb recovery program.'"

"How did you know?" Pete smirked. "That's setting number one on
the remote, because it's the first thing you did to me. Number two is 'the

bonfire with no sprinklers insanity setting.' And number ten is the 'ICU kiss death on the lips recovery program' because I hope it's the last."

"You do realize there are five more settings on the remote, don't you?" Markus chuckled. "I'm dying to tell you about numbers three, four, six, eight, and nine."

"Right. You just made that up."

Markus didn't reply. Although the mechanism in the massage chair whirled and churned, running gently up and down his spine, perfectly kneading his shoulder blades, Pete began to tense up over the fact that Markus didn't answer.

"Did you hear what I just said?"

"I heard."

"Well, you just made that up, right?"

"Name me one time since we've known each other that I just made something up."

Pete thought about that for a minute. Then he turned off the chair and sat up. There was a look of discomfort on his face.

"Why did you shut down your magic massage chair?"

"Because you just stressed me out again."

"Relax. My job is to shake things up. I'll tell you what. Turn the chair back on and use setting number nine for the next thirty minutes."

"Why nine?"

"We'll name that one in January."

"What happens then?"

"Do you really want to know?"

Pete thought about the answer for a moment. "No, I don't. I'm supposed to be on vacation."

"Good. But I'll tell you anyway. In January, you're going to slay the zombies."

Pete cracked up. "Oh, that's good! That's my favorite one yet. Where do you come up with this stuff?"

"Inspiration hit me during my quiet time yesterday."

"Seriously, you were praying to God and He told you to tell me we were going zombie hunting? Vampires are more popular, especially with the teenage girls. Why don't we slay some of those while we're killing things? And why stop there. Let's go after some werewolves and everything else that goes bump in the night."

"I admire your zeal." Markus laughed. "But the zombies will keep you busy enough. Just sit back and enjoy number nine—the 'zombie preparation program.' I need you to get ready for the final adventure. Then I can wrap things up and get back to being a husband once again."

Pete zeroed in on the last statement. He sensed something he wanted to probe more deeply. This was the perfect opportunity.

"Markus, may I ask you a personal question?"

"Shoot."

"Why don't you ever talk about your wife?"

"That's a difficult subject, Pete."

"Will you be bothered if I pry into that area?"

"Talking about the situation isn't as painful anymore."

"I didn't know there were any problems."

"Pete, I think you know how stressful ministry is on our wives."

"So what's the story? You just prescribed thirty minutes on setting number nine. I promise not to fall asleep counting zombies."

Markus reminisced in silence for several seconds. He never delved into his own personal issues with clients. But Pete had become more of a friend than a patron. "Only a true friend," he often said to others, "grants someone the freedom to unload their painful memories." He felt certain Pete would never lose respect or judge him for the mistakes he'd made.

"A long time ago, I pastored a church in Florida where things were going extremely well. Shirley loved the church. She flourished. All of her gifts were in play. She taught a very popular Bible study for women and served in a children's ministry that was growing like gang busters.

"Then a very large church in Tennessee noticed my track record and called us to relocate. Shirley saw every red flag. She was suspicious, but I refused to pay attention or listen. I chalked up her concerns to the fact that she didn't want to leave her friends or the ministries that were thriving under her leadership.

"I, however, saw a larger church, a bigger salary, and greater possibilities. The situation all felt like God but really was all about me. I ignored every warning sign and swallowed the bait. I've never made a more blind decision in my life."

"So what happened when you arrived?"

"The church wasn't anything I expected or hoped for. There were problems with the finances, problems with the staff, and problems in the membership. Everywhere I turned, things were melting down around me. Shirley was betrayed by several ladies who befriended her early on, and things just kept getting worse for her. She cried every day. Finally she had enough."

"You're singing my song, Marcus."

"Ironic, right? Having lived through the experience myself, I can empathize with people who are experiencing the same thing. The pressure was so great on me and the experience so bad for Shirley that she didn't want to be a pastor's wife anymore. She came to me one day and said, 'I love you, but I hate your job. Find something else to do that doesn't require me to fake being happy all the time.'"

"What did you do?"

"I resigned my church for starters, which was the most painful experience of my life. I felt like I let God down. I wondered if He was punishing me for some unconfessed sin. The rumor mill spun into high gear. People made up stories about why we left. Some suggested I was seeing another woman. There were even allegations that Shirley had lost her mind and had become unstable. It was a mess."

"I'm sorry, Markus. I never knew you went through all that."

"Most days I keep it in the rearview mirror. A man has to learn to forgive and move on, or he'll go insane."

"So what did you do after you resigned?"

"Nothing at first. I sat in shock on my sofa and watched TV for a few weeks, lots of old black and white zombie movies if I remember correctly."

Pete opened his eyes and regarded his friend warmly.

"I tried to find another church to pastor, but no one was interested in a man who failed his last church. My friends in the ministry were interested in what happened initially, but then they stopped returning my calls. I was alone. I never thought I'd end up in a place like that. I saw others walk through the valley of the shadow of death and then crash and burn, but that was never supposed to happen to me."

"What happened to you, Markus, nearly happened to me. Monica was finished with our church. I was still fighting hard to turn things around. Then I was blindsided by Gary's request to resign from the pulpit. My story ended differently because I called you."

"You're right," Markus acknowledged. "My life verse has become Romans 8:28: 'in all things God works for the good for those that love Him, who have been called according to His purpose.' God doesn't say everything is good. Some things in life just plain stink. Death is bad. Cancer is bad. Divorce is bad. When a church disintegrates, that's bad too. God has recycled all the garbage from my past into blessings for others."

"What made you decide to become a church consultant?"

"Consulting wasn't something I planned to do at first. I just knew

I still loved the Lord and believed in His calling on my life. I couldn't imagine selling insurance or real estate for a living. I started attending another church in the same town, but they had all the same problems we had. I began encouraging that pastor and helping him lead the congregation past their difficulties. Together we were able to turn the church around. He was the first person to suggest to me that I should help struggling churches.

"So I developed a strategy to market my new idea. I discovered most pastors are facing the same issues in varying degrees. They need someone to come in from the outside and help them understand the situation. Once they gain perspective, they find moving forward easier. There's no better person to give them counsel than someone who's walked in their shoes."

Pete sighed and nodded. "That's an amazing story. I think I understand now. You're on a mission to write a different ending to your own story. You want to help guys like me avoid what you experienced."

"You've said it better than I could say it myself. When I think about your situation, I remember what I went through. When I see Monica, I think of what Shirley experienced. If I can help someone avoid the pain I felt while sitting on the couch after resigning my church, I'll die a happy man."

"You've been quite successful as a consultant. How do you explain that?"

"God deserves all the credit. The best way to describe what's happened is that God turned my thorns into a crown. Out of pain came triumph. There are so many scriptures that speak of this reality. Our God gives beauty for ashes and enables us to soar on eagle's wings.

"God worked on me in Tennessee even though things were falling apart all around me. I didn't see His hand at the time. But looking back, I understand I would never have been able to help guys like you unless

I experienced what happened to me first.

"There was a day I used to think that when God wants a work to be done, He calls a worker. Then the worker goes out to do the work. I've come to realize how wrong that really is. What actually happens is that when God wants a work to be done, He calls a worker. Then He goes to work on the worker so the worker can do the work."

"Nice, I like that. So how's Shirley doing now?"

"Better, actually. When I'm not on the road, we attend the same church together in Miami. The kids are grown and married now, and Shirley's teaching again. Her confidence is returning. The ladies absolutely love her, and the parents appreciate her involvement in the children's ministry."

"There are times I ask Shirley for her advice on how to help a particular pastor's wife since so many are going through the same things she experienced. Not only is she a great prayer warrior, but she helps me understand ladies like Monica."

"Funny," Pete said. "And here I was giving you all the credit for helping us navigate through our challenges. Maybe I should call Shirley and thank her instead."

"There's no *maybe*. Here's her phone number. Write it down."

Chapter 34

He who mocks the poor shows contempt for their Maker
(Proverbs 17:5, NIV).

Bob and Georgette Freeman arrived at Hands and Feet Ministries in
the heart of downtown Ft. Worth. The building had once belonged to an
old Episcopalian church. Many decades earlier, the small remnant who
hung on until the bitter end finally lost their grip. They were forced to
turn out the lights and shutter the stained-glass windows. The property
sat vacant for years. Over time, the once-beautiful church transformed
into a dilapidated eyesore in a rundown section of the city.

The last two surviving members met for lunch one day. Each
confessed to feeling grieved when they drove past their old house of
worship. Something had to be done. That's when a young seminary
student by the name of Mike Murdock caught their attention.

Mike wasn't looking to acquire property when he was approached
by the two men. He was just doing what he always did between studying
and attending classes. He had a passion for the homeless. He shared the
life of Jesus with drug addicts, gang members, runaways, and just about
anyone who fell on hard times. Not only did he love sharing, but he was

anointed in the work.

As Mike often told the story, "A car circled the block one Saturday afternoon while I was witnessing to a homeless family. Two white-haired men held up a set of keys and pointed to this building. God worked a miracle, because the building didn't cost a dime."

When others heard the story and saw what he was doing, they came alongside Mike. Seminary students, businessmen in the community, and other churches started lending their support. Some showed up with a check in hand, others with a set of carpentry tools.

Why Mike would give his life to this kind of ministry often puzzled people. He heard the same questions time and again: "Why are you here? Why are you doing this?" His response was always the same. "I'm just trying to be the hands and feet of Jesus."

Those words spread like *kudzu* throughout the inner city. When Mike decided to stay in Ft. Worth after graduation, he founded Hands and Feet Ministries. Support grew as lives were transformed. Churches all over the city gave Hands and Feet a line item in their annual budget. While Mike appreciated all the financial support, what he desired most were more souls to equip and more workers to send into the harvest.

Bob and Georgette showed up on a day when Mike was eager to recruit fresh blood. He met them outside his office and invited them to have a seat. If the chairs in his office had possessed the ability to speak, they'd tell an amazing story of what happened when people sat and conversed with Mike. One thing was for certain: Bob and Georgette were not prepared for how their lives would soon change.

"How do you feel about poverty, Bob?" Mike's question was blunt.

"Excuse me? I'm not sure what you mean by that."

"When you see a homeless man or woman on the street, what goes through your mind? Everybody has an opinion about that."

"I guess I wonder why they don't walk to the hamburger joint down the road and apply for a job. I see signs saying 'We're Hiring' all the time."

"Bob's family was poor when he was a child," Georgette added. "I think what he means is that people should be encouraged to overcome their difficulties like he had to. He's really a very sensitive man."

"I understand. But what if I told you the hamburger joint down the road won't hire a homeless person? A homeless woman doesn't have access to showers, shampoo, clean clothes, or a healthy diet. If she served you food in that condition, would you eat it or would you walk away?"

"I never thought of it that way."

"Most people don't. Pardon me for being blunt, but did your father ever do drugs?"

Bob was visibly stunned by the question. "Heavens, no! Not once. He was a respectable man. He didn't make much money, and we never had the things other kids did, but my dad always made sure that we went to church on Sunday."

"How would you have been affected in that home to see your father slap your mother until she was unconscious?"

"Oh, my," Georgette exclaimed. "Bob's father was a southern gentleman from the old days. You should have been at his funeral. I've never heard so many nice things said about another man."

Mike could tell his guests were becoming defensive, which was exactly what he intended. He always probed a worker's heart before he let them get involved in Hands and Feet.

"The point I'm trying to make is this," Mike went on. "The people we minister to every day didn't grow up in the same America you did. You have to ask yourself, 'What would cause a man to throw his life away to alcohol and drugs? Why would a woman sell her body to a stranger?'"

"Sadly, the world is filled with sin," Georgette said softly.

"That's the general answer we were taught in Sunday school," Mike replied. "But sin's not descriptive enough. Why would a mother drop her little kids off with a social worker and decide to sleep in the field behind this building?"

"Oh, my," Georgette said a second time.

"The answer to these questions is really very simple. The problem isn't just sin. The problem is what the sin causes. The answer is pain. We minister to people who are filled with deep reservoirs of the stuff. Many of them have hurt for so long they don't know what normal feels like anymore. For some the pain started before they knew how to walk or say the word 'mommy.' The pain has accumulated for so long that they never developed the character qualities or skills necessary for survival, let alone a normal life.

"You were raised in a poor family, Bob. But you weren't raised in that kind of family. Because of the grace of God, you will never live on the streets around Hands and Feet."

Bob was undone. His bottom lip began to quiver. He tried to hide the trembling by saying something, but his voice shook too. "I didn't mean to sound insensitive when I made the remark about the hamburger joint. The reason I'm here is because I'm bothered to see so many people living underneath bridges around our church. At all the major intersections surrounding Green Street Baptist Church, people hold up signs and beg for food.

"Most days I feel guilty that I have so much. I don't understand how others have missed the opportunities that were given to me. I really didn't know what to expect in meeting you here today, but I see now. I have a lot to learn."

Mike pondered Bob's confession. He needed to hear exactly those words. He'd listened to different versions of those words over the years.

The essence was always the same, especially from those who helped Hands and Feet shine as a community of hope.

"Bob, I know I came at you aggressively. Please forgive me if I offended you. I've learned over the years that I need to probe the motivations of someone who wants to work in our mission field. The wrong kind of person can do more damage than good. I try to keep that from happening from the start.

"And you're absolutely right." The enthusiasm in Mike's voice hit a high note. "We all have a lot to learn. I was glad to hear you say that. The kind of learning required to be effective here, however, is what I call 'heart-learning.' In this environment, you learn when your heart breaks in the same way the heart of Jesus broke. He was a man of compassion, through and through.

"We're not the type of ministry that fills your head with knowledge. Our vision is to give you a brand new set of hands and a beautiful new pair of feet. We want you to look just like Jesus when you enter the harvest."

Mike gazed out the window for a moment. "Do you remember the woman I mentioned earlier?"

"The one who gave her kids to a social worker and slept in a field behind your building?" Georgette asked.

"Yes, that's the one."

Bob had a curious look on his face, as though he wanted to hear more of her story. "What about her?"

"She's there right now. I talked to her for the first time this morning. Let's go see if we can help her."

"Oh, my!"

Chapter 35

If any one of you is without sin, let him
be the first to throw a stone at her (John 8:7, NIV).

She didn't feel safe telling anyone her real name. They might trace her back to Jackson, Tennessee, and call her family. Someone would send a rescue team and return her to what she'd finally had the courage to escape a few months ago.

On the streets, people called her Adelaide—an old name that her great aunt was given. Though she died many years ago, the original Adelaide was a kind and compassionate woman who'd cared for Cindy when she was a little girl. Cindy never knew a lovelier person. Adelaide was the woman she most wanted to be like, so she changed her name.

Cindy was abused. Adelaide was never abused. Cindy had two children from fathers who took what they didn't deserve. Adelaide never married and never bore children. Cindy was offered drugs by strangers and friends alike, usually for one purpose alone. Adelaide never took a sip of alcohol during her entire life. Cindy died a little each day. Adelaide was deceased but lived on in Cindy's memories.

"Adelaide," Mike called out. "I came back with some food and two of my friends."

"Food? I'll take it. Just put it down and stay away."

Georgette's heart shattered into a thousand pieces over the sight. Adelaide was young and vulnerable, with blond hair and pretty dark eyes. There was no reason for her to be living here. Not with a five-bedroom home and four empty beds just down the road. Her house was safe. This place wasn't.

Bob thought of his own daughter, Sarah. She'd graduated with a degree in education and taught at a local elementary school. She was about the same age as Adelaide, but that was the only thing the two had in common.

"Adelaide," Mike said tenderly, "I think I know what you're looking for."

"You don't know anything about me."

"You're right. I don't know what you're running from, but I know what you're running to."

"You have food. I don't want anything else from you. Leave me alone."

Bob had a father's voice. His own daughter melted when he spoke to her. She trusted him and searched for years to marry a man like her dad. "Hello, little girl," he said.

Something in the tone of his voice caught her attention and she burst into tears. "My little girls," she sobbed. "I deserve to die."

"How old are your little girls?" Bob asked.

"One is three. The other just turned one last month. But they're not mine anymore. There was no food."

"Adelaide. That's a pretty name," Georgette said. "I haven't heard that name since I was a little girl. My great-grandmother was named Adelaide. My mother told me once that the first Adelaide was the patron saint of abuse victims. She lived centuries ago."

"Abuse victims?"

"Yes, honey. There are people who remember her for all the good she did in spite of the cruelty she endured."

The blonde-haired girl looked up for the first time, and Mike watched another miracle unfold. He was no longer surprised by such occurrences. Though he knew nothing about the patron saint Georgette spoke of, he knew God always orchestrated things to reach a crescendo in someone's life. This happened all the time at Hands and Feet. The ministry was anointed. The right people were always there at the perfect moment.

"Why would God let that happen to a saint?"

"I wish I knew the answer to that, darling girl," Georgette responded. "But I do know what I read the other day, 'The Lord will maintain the cause of the afflicted, and justice for the poor.' That's Psalms 140. It's in the Book."

"What book is that?"

"The words are in the Bible, sweetie. God loves you."

"How can God love me?"

Bob didn't stop to consider the implications of what he was about to say. Compassion overcame reason and reservation. "Come stay at our house tonight. I'm going to figure out a way to get your children back, Adelaide."

"You would do that for me?"

"Yes. You remind me of my daughter."

"What's her name?"

"Sarah."

"That's a pretty name. You can call me Cindy."

Chapter 36

The unfolding of Your words gives light;
it gives understanding to the simple (Psalm 119:13, NIV).

Markus experienced a dramatic uptick in the traffic to his daily blog. He was amazed at the number of comments posted in his Green Street journal. They ranged from the poignant to the comical. After dining with Pete and Monica one evening, he replied to a few from his laptop. He typed away while relaxing on their living room sofa.

From Becky in Cincinnati: *Can you think of a good substitute for Ripper? I'd like to try something like that at our staff retreat, but all I can seem to get my hands on is a three-toed sloth.*

Dear Becky: Ripper was managed by John Dewayne. He's a personal friend and a trained professional. Please don't try this in your home church. I can think of several possibilities for a sloth, however. The pews of the modern church are filled with them.

From James in Mississippi: *Can you post a video of the secret shout of the Imaginators? My youth minister here hooked me up with your blog. He's got all the teenagers making weird noises in our church. If we could hear the real thing, I might be able to put a stop to the awful sounds bouncing off the walls of our church.*

Dear James: I'll pass the request on to Buck. I'm pretty certain he doesn't know how to post a video to the web. I can also assure you, nothing your youth have come up with could rival the shrieking sounds coming from that man's mouth. He's got a great set of lungs. I'd stick with what's originated in your culture and context, which will be more meaningful over the long run. One more thing: don't quench the Spirit.

From Anonymous in First Dead Church: *We need you to come here quickly. Bring the bomb. Show up with whatever is left over from the abyss. Bring Pete and Monica too. Hurry! I don't know how much longer we can last.*

Dear Anonymous. Send me an email privately. For the rest of the readers out there, let me state that each situation is different. There's probably something creative that we can latch onto in your area. Consultants with notebooks of prepackaged materials have always annoyed me. Keep the methods fresh, Anonymous. That way you won't stink up the place.

From Church Mouse in Kentucky: *Dear Markus. Does Monica have a sister? I'd like to meet her if she's single.*

Dear Church Mouse: I don't know, and I'm at a loss over how to respond to your question. You frighten me a little to tell you the truth. You might be one of those guys Paul said should stay single. Just sayin'.

From L. Frankfurt Hogwell, III in Georgia: *Someone in our church told me about your blog. I didn't believe it at first. But after reading it, I'm convinced you need to stop the ridiculous antics you're pulling over the sheep's eyes at Green Street. Please stay away from our church.*

Dear Trey: I have the feeling a lot of people are staying away from your church. I'll pray for your pastor. If you're the pastor, I'll pray for your people. Hang on to that attitude, buddy, and I may be called in sooner than you think.

From Ian in California: I think our church is a morgue. Everyone else says it's a movement. Who's right?

Dear Ian: Since you've given me so little information with which to make a diagnosis, I'll need to consult my crystal ball. I didn't bring it with me to Texas. You'll have to wait until I get back to Florida. Until then, chill. Don't stir up the dead bodies.

"Markus, you seem focused," Pete commented.

"Just responding to some of the comments posted on my blog."

"I remember Sam mentioning your blog at Furniture with a Cause. That was the first time I heard anything about it. Anything interesting being posted?"

The consultant's eyes stayed fixed to the screen. "The blog's more entertaining than interesting. I believe social media is more about the need to connect than the need to inform. I use it to link up with people who are interested in what I do. Blogging's part of the marketing strategy."

Pete studied Markus. He considered whether now would be a good time to share something that was percolating in his head. Pete always liked to test-drive a new idea before driving the concept off the lot.

"I've been reflecting on something you said awhile back."

Markus looked up and latched on to Pete's eyes. "What was that?"

"You said, 'The real work begins now. But first, it must begin in you!'"

"I remember. That was right after you told the sweet Christians at Green Street that they were a bunch of snakes."

A surprised look appeared on Pete's face. "I was preaching about the snake that Hezekiah smashed. I made no such connection."

"Relax, Pete. I'm only playing with you. Go sit in that magic chair and resume setting number nine."

"'Playing?' I believe 'tormenting' is the word you're searching for."

"You're right. Reading all those comments in my blog has a strange effect on me. My mind goes to a weird place. So, tell me what's on your mind."

"I've been thinking about where my passions lie. When this season is over, I want to be part of something that can be described as a real movement of God. That's the reason I came here so many years ago in the first place. If we go back to business as usual, I'll not survive another year."

"You're actually in a good place, Pete. And that's exactly what I wanted to hear you say. You said you wanted to be part of *something*. Do you know what that something is?"

"I believe I do."

"Care to share that with me?"

"I've been reading the Bible..."

"Hallelujah, we're saved!"

"Watch it. You're getting weird again."

"Sorry. I'll be good."

"I've been analyzing the life and ministry of Jesus for the last several weeks," Pete explained. "I want to duplicate His strategy in our church. I think I have his ministry boiled down to four simple words."

"Now that sounds fascinating. You definitely have my attention on that."

"I thought you might be interested. The first word is 'gather.' Jesus gathered people. There was no one better at pulling people together. Movements don't take off unless this happens first."

"I would agree with that."

"The next word is 'deliver.' After Jesus gathered His twelve disciples, along with many others from the crowds, He delivered them. The way I see things, Jesus delivered people from crisis and darkness. Often the crisis was a result of their physical condition. As the King James Bible phrased it, many were lame, halt, and blind. Others were delivered from leprosy, deafness, bleeding disorders, and even death itself."

"Don't forget His first miracle at Cana of Galilee," Markus interrupted. "Do you remember how Jesus delivered the guests from that lame wedding party?"

"You mean by turning the water into wine?"

"Precisely. If I remember correctly, the Master of Ceremonies said, 'You saved the best for last.' John, Chapter 2. It's in the Book. Be sure to use this example when you're explaining what delivering people means. You'll have one big happy hour at the Baptist church during that Sunday morning."

"I thought you were brought here to help me keep my job."

"They'll like you more if they're tipsy."

Pete smiled deviously. "'Get thee behind me, Satan.' That's in the Book too."

"Ouch!"

"Serves you right." Pete chuckled. "I might have to read that blog of yours just to see what you're writing about me."

"You probably won't recognize yourself."

"Why's that?"

"I've given you a long red cape, blue polyester tights, and a big letter S."

"Superpastor! Monica would like that. Humble Pete Blackman on weekdays, invincible man of the Word on Sundays. But I'm already that person."

"Okay, now you're embarrassing me, Pete. Please start talking about Jesus again."

"I wasn't the one who stopped being serious. Too bad you didn't portray me as Batman. He had a sidekick. You could be my little sidekick as we enter morgue-class churches, kick the devil's butt, and start new movements. We'd make a great duo."

"A little sidekick? I want to be Batman. You be the sidekick."

"Excuse me." Monica entered the room. "Would you little boys like some coffee?"

"I'm okay, sweetie. Markus?"

"I'll pass."

"I didn't mean to interrupt your brilliant conversation, but it's getting late and I'm off to bed. I just thought you might need some caffeine. You don't sound like you're getting much work done."

"See there, Markus? You just got me in trouble."

"I didn't do anything."

"Don't stay up too late, Superpastor. I don't want to be lonely all night." Monica left the room.

"I'll be there shortly," he called to her then turned to his friend. "All right, Markus, let's hurry."

"Yes, my little sidekick, you were talking about Jesus."

"Right. I'm going to ignore that and move on. As I was saying, Jesus gathered people and then He delivered them from crisis and darkness. The darkness was pretty intense. Sin was rampant. All the demons of hell seemingly gathered in the ancient Holy Land during the ministry of Jesus Christ. My point is that He had power and authority to drive them away. We've been given the same power—the power to deliver people."

"I like it. Gather, deliver... What's next?"

"This is where it gets interesting. The next word is 'train.' A great portion of the New Testament is devoted to the teachings of Jesus. But this is where most churches get stuck and ultimately become a morgue. They stop the work of gathering and delivering, and spend all their time offering endless training opportunities. The problem is that we only train them to be smarter Christians, but we don't train them to accomplish the fourth thing in Jesus' strategy."

"That's brilliant, Pete. That's why I have a job. If you discover the solution to this problem, my career as a consultant is over. So what's the fourth word?"

"The word is 'send.' Jesus sent the ones He gathered, delivered, and trained into the harvest. Then the cycle repeats itself and starts all over again. This is why Christianity spread throughout the world so quickly. If we gather, deliver, train, and send, then we'll multiply."

Pete shook his head. "I haven't figured out how to implement this yet. Plus we have a lot of members in the field discovering new ideas. My biggest question is whether this four-point strategy will interface with your brilliant scheme to slay the zombies."

"Great question, Pete, and the answer is yes. Once we slay the zombies, you'll be sailing on smooth seas underneath a clear blue sky. This is all coming together nicely. You're the best sidekick I've ever had the opportunity to partner with."

"We'll talk about who's the sidekick later. I'm done, and I'm gone. Superpastor needs to go rescue a damsel in distress."

Part 4

Chapter 37

From the ends of the earth we hear singing: "Glory to the Righteous
One." But I said, "I waste away, I waste away! Woe to me! The
treacherous betray! With treachery the treacherous betray!"
(Isaiah 24:1, NIV)

The doors of Green Street Baptist church remained closed throughout
the entire month of December. In the lengthy history of the church,
nothing like this had ever happened before. If someone were to drive
by on a Sunday morning, they might wonder if something terrible had
happened. Nothing could be farther from the truth.

The members spread out all over the city of Ft. Worth, watching,
learning, and growing. Everyone who participated was waiting to
share their story. Anticipation was building for the return. For certain
there'd be enthusiastic conversations spiced up with a whole new set of
vocabulary words, words like "incarnational," "communal," "tribes,"
and "teams." New phrases would emerge as well: "house church,"

"church plant," "evangelistic tools," "volunteer process," "non-threatening environments," "*be* the church," "not fans but followers," "portable not permanent," "rocking the pool hall for Jesus," and "we all have a lot to learn."

Members would need a long time to exchange their stories about other places they visited, such as Cowboy Church, The Gospel Soup Kitchen, Slave Trade Rescue House, Multi-Housing Mission, and Marketplace Ministry. One short month did more to revitalize the enthusiasm within Green Street Baptist Church than an entire decade of Sunday services.

The idea was crazy and full of risk. Success was not guaranteed. Not everyone agreed the idea was a good one. But Markus, Pete, and Monica had nothing to lose. People don't gain anything of value while trying to save their own skin. Leaders who aren't afraid to lose usually don't. People who take risks eventually win.

They were off to a fantastic start, but their work was far from over. In fact, everything seemed to be going a little too smoothly. Monica had an uneasy feeling that something was brewing.

Shortly after Christmas, Pete heard a knock on the door. Josh Duncan stood on the front porch with an umbrella in his hand. The winter night was cold, and the rain had been pouring for hours.

Josh had served as the education minister of Green Street for ten years, five of which were during Pete's tenure. Monica often wondered why the two weren't more social. They hardly spent any time with each other outside the office. When the leaders made the journey to the Jan-Kay ranch, Josh had pulled out at the last minute. Monica remembered Pete mentioning some story about Josh recovering from a bad stomach virus. That being the case, everyone made allowances for the fact that Josh wasn't there.

But when he took a two-week vacation following the retreat, Monica grew suspicious. Even though he tossed his job description into the bonfire, his conspicuous absences were a cause for concern. Her senses were on high alert.

Now, knowing that Josh had come to see Pete, Monica opened the door to her bedroom so she could hear the voices drifting down the hallway. She didn't want to intrude on what appeared to be official business, but she did want to hear the conversation. She could tell by the tone in her husband's voice that he was a little uneasy with the surprise visit.

"Hey, Josh! Come in and have a seat. Would you like to try out my new massage chair that Monica gave me for Christmas? It has ten different settings."

"No, I'm afraid I can't stay long."

The two entered the living room and found a seat. Monica sat very still on her bed just around the corner. From this vantage point, she could easily hear every word without straining her ears. *It's not eavesdropping when it's your own home.*

"What brings you over here on such a miserable night?"

"I wanted you to be the first to hear the news from me...personally."

"Okay. Would this be good news or bad?"

"I'll let you decide. Pete, I feel very uncomfortable about the things that are happening at Green Street. And apparently I'm not the only one who feels this way. Several people have called me and asked questions about what I think of all the changes taking place."

"How long has this been going on?"

"The calls started on the first night Markus spoke to the leaders of the church. He offended several of our members with all that talk about death."

"Josh, you mean to tell me you've had private conversations with church members about emerging problems, and I'm just now hearing about them?"

"At first, I really didn't know what to do. You understand what it's like. We've all had plenty of conversations with disgruntled people over the last several years. We just do our job and move on."

Pete cut straight to the point. "So tell me. How did you do your job in this case?"

"Well, in this case, I'm sorry to say that I agreed with them."

"That's disappointing." Pete rubbed his eyes. "You should have let me know immediately whom you were talking with and what you were doing."

"Here's the difficult part I need to tell to you. There are about twenty-five people planning to leave and start a new church in another location. They've asked me to be their leader."

Monica could restrain herself no longer. Hopping up from her bed, she quickly appeared in the doorway to the living room. "Sorry, Pete. I overheard the conversation. How dare you, Josh! Leave my home right now."

"Monica, let me take care of this," Pete chided.

She relented for a moment. Then she changed her mind. "Josh, I said you may leave my home right now. And by the way, you're fired as of today. Clean your office out tomorrow."

"Excuse me, Monica, but I'm resigning, and besides, you have no authority to fire me."

"You know what, Josh," Pete said, "you're wrong. I want it to be known that the pastor's wife is the one who terminated your job at Green Street."

Josh appeared sincerely regretful. "I didn't want things to end this way between us, Pete. We've worked together for five years."

Monica's face burned. A few months ago she'd have bitten her tongue and said nothing. Then for years, she'd have rehearsed what she really wanted to say. Her next words were a pretty good indication that things had changed of late.

"Josh, the reason we're ending this way is because what you've done is wrong. If you'd come to us from the beginning and expressed your concerns, we might have dialogued. If you wanted to start a mission church from Green Street in the proper way, we'd have supported you. But you went behind my husband's back. You conspired against him, and now you're the leader of a split. The only way to undo what you've done is to confess your actions and ask forgiveness. That's in the Book somewhere, you little coward."

"Monica!" Pete's voice was assertive.

"I'm not backing down anymore, Pete. This is the first time I've been excited about church in a long time, and this man is a Judas. Trust me. You should have been the first person he talked to, not the last."

"She's got a point, Josh. I hate to end this way, but until you acknowledge your actions, our relationship can't continue. And I'd be careful. What you do to others has a way of bouncing back."

"Like karma," Monica said. "You do believe in karma, don't you, Josh?"

"Excuse me, but that's not a biblical word."

"Then here's something biblical for you to consider. You will reap what you sow. Not only that, but you always reap longer than you sow and more than you sow, and reaping is more difficult than sowing. So remember that when one of the grumbling twenty-five begins to question your leadership."

The fire moved to her eyes now. "You can see yourself to the door. And please don't leave your wet umbrella on my living room floor."

Monica turned her back and marched into the bedroom, slamming the door shut behind her.

"I'll tell you what, Josh," Pete said. "Spend some time meditating on what you've heard tonight. I'd like to redeem this situation after we've had a chance to process what's going on here."

Josh nodded silently, picked up the umbrella, and stepped outside into the cold driving rain.

"Is he gone yet?"

Chapter 38

The man who plants and the man who waters have one purpose, and each will be rewarded according to his own labor. For we are God's fellow workers; you are God's field, God's building
(1 Corinthians 3:8-9, NIV).

Markus was stunned. "She said what?"

"Monica called him a coward right to his face."

"Ouch! When a woman calls a man coward, that's like asking him to hand over his man-card."

"She kicked him out of the house so hard, I believe he left with a numb bum."

"A numb bum? That's hilarious. Where did you hear that?"

"I watch PBS. It's mostly British, you know."

"That's right. I forget you're the highbrow among us common movie-going types."

"I've never seen her that aggressive before."

"She's a surprising package, Pete. But what she did was right. She called the situation for what it was. The Apostle Paul had a reputation for doing that too. If he'd met Monica back in Corinth, I don't think he'd have stayed single for long. Paul would have married Monica and set her loose in the pews. All those Corinthian problems... solved!"

Pete grinned. "I'm not sure about that. She only goes for the handsome superhero type."

"Are we back to having that discussion again? You're the sidekick, remember?"

"Actually, I felt a kick in the side when Josh delivered the news."

Markus offered Pete a sympathetic smile. "I'm one of the few people who understands what that feels like. What I'm about to say may not provide much comfort during this moment, but you need to hear me. He's done us a bigger favor than Ripper."

"Now that's a revelation. How do you figure that?"

"Chances are that Josh has been a bigger problem for more years than you've realized. His decision wasn't made overnight. He's been chewing on this bone for a very long time."

Pete's eyes widened. "Finally... this is starting to make sense. I knew there was grumbling going on in the church, but I couldn't figure out where the noise was coming from. I felt the effects every day. Unfortunately, I never got a handle on it."

"You have more than a handle now," Markus affirmed. "You have the whole shovel too, and he's just been busted in the act of trying to dig your grave. In every grumbling scenario, there's always one person standing at the epicenter. Numbers, Chapter 16. It's in the Book. Remember Korah's rebellion? He incited two hundred and fifty leaders to stand against Moses and Aaron. Be thankful you only have twenty-five.

He leaned toward Pete. "Listen to me very carefully, my friend. Make certain you do what Moses did when faced with a similar situation. Let God take care of it. He does a better job."

Markus paused, wanting to see the spark in his friend's eyes once he connected the dots. Pete's eyes finally lit up. Then Markus smiled and whispered for maximum effect, "Don't swing at dirtballs."

Pete laughed. "Dirtballs? Where do you come up with these sayings of yours?"

"From doing the same thing you do—getting up to bat every day and striking out one too many times. The chances of you connecting with a dirtball and knocking it out of the sanctuary are slim."

"Korah's Dirtballs. How ironic! I'm just now remembering how God caused the ground to open up and swallow those men alive. That's one of Monica's favorite stories. In fact, I wouldn't place her in first-century Corinth with Paul. I'd put her in the wilderness with Moses. Monica would be the one standing over the edge of the pit making certain no one crawled back out. She may even have provided the special music while they descended. Something from John Lennon like 'Instant Karma's Gonna Get You' or 'Imagine There's No Heaven'... at least not for you."

"*At least not for you?* You crack me up, Pete, but that's not how the song goes if I remember the '70s correctly."

"She wouldn't care. Besides, no one remembers the '70s correctly."

"You have a point, but now back to mine. The children of Israel kept facing death in the wilderness because they wouldn't stop rebelling against God and Moses. The same is true with churches. They never get near the Promised Land until they're willing to make the journey with one heart and one mind.

"I remember an old preacher from my childhood who had a flair for the dramatic. I'll never forget what he preached one Sunday morning in my home church. 'Why, you ask, is there no harmony among the sheep? Listen very carefully, and you shall hear. Their faith only runs one inch deep.'"

"That's good, Markus. I need to write that down and use the

illustration in a sermon one day. You mentioned he was a preacher with a dramatic flair. He must have been your Jedi Master."

"Not quite, but he did teach me a few things, my young Obi-Wan. The reality is that Josh and company have no faith in what God's doing here. We'd have spent too much time trying to convince them to get onboard and wasted all our emotional energy. That slows down the pace of change. With their exodus, moving forward will be so much easier. I know their departure's painful, but trust that God knows what He's doing right now. This isn't bad news."

"Markus, what am I going to do without an education minister, especially when we implement this new strategy I'm working on?"

"I know a few people I could call. I'll have some send their resumes to you. We can go over them together."

"Please don't do that."

"Why not?"

"Because I need a new sidekick, and I want you."

Markus studied Pete's stoic face. It was obvious he was completely caught off-guard. The thought of going back to work full-time in a church rarely crossed his mind. His home situation was still very complicated. His wife was glad to be out of the spotlight, and they lived in another state. And besides, he'd never been a sidekick in the number-two slot before. He'd always been the senior leader.

"Pete, remember me telling you a long time ago that I'm a solo act?"

"Yah, you said, 'I blow in, blow up, and blow out,' if I remember correctly."

"You have a good memory for someone who's unstable."

"Unstable?"

"Any man who'd ask me to work for him has a great big pile of leaves in his head."

"Markus, come share this load with me. I'm only asking you for one year of your life. Think about all the crazy things you've asked me to do already. We dropped a bomb, lit a bonfire, stared into the abyss, and kissed death on the lips."

Markus thought to change the subject. "You know what, Pete?"

"What?"

"I think somebody should write a theme song about what we've done together."

"Who'd sing it?"

"I'd find some rapper. I don't think the words sound very Country-Western at all. Maybe U2 would do it. They need to make a comeback."

"That's perfect." Pete jumped to his feet. "I still love U2. Let me take a stab at the lyrics for our new theme song."

Pete went deep into thought. His mind churned until he crafted the perfect lyrics to put their story into a song. Then his eyes sparkled.

"Got it. I'm ready to jam.

"It was a 'Beautiful Day' when I dropped the bomb. I stared into the abyss and 'Still Haven't Found What I'm Looking For.' So one 'Sunday Bloody Sunday,' I kissed death on the lips. That started a bonfire on 'The Street with No Name.'"

"Pete, never sing that to anybody again. It was absolutely awful. How could I ever work for a guy who came up with something like that?"

"You were the one who suggested a song. Now you want me to slay the zombies. I don't even know who or what they are yet. Markus, help me, please. I'm afraid of zombies. But with you as my partner, I'd be fearless."

"I thought you wanted to hire me as a sidekick, not a partner."

"Superheroes pair up on occasion, like Batman and Catwoman."

"There's a problem with that comparison, Pete. You would make one ugly lady. Besides, this is a crazy idea."

Pete became more excited. "Look at who's afraid of crazy now. What's the matter? Did the fearless consultant get a little too close to the kryptonite? Let's turn everything upside down. I could use a partner who would share the responsibilities of preaching and leading with me. We have a missionary house that's currently vacant. All I'm asking you to do is pray about what I'm asking."

"I'll pray because you're my friend, but I can't make any guarantees, so don't get your hopes up. But if you write the lyrics to any more songs, we're through."

"I can live with that. I'm Batman."

Chapter 39

She named the boy Ichabod, saying, "The glory has departed
from Israel"—because of the capture of the ark of God and the deaths
of her father-in-law and her husband (1 Samuel 4:21, NIV).

The first Wednesday in January was scheduled as the Homecoming
Celebration. The evening was designated as open mic night, a strange
ritual that always made Pete uncomfortable. Markus told him to spend
an hour in his magic massage chair before meeting.

"You want me to do the Zombie preparation program?"

"Sure. It's still awhile before we slay the zombies, but I think that
setting will do. If I recall, that was number nine, right?"

Pete nodded. "Yep. Number nine. I rotate the settings. I don't want
to wear this thing out."

"I talked to Shirley."

Pete sat up and turned off the chair. "What did she think?"

"You never told me you called her."

"You asked me to, remember?"

"I do, but I didn't know you'd do it so soon."

"We had a really good conversation. You married up, just like me."

"What you said moved her deeply. She couldn't stop talking about all the nice things you said about me personally. She claimed you used words like smartest, most courageous, funny, inventive, and needs his head examined."

"She laughed when I said that, but she also agreed."

"The prayer you spoke over her was powerful. She couldn't stop talking about your conversation. This was the first time she's had a phone call from a stranger who blessed her like that. It's a powerful gift you have. Not only that, you paved the way for our next conversation."

"About coming here?"

"Exactly. She said she was ready for a new adventure. To say that I nearly had a heart attack would be an understatement. I guess what I'm saying is… the answer is *yes.*"

Fanny Mae sat on one side of Kittens. Kate Shoemaker sat on the other. All three had spiked hair. Fanny Mae wore a sporty black-leather jacket. She'd made a return visit to the Hog Barn during the recent cold snap. The cold weather offered her a great excuse to find a replacement for her old powder-blue fabric jacket, which Kate said smelled like mothballs. The one she purchased had pink leather details that formed what the clerk called "a racer pattern." After she'd tried it on, the saleslady offered her a bit of advice.

"With this jacket, your hair would be dazzling with a pink wave. Here's the card for the lady that does my hair. You'll be the talk of the town."

Fanny Mae made an appointment within the hour.

Kate was surprised when she picked up Fanny Mae for open-mic night. "Darlin', you've only been gone a month. People you've known for decades will mistake you for a guest. You look radiant!"

When Pete walked into the fellowship hall and laid eyes on his administrative assistant, he stopped blinking altogether. He was speechless too. The hulk of a man sitting beside her appeared to be looking his way. He stood to his feet and walked straight in Pete's direction.

"My name is Kittens." He grabbed Pete's hand and squeezed so hard Pete wanted to squeal. But he couldn't. He also wanted to laugh.

"Did you say Kittens…or something else?"

"Yes, Kittens. I'm here with Fanny and Kate."

Bender was also in the room. He'd not sat in the fellowship hall of Green Street Baptist Church for a very long time. The memories flooded over him like a second baptism. Seated next to him, Gary Lovejoy grinned from ear to ear as he introduced his guest. When asked, "Where did you get that name?" Gary answered the question for him. "Because he bends the rules of man to follow the heart of God. I taught him in Sunday school when he was a little boy."

Bob and Georgette Freeman sat with Cindy. No one would have known that just a few weeks ago her name was Adelaide. True to his word, Bob was launching an offensive to recover her little girls. Progress had been made, but they were still waiting.

Pete scanned the room. There were so many people he wondered if he was in the wrong place. "Markus, who are all these people?"

"I thought you'd know the answer to that by now. These are the children of the new movement. Anytime you stop doing business as usual, people sense God is ready to do something new—happens every time. My only advice to you is relax and don't try to control the outcome. Let this moment be wild and untamed. You never know what's going to happen in meetings like this. I've seen a lot but never the same thing happening twice. Remember what you said at the Jan-Kay ranch. 'Our

God is never boring. He's new each and every day.' Live your own sermon, Pastor."

Markus stepped to the microphone intending to begin the meeting. At that precise moment, an intruder burst through the doors of the fellowship hall and began shouting.

"You can write Ichabod on the walls of this church. God's glory has departed. You've been invaded by evil spirits. Cleanse yourself from this consultant and the pastor who leads you astray. Come with us. We're starting a new church."

Pete was stunned. Markus was perturbed. Bender was frustrated. Bob and Georgette were disappointed. Cindy was confused. But Fanny was flaming mad. Her pink wave transformed into a burning fire.

"Sic 'em, Kittens! Go show that man how we deal with nuts at Heaven's Angels."

Kittens went to work. For a man of such enormous size, he moved surprisingly fast. When the heckler got one look at the hulk of a man barreling down on him from the other end of the fellowship hall, he turned tail and ran for his life—back through the door and down a long hallway. But the poor guy wasn't fast enough and far too clumsy. In his haste, he stumbled over his own feet and made a hard landing just inside the main exit.

In an instant, Kittens was hovering over the trembling man who now sported a fresh set of carpet burns on both forearms. Starring into the whites of his eyes, he asked, "May I offer the gentleman a hand up?"

Reluctantly the intruder reached out his hand. What he felt next was the strength of the other hand effortlessly hoisting him back to stand on his weak knees. "Thank you, sir," he responded timidly.

Kittens reached down and covered the little man's shoulder with his right hand as they exited the building together. In the parking lot he asked, "Do you believe the Bible?"

"Yes, sir, very much so."

"Very good! Have you ever heard about Elisha?"

"The Old Testament Prophet? Yes, sir."

"Do you know what happened to those name callers who mocked him?"

"I don't believe I know that part of the story, sir."

"You should, especially since you like that one about Ichabod so much. In fact, I suggest you go home tonight and look up the passage for yourself. You'll find it in 2nd Kings, Chapter 2. Would you like me to write that down to help you remember?"

"No, sir. I won't forget."

"Good, you have a skill that will help you in life. I personally don't like spoilers, but I'm going to tell you how the story ends anyway. Are you okay with that"

"No problem, sir."

"Unfortunately the mockers were eaten by bears. Do we understand each other?"

"Yes, sir. We understand each other."

"By the way, they call me Kittens."

Back in the conference room, Pete thought layers of crazy were folding in on themselves. Never in his wildest dreams had he imagined the grand homecoming would go down like this. Pete observed that the whole audience had turned around in their chairs, and every eye was still focused on the door that Kittens had bolted through only a few moments ago. No one really knew what was happening in the hallway. They half expected to hear shouting of some sort or even pleas for mercy. Truth be told, a few had their hopes strongly leaning in that direction. Only a handful of the members present had ever seen Kittens before. But like

Pete, they were glad he was on their side.

After a few moments, nearly everyone turned back around to see how their pastor planned to handle this strange turn of events. They did so just in time to see a wild expression emerge on Pete's face, which caused them to turn back around and look in the other direction again.

Now a second commotion began. The church members sprang to their feet and gasped in unison, much like crowds do in wedding ceremonies when a lovely bride commences her march down the aisle. Pete was so moved by what he witnessed that tears rolled down his cheeks every time he blinked. In moments like these, there was only one thing to do. He offered a joyful prayer to the God of the heavens for divine intervention. Then he thanked God for the uncanny influence pastors' wives have on the churches they serve.

Monica had suddenly entered the room, holding the hand of Frances Jake.

Chapter 40

Charm is deceptive, and beauty is fleeting; but a woman
who fears the Lord is to be praised (Proverbs 31:30, NIV).

Monica had hardly slept two winks the evening of Josh Duncan's visit. She tossed and turned in bed while Pete snored without remorse. Typically her husband was the one with sleep issues. Whatever noises he made were usually lost as she dreamed the night away, but not that night. After watching the ceiling fan whirl for what seemed like hours, she decided to walk through the house and pray. Prayer always worked better for Monica when she was on the move.

She'd stepped into Zane's room. The day he left for college flooded her memories. She recalled spending that entire morning helping him pack. Suddenly the room was filled with cardboard boxes once again. Within each were the memories of a lifetime. She knew that was true because she sealed each one with packing tape herself. On that day, she'd accidently released a few tears on the last box. The discolored cardboard revealed more than she wanted Zane to see. He gave her a big hug and pretended not to notice. Now leftover tears reserved from that memory rolled down her cheeks once more.

Dustin's room was half-empty. Her baby was the last to fly from the nest a little over a year ago. He'd made a short visit during Christmas, but he had to return early. He had a job and a new girlfriend now.

"Mom, she has the brightest eyes you've ever seen," Dustin beamed. "We're getting pretty serious."

Monica desperately wanted to meet this little bright-eyed girl. The way Dustin talked about her made it sound like she might become part of the family. Monica smiled at the thought.

She walked into the living room. Her father's old wooden cross still had four little pieces of paper attached to it. Moonlight spilled though a bare window, causing the nail heads to shimmer. Words she'd written on each paper square now stared back at her: Anger, Fear, Frustration, Depression. She smiled because they no longer represented the names of strongholds that waged war in her heart and soul. No. Not incriminating words at all—just simple instructions on what she had to do next. *Monica, act against your anger. Step into your fears. Fight frustration with a plan. Say goodbye to depression.*

The Voice had clearly spoken once again. She knew what she had to do next. The idea first came to her when she spoke at the Jan-Kay ranch. Something she'd said caused everyone to look at the door. The leaders of Green Street had hoped Frances might walk into the room that afternoon. She remembered saying, "No, I don't have the scheming mind of a Markus Cunningham."

She still didn't. She had something even better. She was the girl who cheered from the bleachers when her husband was giving all he had— like now. She was the girl who made a promise to the ladies of Green Street. She was still the little girl who liked to talk with God. And His voice was always sweet, especially when He spoke so clearly.

Who Killed My Church?

Most people were still trying to process the twists and turns that had already taken place during their homecoming celebration. Had the heckler along with Kitten's response been the only dramatic highlight of the evening, surely this would have been enough to fuel conversations for months to come. Now that Frances had arrived, epic events were unfolding before their eyes.

"I had nothing to do with this, Pete." Markus seemed genuinely surprised.

"Monica, was this your plan?" Pete asked.

"I called Frances right after that coward— Sorry. That *person* left our house. We devised a plan to deal with the possibility of fallout. Frances had the idea to jump on a plane and offer a little moral support. At least I believe she came up with the idea, though I might have been the one to suggest the visit first."

"Frances, how wonderful to see you again," Markus said. "How's Jim doing?"

"He still acts like Hercules. One day he'll realize he has an Achilles heel. When he shared the story about his reception last month, I decided it was my turn to enjoy a family reunion and his turn to take care of the dog."

A line began to form quickly where Frances stood. Most of the ladies who knew her hadn't seen Frances in six years. Misty eyes sparkled all across the room. Frances picked up a wireless microphone and did what came naturally for her.

"Surprise!"

Responses ranged from, "Why didn't you tell us that you were coming," to "Please stay for a while."

"Ladies, it's so good to see you again. For those of you I don't know, welcome. I'd like to thank Monica for extending an invitation for me to be here tonight. She's my precious sister. How I've grown to love her. We connected the first time I heard her voice. What a blessing she'll be for you over the coming years.

"For the men in the room, you'll have to pardon us for a moment. The girls in the house need a little time to say a few things."

At that point, Frances noticed Fanny Mae and Kate sitting next to Kittens, who had returned to his seat merely seconds ago after exercising a little church discipline. "My heavenly stars! Who's this big handsome man? You can't be here together. Three's a crowd."

"Kittens, madam." He rose to his feet still breathing rapidly. "They call me Kittens."

"I need to hear your story later. Fanny Mae, you look stunning. Let me know who did your hair. I want to give Jim a big surprise when I get back to Florida."

Fanny Mae beamed with delight, as Monica watched Frances survey the crowd. She wondered what thoughts rolled through her mind. Monica tried to place herself in Frances' shoes. This domain once belonged to her many years ago. She'd raised a family here, shared so many friendships, and lived her life right here on the ground beneath her feet. How did she feel returning, especially on a night like tonight with all that had transpired? And what did she plan to say during such a time as this?

Frances never let anyone guess for long. She went straight to the point. "I heard someone shout the name Ichabod as I approached the room. That never happens on a normal day. But then again, we didn't have many normal days if I remember correctly."

"No, we didn't," Kate responded.

"Thank you, dear. How I've missed seeing you and hearing you play that organ. No, we didn't have many normal days, but I still treasure each one. There are so many precious memories and oh, how they linger!

"During my quiet time a few days ago, the Lord promised to give me a word tonight. I was about to panic as I walked through the door, but then I heard that wonderful name, Ichabod. The heckler may not have intended to inspire me, but God works in mysterious ways, doesn't He?

"So let me begin by telling you a story."

Chapter 41

One day Jesus told his disciples a story to show that
they should always pray and never give up (Luke 18:1, NLT).

Jim Jake had written several books about the Christian life. They were practical, inspiring, but most of all, creative. People enjoyed reading what he wrote. What they didn't know was that Frances worked behind the scenes as his editor-in-chief. If not for her, most of what Jim wrote would have sounded like the sermons he preached. While he was greatly admired for his ability to parse the Word in the pulpit on Sunday morning, his sermons didn't make for very exciting reading. That's where Frances applied her skills, the same skills she would draw upon tonight.

"Sweet little orphan boy, I think about you night and day. The first time I read your story in the Bible, your name made me smile. I wish I knew so much more about you, but the story of your life ended after you were born. For me and so many others, you seem frozen in time.

"Your mother was so weak on that day. She never had the chance to hold you in her arms. That she would die just moments after you came into the world was totally unexpected. She used the last remaining breath in her lungs to cry out your name. Sometimes I imagine the sound of her voice, so helpless and frail.

"Ichabod!" she cried.

"Then she closed her eyes for the very last time. That your mother's name was never mentioned is so very strange. Most of the characters who played a role in the misfortunes of that day had names, but not her. I wish the world had something more to remember her by.

"One day I tried to decide on a name I'd give her. I had this picture in my mind of what she looked like. I can almost see her now. She had delicate features, long dark hair, soft brown eyes, and the most playful smile imaginable. It may sound a little unusual, but I wanted desperately to connect a name with her face.

"Then it dawned on me that perhaps she wanted to remain anonymous. There are too many instances throughout history where a personal name became a synonym for the tragedy someone endured—kind of like yours did, Ichabod. Sometimes circumstances allow that to happen. Perhaps it's best to let your mother remain in the shadows, to be remembered as a simple woman who brought a sweet baby boy into the world, and then quietly slipped away.

"Ichabod, my sweet little orphan child, there's so much more to share about that day. Telling the story is hard, but still, it remains a part of who you are. Now that you're old enough to hear the truth, let me paint a picture of what happened one tragic day not so very long ago.

"You'd have loved your grandpa. I wish you'd known Eli. He was a prominent man who served as the High Priest of Shiloh. Your precious mother was married to his son.

"Tragically, on the same day you were born, your grandpa fell over backwards from a chair. He was nearly a hundred years old, and his aged body couldn't absorb the impact. Your mother was heartbroken when she heard the news that Eli's neck had broken. The reality must have settled in her mind that her father-in-law would miss holding his grandson by just a few hours. She was devastated.

"Your father's name was Phineas. On the very same day, a man was seen running toward the city gates of Shiloh. He arrived with torn clothes, dust on his head, and disturbing news from the war against the Philistines. Your father had been slain in battle. Tragically, his brother—your uncle—died as well. Thirty thousand men perished on that day. Even the Ark of the Covenant, which contained the Ten Commandments, was captured and became part of the spoils of war.

"My dear Ichabod, this is how your life began. This was the news that caused your mother to begin labor. Her world came crashing down on a day when a young woman needs every ounce of strength she can muster. Birth pangs alone were enough for her to endure, but there was so much more…too much more.

"She must have felt like her entire world was ending. Her nation had just lost the war. The Philistines were descending upon Shiloh. Her husband was dead. The uncle who could have taken the place of your father was cut down by the enemy. The grandfather who might have provided security for the two of you was lying on the ground. But the greatest fear of all was that God had forsaken His people.

"She grieved and she pushed. Each time her womb contracted her tender heart grew a little weaker. I don't know how long she labored to bring you into this world, but I do know this: she never stopped.

"My precious child, you were named on that tragic day. The day was like none other. Your name means 'no glory.' But it merely describes how everyone felt when the man with torn clothes and dust on his head delivered the chilling news.

"But listen to me very carefully, Ichabod. Nothing that happened on that day was your fault. You were just a tiny little baby when Shiloh fell. My sweet Ichabod, you are innocent."

Georgette Freeman paused and glanced at Cindy. She saw the emotions building. Cindy wasn't raised in church, and clearly her knowledge of Scripture ranged from limited to nil. However, the way Frances told the story connected in obvious ways. Until a few days ago, Cindy didn't want anyone to know her real name. Her little girls were orphans now, just like Ichabod. Georgette wasn't surprised when she saw the first tear. Frances noticed too.

"Today someone walked into this church and called you Ichabod. Be very leery of people who value their opinions more highly than the Word of God. Like Ichabod, there's no reason for you to live under the yoke of disgrace, especially over your willingness to start a new journey. What the heckler meant as a curse, I challenge you to embrace without shame. Keep moving forward!

"In Christ, you are innocent. 'There is now therefore no condemnation for those who are in Christ Jesus, who walk not after the flesh, but after the Spirit.' Romans, Chapter 8. It's in the Book!

"Neither are you orphans any longer. You are sons and daughters of the King. 'Behold, what manner of love the Father has bestowed upon us, that we should be called the sons of God.' First John, Chapter 3. It's in the Book!

"Tonight the devil wants to lay a foundation for a new stronghold. He would have you believe the glory of God will never shine in this church again. But I say to you, 'Arise and shine for your light has come. The glory of the LORD has risen upon you.' Isaiah, Chapter 60. It's in the Book!

"Ichabod, others may believe you're marked with a curse to be carried for the rest of your life. But I say they don't understand the power of God. For 'we know that all things work together for good for those who love God and are called according to His purpose.' Romans, Chapter 8. It's in the Book!

"Green Street Baptist Church, I challenge you to keep searching this city for all the little Ichabods out there whose hopes have been shattered by the modern-day Philistines. I am so proud of what you're doing to revitalize this church. Not only do you know what's in the Book, but now you're living the Book! Don't give up, Ichabod. Your life has just begun."

Cindy was no longer crying, but neither was she sitting. She was moving toward the pulpit, eyes sparkling, face smiling. Frances received her with open arms. As they embraced, she whispered in Frances' ear.

"I want to believe all those things you said were in the Book. I think her name could have been Cindy. That's my name too. Can God help me?"

"My sweet little child," Frances whispered back. "He sent me here tonight. How would you like to know Him personally?"

"I'd like that very much."

Everyone watched the drama unfold as Frances prayed with Cindy. There was just something about that girl. Kittens knew what it was. And for the rest of the evening, his eyes never looked elsewhere.

Chapter 42

My lover is mine and I am his; he browses among the lilies
(Song of Solomon 2:16, NIV).

Monica sat on the bed laughing. Pete stood in the open doorway of their bedroom. The evening had been full of surprises, and she felt very alive. Everything that transpired from the gathering in the fellowship hall to dropping Frances off at the hotel made for one unforgettable day. She was curious to know how Pete felt about the events of the evening.

"Did you see Kittens gawking at Cindy?" she asked.

"He's a goner." Pete moved into the room and sat beside her on the bed.

"I believe you're right. I think I heard Kittens purring," she giggled.

"That's one big man. He tried to look inconspicuous but ended up lumbering around after Cindy like a badly-wrapped mummy. She was so happy after praying with Frances, I don't think she noticed."

"There could be wedding bells," she said with a lilt. "And who was that mindless heckler that Kittens went after?"

"He hardly ever comes to church on Sunday morning. Josh goes out with him to lunch about once a week. He won't try that again. If he does,

I'll get Fanny Mae and Kate to call up our new hit squad."

"And the guy Gary Lovejoy introduced—what was his name again?"

"That was Bender. He's been friends with Markus for a long time. In fact, I'm supposed to meet him at a coffee shop tomorrow. Markus said Bender is doing some pretty exciting things that are part of our plan to slay the zombies."

"Who are the zombies?"

"I don't have a clue. Markus hasn't told me much about it yet. He likes me to believe he's got everything mapped out in vivid detail, but he's still trying to figure this one out. At least that's my opinion."

"I wish you could get someone like him to replace Josh."

Her comment triggered Pete's memory. "Oh, you're not going to believe this! I almost forgot to tell you. I've already asked, and he accepted my offer."

"Pete, are you serious? That's too awesome! Will he move here with his wife?"

"I plan to let them stay in our missionary home since it's vacant right now."

"Yikes, Pete! That place needs some help. I'll call his wife and find out what we can do to get the place ready for them. You guys always think about the job. For the woman, it's about the home."

"Good catch."

"Frances told me on the drive back to the hotel that she loved hearing all the testimonies of what people did in December. She said her husband would have enjoyed leading something like that. By the way, I'm going with her to the beauty salon tomorrow."

There was something in the tone Monica used to state her intentions that made Pete feel a little cautious. If he said nothing, he risked the accusation of being insensitive. If he said something, he usually didn't get it right. What to do?

"You two seem to really enjoy each other," he said, offering what he considered a safe statement. "I'm glad you're going."

"Do you think I'm still pretty?"

I knew something was coming. "You look better than the day we first met."

"That was so predictable, Pete. You said that just to stay out of trouble."

"Sounds like I just got into trouble."

Monica spoke the next words very slowly. "A girl needs to hear the particulars... like what you find attractive, and how she makes you feel. Haven't you done marriage counseling before?"

"I get it. When you strolled into the fellowship hall tonight holding Frances' hand, I was so surprised. My knees grew weak. My heart skipped a beat. I couldn't even think straight. I felt like Kittens did after seeing Cindy for the very first time. Then I thought to myself, who is that gorgeous woman? Several ladies called out the name Frances. That's when I knew."

Monica slapped Pete's shoulder.

"Ouch!"

"You're not funny." She stood to her feet and sashayed toward the bathroom.

Pete laughed, half nervously and half because he thought he'd been clever. Then he bounced after her. "Monica, wait a second."

She turned around and beguiled him with a smile. "Do you want to try again?"

He reached down and wrapped his fingers between hers. Pulling her close, he closed his eyes and inhaled deeply. "You smell like happy feels."

Monica giggled and then burst out laughing. "Where did that come from? It sounds like a sad pick-up line from a B movie."

"I said it because I love to hear you laugh…" He released her hands and ran his fingers through her long strawberry-blonde hair. "…and it worked too." He loved how her hair cascaded down her back. "You should have let me finish…" he continued. She tilted her head as he caressed her neck. "…because there's more I want you to hear."

He gazed into her eyes, a deep-blue sea, then brushed her lips with a delicate touch. "As I was saying…" He smiled. "That's when I knew once again that I can't live without you.

"I've never seen you walk through a door that you didn't grab the attention of every eye in the room. Your laughter fills up the empty spaces. From the very first time you smiled at me, you cast a spell that's never been broken. I'm more alive when you're around. There's not another girl like you.

"Your beauty…" He kissed her with all the longing and passion he felt. "…is both skin and soul."

Monica took a deep breath. "That was sweet." There was a slight flutter in her voice. "You should have gotten the words right the first time, but you're not in trouble anymore.

"Now let me ask another question, and I want an honest answer. How are you doing?"

Pete's eyebrows shot up. "Me?"

"Yes, you! And don't feed me a bunch of bull. I need to hear you convince me that things are good on the inside of Pete Blackman."

Pete considered the question for a moment. Memories accompanied by emotions raced through his mind. He remembered how he felt while sitting in Room 212b. Not so very long ago, his future at Green Street was careening out of control towards a jagged cliff. The day he decided to visit the lake and ended up in the water flashed through his mind too. Then there was the sense of uncertainty that descended upon him each time Markus came up with another crazy idea. Josh's surprise, Markus' yes, Cindy's transformation, Ripper, the zombies on the horizon, all swirled around him like he was the center of a large vortex. *How am I doing?*

"Pete, what are you thinking?"

"I'm thinking the magic massage chair has solved all my problems."

"Be serious. I need to know that you're okay. You've always stayed in a race whether you felt like it or not, whether you were injured, or about to collapse from exhaustion. You haven't changed since the day we met."

"You're exaggerating."

"We can argue that later. Here's my point. If you're running for a goal you believe in, I'll keep cheering in the stands. But stop doing this if it makes you miserable and puts you in an early grave. I can't live without you, either."

Monica lifted a hand and gently rubbed Pete's forehead. "If you ever desire to go somewhere and live a less complicated life, I'll follow you to the ends of the earth. Don't think for a moment that I need all this stuff. The only thing I want is for us to enjoy our lives together. You're the best man I've ever known. I need to know how you're doing."

"To be honest with you, I don't think much about how I'm doing."

"Then be very thankful that God gave you a woman. 'Know thyself,' Pete, 'and to thine own self be true.' If you want this with all your heart because you believe God has planned this for our lives, then we're doing the right thing. But if you're just trying to save your reputation, career, or anything else of less worth than your sanity and joy, then stop. Under God, the responsibility you bear is that I will follow you over a cliff. I trust you to be in this for the right reasons."

"I…" Pete struggled to gather his thoughts. "This conversation got real deep real fast."

"You believe I light up a room when I walk through the door. The truth is I light up when I see you in the room. If you want to start a church on a tiny island and move me into a one-bedroom hut, I'll go. Let the fruit of the Spirit guide your heart in discovering the path of God, whether that's here or elsewhere. If you *love* what you're doing, find *joy* in it, and experience *peace*, then you're rooted in the will of God. When the fruit is missing, the roots are in the wrong place.

"As you and Markus forge ahead, don't forfeit love, joy, or peace. Fight courageously for what you believe in, and don't let the creeps grind you down. Does this make any sense?"

"Monica, you'd have made a fantastic preacher."

"Silly boy, I'm just repeating a sermon you preached a long time ago. You also said it's far better to fail at something you're not supposed to do than to find success at doing the wrong thing. Preacher, hear thyself!"

"I've never desired to sway the masses like you dream of doing. All I care about is swaying your heart to be true. Then the masses will fall in love with the man I know you to be. Do you understand?"

"Absolutely."

"Why are you being so agreeable?"

"I was just wondering if you wanted to say anything else before I jump into the bleachers and carry you away."

Monica giggled again. "Don't get your hopes up, Champ."

"You wouldn't want to deny me love, joy, or peace, would you?"

"Stop being so theological and just kiss me."

Chapter 43

Bear with each other and forgive whatever grievances you may have
against one another. Forgive as the Lord forgave you
(Colossians 3:13, NIV).

Gary Lovejoy, Pete Blackman, Markus Cunningham, and Shawn
Davis, aka Bender, sat at a table. Bender's coffee shop was hopping
with business. Several baristas worked the counter handing out signature
drinks, much to the delight of the clientele. Not only was the place
packed, but Pete thought everyone had one thing in common—they
were all happy people.

"Nice environment," Pete remarked. "Markus told me about your
background and how you got your name. I was inspired."

"He and I go way back. But listen. What an honor for me to have the
one and only Pete Blackman in my coffee shop. We're all on pins and
needles wondering how this story will end. Do you read Markus' blog?"

"No. Why read it? I'm living it."

"Right! Hey, Markus, our tribes are studying your notes on the life
of Ichabod this week. I don't think you missed anything Frances said.
Did she really come up with all that on the fly?"

"That would be Frances' special gift," Gary responded. "Sometimes I wonder whether she helped write some of Pastor Jake's best sermons. When Monica led her into the fellowship hall, I knew God had something special in store for us."

"I'm glad she rescued Ichabod from the cartoonish images I remember from childhood," Pete added. "Every Halloween our family piled on the couch in the living room and watched 'The Legend of Sleepy Hollow.' I can still see poor Ichabod Crane with his oversized Adam's apple trying to escape the headless horseman. My older sisters loved to spook me when that decapitated ghost started swinging his terrible sword. At the most frightening moment, when he threw that pumpkin across the bridge, one of them would always pop the back of my head."

"That's messed up," Bender said. "Did you ever get therapy for that?"

Markus laughed first. Gary joined in cautiously.

"No, but after this is over, I'll add it to the list of things Markus has put me through."

"Good call!" Bender laughed. "When I went to see a counselor once, I put all my lost marbles on the table and said, 'I'm more broke than I am broken, so you've got one hour to fix me.'"

"That's good. I might try that myself."

Markus shifted the topic abruptly. "Bender, a few nights ago Pete and I had a discussion that reminded me of your ministry. Pete's working on a plan to implement the disciple-making strategy of Jesus. He's got the process nailed down to four steps. If I remember correctly, they were gather, deliver, train, and send."

"The process is elegant and simple. In fact," Markus said with a smirk, "it's too brilliant for him to have come up with this on his own. Monica probably did the lion's share of the research."

"*Et tu*, why don't you step into the kitchen and roast some beans since roasting me isn't working for you? I'm adding your funky brain to the list of reasons I need therapy." Pete leaned back and laughed at his own joke.

"Perhaps you really should read my blog, Pete. You might enjoy the list I've started on you."

"That's not true. There's no list. Bender, he just made that up, right?"

"Like I said earlier, you're the one and only Pete Blackman. I wouldn't worry, though. Everyone knows Markus exaggerates the truth."

Pete pulled the phone out of his pocket and started searching the internet. Markus exchanged a wicked smile with Bender. Both started laughing.

"What?" Pete looked up.

"Young man," Gary chimed in, "they're playing you."

Pete sighed. Then he chuckled. "Maybe I'll write a book when this is all over. Somebody needs to set the record straight." Pete sipped his white chocolate cappuccino. "Wow, this is fantastic!"

"Thank you. You've just made my day. Now, did I hear correctly? Gather, deliver, train and send? I like the way that flows. Where did you come up with that?"

Pete placed his coffee cup on the table and leaned back. The room was already full and over a dozen people were still standing in line. Something about the room felt very familiar. He gathered his thoughts momentarily and answered the question.

"I started under the assumption that Jesus was the best disciple-maker who ever lived. His strategy was flawless as well as timeless. My goal was to read through the New Testament and condense His methodology into a transferable process.

"After a lot of reflection and prayer, those four simple words emerged. I believe they describe how Jesus launched a disciple-making movement that spread across the world. Now I'm trying to figure out how to build our new ministry structure around His strategy. As you know, our church is undergoing a massive overhaul."

"Yes, that's an ambitious plan," Bender responded. "As I was listening, I realized we use the same strategy in our house-church network. We *gather* people from every background into tribes that meet in homes, although some prefer to meet in a different setting. In fact, three groups are meeting here right now."

Pete scanned the room again and noticed open Bibles on half the tables. "Brilliant," he exclaimed. "How did I miss that?"

"We flow with the natural rhythms of our age groups. Through the course of getting to know them personally, we come to understand how sin is manifesting in their lives. We're intentional about *delivering* them from bondage. Next, we *train* them in the Word and *send* them out to plant more tribes in other locations. Gather, deliver, train and send—a simple strategy but a workable one."

Pete looked through the windows to the tables on the sidewalk. Several people were enjoying a resting place in the cool afternoon breeze. He noticed animated conversations taking place over open Bibles. His eyes found Bender's. "I'd enjoy leading something like that at Green Street."

Gary's face lit up. "Pete, I need to share something with you. I attended one of those tribes during December. The first time I went, I was reminded so much of how our church began when I was a young man. The memories flooded..."

Gary choked up. He couldn't speak. He tried, but the tears just rolled down his face more rapidly. "Excuse me," he said. "I'll be back in a minute."

Pete observed Gary moving a little slower than normal as he made his way to the back of the coffee shop. "I've known that man over five years now," he reflected. "That was the first time I've ever seen him get emotional. He's always been the epitome of courage under fire."

"He has a lot going on right now," Bender said. "There are some pretty serious issues he needs to get off his chest, but I'll leave that for him to say. I don't mean to change the subject so abruptly, but I have an idea that I need to share with you, that is, if you have the time."

"Of course he does," Markus said. "Pete and I are partners now. My vote is that he doesn't leave until he's heard every last detail."

"I'm still getting used to my new sidekick." Pete grinned. "Fire away, I'm interested."

"Something's been bothering me for a very long time. I didn't know how to put what I was feeling into words until I sat in the fellowship hall on the night Frances led Cindy to Christ. The door beside my chair opened into a small Sunday school room where Gary first taught me how to become a Christ-follower. In that moment, I felt both sadness and joy—joy over the memory of finding salvation just a few feet away from where Cindy accepted Christ, but sadness over the growing divide between the old and the new, the young and the old, the affluent and the poor.

"My heart broke while sitting in that chair. American Christianity has become fragmented, less kingdom-oriented, and too focused on catering to personal preferences. Our house-church network is filled with young people who've abandoned all the traditional churches. While we've been very successful at creating an environment that blends with their culture and expectations, I believe we've lost something in the process—almost like we dropped our inheritance in the dust and simply walked away."

"I would agree with that," Pete said. "I spy a sea of gray hair every Sunday morning as I survey the audience."

Bender continued. "Traditional churches like Green Street have vast resources acquired over decades. They once believed they were building a legacy for future generations. Unfortunately, they haven't figured out how to leverage those resources for ministry in the modern age. Someone needs to crack the code on what's causing the rift in the fabric of our faith. I believe the next movement of God will happen when we allow Him to throw down the strongholds and bridge the great divide."

"What would that look like?" Pete asked.

Bender was about to reply when he noticed Gary returning from the bathroom. The aging saint's eyes were glossy-red. So was his nose, an obvious sign that he was far from getting a handle on his emotions.

"Welcome back, Gary." Bender's eyes were filled with sympathy. "I was just about to tell Pete about my idea."

Gary nodded but didn't say a word.

"There are two challenges I face every day in my ministry," Bender said. "The first is making sure we have a place to meet on the weekend when our tribes all gather together. The second is discovering and training enough leaders who can plant more tribes."

Bender paused. His eyes intensified their focus. He leaned into the table and said, "Imagine if I became a third partner with you and Markus."

Markus jumped back into the conversation. "Pete, I'm ready to reveal the plan for slaying the zombies."

Then Gary spoke. "Pete, will you forgive me?"

Pete remembered sitting in a room once as a little boy with his mother and two older sisters. He couldn't seem to figure out how their conversation worked. Each appeared to be talking about something different, and yet they were still talking to each other. He was confused as to why they weren't confused. He grew frustrated just trying to make sense of it all. His mind swam in circles on that day. The only thing different about this day was that he happened to be older now.

"Gary, I'll start with you. What's wrong?"

Chapter 44

I know that there is nothing better for men than to be happy
and do good while they live (Ecclesiastes 3:12, NIV).

The announcement that there would be another special meeting at Green Street Baptist Church blasted through the prayer chain. Word traveled fast. All Fanny Mae had to do was call up the captains and let the process take care of itself. The prayer chain was an old tech marvel that could hold its own against any newfangled method one might find in other churches, at least in Fanny Mae's humble opinion.

The leadership was no longer surprised to hear a meeting had been called on such short notice. Truth be told, they kind of enjoyed the marvel and mystery of what was happening. Of late, their meetings had become a showcase for wonders to behold, just like in the good old days. Only now, the new days were the new rave.

This meeting was supposed to be for church leaders only. A few curious non-leaders, who fancied themselves to be in the know, attended anyway. While most in the room knew nothing, a spoiler alert had gone out that Gary Lovejoy might be the main feature of the evening. Since he'd never served on staff, they were puzzled as to why this would be the case. Perhaps he was a smokescreen for someone else who planned to show up and astound everyone, although who that might be was hard to imagine. Anyone of note had already done that.

Pete, Markus, Bender, and Gary sat in the choir rehearsal room as people assembled in the sanctuary. Pete noticed Gary was shaking. He could be nervous, or he might be suffering from his latest chemo treatment.

When Gary told Pete he had an aggressive form of pancreatic cancer, Pete was shocked. "They don't give me much time to live, Pastor," Gary had said. "There's little they can do but throw a few Hail Marys in the IV and hope for a miracle."

Pete wept with Gary when he'd shared the news at Bender's coffee shop. Despite everything that happened between the two a few months ago, Pete was still a minister through and through. *There's no reason to hang on to a root of bitterness,* he thought, *especially when there's an opportunity to comfort a brother in crisis.*

Gary asked Pete to forgive him at least five different times, twice in the coffee shop and three times on the sidewalk after Markus and Bender left. Pete's response was kind and genuine. "Let go of the guilt, my friend. God used it for His glory. What our enemy meant for evil, God intended for good. We wouldn't be here today if that meeting had never taken place."

Pete would never forget Gary's reply. "I've been torturing myself for what happened in that conference room. I don't like revisiting the memory of that cold November morning, but there's no other way of getting it off my chest. I remember saying back then, 'Pete, you're a good man with a good heart, but we need more than that right now.'"

Gary's eyes turned into a puddle of tears after he repeated those words. What he said next was punctuated by sobs. "I've never been so wrong in all my life. You're not just a good man, Pete. You're the godliest man I've ever met. We've never needed more than that. Please share my heart with Monica. I know I caused her pain too."

The only surviving charter member had one final wish. He wanted to address the committee leaders, Sunday school teachers, volunteers, and staff about something God had branded on his heart. There was no one in the church who had more influence than Gary Lovejoy. He'd been there from the very beginning. He was there every Sunday. He'd been there longer than any pastor or any other church member. He was older than the buildings and even the name on the church sign. No opinion was more highly respected. Such men have the ability to make things happen or make them go away. Sadly, he was about to go away but not without leaving something behind—a stronger church with a brighter future.

Pete, Markus, and Bender were now working side by side. When they heard Gary's proposal, they seized the opportunity without hesitation. The plan fit perfectly with what would be necessary to slay the zombies. The details and timeline were still being hammered out daily in Bender's coffee shop. Bender referred to these meetings as 'jam sessions.' Pete really liked the phrase, but what he liked even more was Bender's new role at Green Street.

Without revealing the more sensitive aspects of the plan, Markus shared a few details in his blog. The number of unique visitors had nearly doubled since the last week. Someone wrote a comment that the three thought was fascinating.

From Bradley in Vancouver: *All the interesting things in life center around the number three. Our one God is a triune being. Jonah was in the belly of the whale for three days and three nights. There were three disciples in Jesus' inner circle. His ministry lasted three years. Jesus prayed in the garden three times before He was arrested. Then Peter denied Him three times shortly thereafter. Capping everything, Jesus was in the tomb for three days before the Resurrection. To the three men named Pete, Markus, and Bender, who are rocking the Christian community from Ft. Worth to Canada, I have three things to say: Keep going. Don't Stop. Write a book.*

The three men did the first two things without flinching. The third would have to wait. Tonight, everything was coming down to one defining moment. Gary was about to do what he did so many years ago. As one of the twenty charter members who founded Green Street Baptist Church over six decades earlier, he didn't want to leave this world without helping to birth a new movement. That was the only legacy he wanted to leave behind. And now he was standing in a place where he seldom stood—a pulpit.

From the looks on the faces of those who'd gathered there that night, everyone was anxious to know what he had to say.

Chapter 45

When I heard these things, I sat down and wept. For some days I
mournedand fasted and prayed before the God of heaven
(Nehemiah 1:4, NIV).

Those who were there remembered Gary Lovejoy walking very
slowly to the pulpit. He'd pulled out a few sheets of paper, and for several
seconds, stacked them neatly before his eyes. Some in the audience
believed his age made him appear tired and frail. Others entertained
the possibility that he labored through a sleepless night in preparation
for what he was about to say. Only Pete, Markus, and Bender knew the
real reason. Nevertheless, what he said that night was of such historical
significance that a word-for-word transcript was made for the church
archives.

Approximately two years later, his great granddaughter heard about
this speech and the lasting impact it had on Green Street Baptist Church.
Knowing Gary never appeared in public again touched her in ways she
couldn't quite explain. She wanted to possess a copy of the transcript
for herself and learn more about the man who was remembered as the

patriarch of the Lovejoy family.

Monica knew exactly where it was tucked away. In the historical archives section of Green Street's church library, she pulled out a loose-leaf binder that bore the title *The Start of a New Day*. Her smile was genuine as she handed it to the bright-eyed girl.

This is what Monica's new bright-eyed daughter-in-law, Gari Lovejoy Blackman, read as they sat together.

Good evening, and thank you for coming tonight. I've never realized how intimidating it is to stand up here. I'm not a very good public speaker, but perhaps my heart will be able to communicate what needs to be said, even if my words fall short.

Some of you may feel like the man whose hanging failed because he was left out of the loop. In his case, being left out *of the loop was a bigger blessing than being* in *the loop. So you'll have to decide when this is all over how important it is for you stay in the loop* [Editor's note: Everybody laughed].

I have many things of importance I need to share. The first one won't be very easy for me. Last month I went to see my doctor because of some troubles I was experiencing. That's never surprising when you're nearly ninety. If someone had told me when I was younger that I'd be spending so much time waiting in a doctor's office at this stage in my life, I would have learned to enjoy crossword puzzles or knitting doilies [Editor's note: More laughter].

Well, after a few tests, my doctor told me I needed more tests. After those tests, my doctor told me I had advanced pancreatic cancer. At my age, or any age for that matter, this isn't good news. When I asked him how much longer I had to live, his tears revealed a genuine concern. "Gary," he said, "you have perhaps six months to get your business in order." The words he spoke sent cold chills up and down my spine.

Who Killed My Church?

News like that will change a man's life. You might think I'd be over and done with changing by now. Many of you remember my sweet wife, Gail. She always tried to get me to change this or that. I was pretty stubborn back then, but she never stopped loving me anyway. How I've missed that woman over the years.

I always wondered what people meant by the statement "My life flashed before my eyes." That's not a mystery to me anymore. In that moment, I saw myself as a little boy riding a red and gold bicycle down the street. Then I was standing before a preacher holding the hand of a pretty girl all dressed in white. Our children were born. I saw flashes of them growing up, leaving home, getting married and having children of their own. All of this spun through my mind like a cyclone.

Other things flashed through my mind as well. I saw myself standing on the front lawn chatting with our neighbors about starting a new church. I watched Gail clean our house from sunup to sundown to get ready for that first meeting we held back in the early '50s. I stood for a picture, holding a shovel as we broke ground for this sanctuary. All of this and more rushed through my memory.

There was one scene, however, that caused me a great deal of sorrow. I saw myself in our conference room here at the church. Other members of the finance committee were seated around me. The looks were grave and tempers were flaring. I put my foot down and forced a vote. It came back three to two in my favor. As the chairman of the finance committee, I asked Pete Blackman to resign as the senior pastor of Green Street Baptist Church.

Our church had been in a steady decline for years. I panicked and took matters into my own hands. I was so frustrated and confused on that day. All of these same emotions came rushing back in an instant when the doctor handed out my diagnosis. But this time they wounded my heart. I realized then as I do now that if God hadn't intervened,

I would have made one of the biggest mistakes of my life. The words of rebuke that Jesus spoke to Peter echoed in my mind: "You are not mindful of the things of God, but of the things of man."

Since then, I've asked both Pete and Monica to forgive me. The day I went to ask Monica personally, she invited me into the living room of their house. She showed me an old wooden cross her father made before he passed away. There were several yellow pieces of paper nailed to the cross. One read "Pete." On two others were written "Zane" and "Dustin."

Gari looked up from reading the transcript and locked eyes with her mother-in-law. Monica knew the place where the bright-eyed girl stopped reading. She also detected a hint of emotions beginning to surface. Gari looked back down and continued.

I also remember seeing words like "fear" and "frustration" written on some of the pieces of paper. I felt so responsible and ashamed. I knew then what my role had been in quenching the Spirit of our church. I saw my ugly pride for what is was, and I broke down in her living room and wept like a baby.

Then Monica said, "Mr. Lovejoy, I didn't show you this to make you sad. Everything and everyone I pray for is on this cross. I always finish my quiet time in the morning standing right here. What you're looking at are people and things I've given to Jesus. Each piece of paper represents a miracle or the hope for one. God has turned my mourning into dancing.

Moments later she took me by the hand and led me into Pete's study. In the top drawer of his desk were more pieces of paper, a small hammer, and a few nails. We went back into the living room. Then she wrote my name on one of them, and I watched her nail it to the cross.

"You see," she said, "Every morning I will pray for you until you go

home to be with Gail. She's waiting for you. Don't be afraid. Like Jesus said, 'All your sins are forgiven. You can go in peace.'"

Gari looked up again. Tears rolled down her cheeks like raindrops sliding down a windowpane. The very sight of her caused Monica to do the same.

"I'll have to read this later. My contacts just quit working. It's so emotional reading about what happened. I remember Dustin telling me once that my great-grandfather restored his faith in God. He never shared the full story."

Monica smiled. "When you nail something to the cross, you're supposed to leave it there. If you don't, you'll run out of nails and lose your mind. We've all learned that together as a family.

"All of this happened around the same time Dustin started dating you. He didn't know about the finance committee meeting back then. When he connected the dots and discovered you were related to one of our church members, he had no cause to be concerned."

"Please tell me…how did the meeting end?"

"As I remember, time stood still. It may have been the longest night in the history of our church. Like the title says, it was *The Start of a New Day*. What your great grandfather did took the kind of courage that's very rare in church life. He entered a season of genuine brokenness. When he removed the mask covering the truth, his own transparency and humility came shining through.

"He gave the most beautiful public confession I've ever heard. He told the truth about himself and the truth about the church. It was like the floodgates opened up after that. Others began to do the same. People were confessing, crying, hugging each other, and even laughing before the night was over. What happened was like the revivals you read about in history. God poured out His Spirit in that room and we haven't been the same since."

"Dustin told me things changed after that. How so?"

"Funny you should ask. All that next week people came knocking on my door. They wanted to see 'the old rugged cross.' Some took measurements. Others asked if the church could make a few hundred and pass them out one Sunday. I've heard that most people in our church have one hanging somewhere in their house."

"I think you started a movement," Gari beamed.

"Funny that you should say that too. For me, the whole thing started when I heard Markus say something to my husband. Though the words were originally intended for him, they hit me pretty hard too."

"What did he say?"

"He said the real work must begin in you."

Monica smiled. "Now, let's go look at some furniture for the two of you."

Chapter 46

His lord said unto him, "Well done, thou good and faithful servant...
enter thou into the joy of thy lord"
(Matthew 25:21, KJV).

Fanny Mae was the first to call Pete when she found out Gary
Lovejoy had been taken by ambulance to the emergency room. The
doctor had been generous when he told Gary how much time he had
left. He didn't have six months—he had more like six weeks.

Pete jumped in his Camry late that night and drove to the hospital
as fast as he could. When he arrived, the nurse ushered him into the
room where the last charter member of Green Street Baptist Church lay
quietly in bed. Pete was surprised to see how much weight Gary had lost
over such a short period of time. Every piece of technology the hospital
owned to monitor a vital sign appeared to be attached to his failing body.
But there was nothing more that could be done. That much was certain.
His physical condition had deteriorated so rapidly that Pete knew he
didn't have long.

"Pastor," Gary whispered, "you didn't need to come."

Before Pete had a chance to respond, another nurse walked through the door. "Mr. Lovejoy, are you comfortable? I have something to ease the pain."

"Please, no…" The words came out weak. "…talk with my pastor."

As she left, Pete struggled to find the right words to say. He remembered Job's friends in the Old Testament who said all the wrong things. Even though Pete had sat with the dying more times than he could remember over the years, he always had a struggle. After searching his heart momentarily, the words he wanted to say finally came.

"Gary, thank you."

The response wasn't immediate. "Why?"

"After all those years of hearing about the church starting two blocks down the road, I never knew it was in your home. At least, not until you mentioned it on the night you spoke before the church."

"Acts 20:20."

"You want me to read Acts 20:20?"

Gary nodded. "Yes… It was our vision."

Pete found the verse on his phone and read it out loud. "You know that I have not hesitated to preach anything that would be helpful to you but have taught you publicly and from house to house." His eyes drifted back to Gary. Pete could tell he was struggling to speak. He put his ear close to his friend's lips.

"We started house to house… began in homes like Bender… like today."

Gary's eyes rolled back as he drifted off to sleep. Pete sat in the chair next to his bed for the rest of the evening. He texted Monica to let her know he wouldn't be coming home anytime soon.

Around five a.m., the heart monitor set off an alarm. Pete woke up to the sound of rushing feet. A doctor came into the room and quietly whispered to the others, "DNR."

"Is there anything we can do for you, Pastor?" a nurse asked.

"Thank you, but no. His family's on the way. They won't arrive in Ft. Worth until this afternoon. I'll meet with them later."

Pete placed his hand on Gray's forehead. "Say hello to Him for me."

Chapter 47

Brothers, we do not want you to be ignorant
about those who fall asleep, or to grieve like
the rest of men, who have no hope (1 Thessalonians 4:13, NIV).

Pete drove past the church on his way home from the hospital and remembered he needed to leave a message on the church's answering machine. When Fanny Mae got in the office that morning, the prayer captains would be notified immediately. In a few hours the entire church would learn that Gary Lovejoy had passed away.

Pete's car pulled into the driveway just before dawn. The front porch light was on, but the rest of the house was dark. He walked cautiously through the living room trying not to stumble over anything. The door to the bedroom opened with a soft pop. Monica's eyes opened. She was a light sleeper, an acquired skill that came in handy when Zane and Dustin were teenagers.

"How are you doing?" She rubbed the sleep from her eyes and reached for his hand.

"I'm okay, just exhausted. I need to crash for a few hours before the family arrives."

"So he's gone?"

"About thirty minutes ago."

"That must have been hard to watch."

"The heart monitor went berserk, but he went peacefully."

Monica observed the dark circles under her husband's eyes. She could tell he was emotionally drained. Even his words sounded fatigued. "Come to bed. I'll help you fall asleep."

Pete slid into bed as if into an oasis of calm. Monica snuggled up close and kissed him on the shoulder. She gently caressed his forehead until his breathing changed. He was fast asleep in seconds.

Monica watched the ceiling fan spin for several minutes. The curtains began to glow as the sun peeked over the eastern sky. She slipped out of bed quietly and entered the living room to pray. The first thing to catch her eye was a little piece of paper nailed to her father's old wooden cross. "Gary Lovejoy," she read.

A few minutes later Monica was in her car. The destination was a place she'd not seen in over four years, but she remembered the way well enough. When they first moved to Ft. Worth to lead Green Street Baptist Church, many social gatherings and special meetings were held there. *We shouldn't have given up so easily.*

She arrived in a matter of minutes and walked to the front doorstep and rang the doorbell. No one answered, not that she was expecting anyone to be home. She turned the door knob and entered through the front door. *They forgot to lock the house before they rushed him away.*

A large portrait of Gary and Gail Lovejoy hung in the entryway. Monica recognized the picture from an old church directory. This was the last one where his wife appeared by his side. In the two directories that followed, he was photographed alone. Those pictures didn't show the same spark in his eyes that this one did. Here he looked so alive and strong. Gail's eyes appeared sunken and distant. The subtle signs of dementia had already begun to reveal themselves. *He missed her so much.*

Monica began to pray silently. *You must have seen him by now, Lord. I'm so happy for him. I've tried to imagine what it was like when he first caught site of Gail. Even though he was devastated when she left him here all alone, he never stopped...*

Her throat tightened. Tears rolled down her cheeks. The portrait blurred before her eyes. *He never stopped serving You. On the night he spoke to the leaders of our church, he honored my husband in a very special way. He told everyone he would be the first to sign up for Pete's seminar on the disciple-making strategy of Jesus. He encouraged everyone else to do the same. My husband was so happy. I never thanked Mr. Lovejoy for that. Please let him know how I feel.*

He made things right between us before You carried him away. Now our hearts are free. He brought healing to our home. Please let him know that I believe he was a great man.

Monica pulled a yellow sticky note out of her pocket. On one side it read "Gary Lovejoy," on the other, "Gail is waiting for you." She took a pen and marked out the words "waiting for." Up above she wrote the word "with"—"Gail is with you." She fixed the note to the portrait, turned away, and locked the door behind her.

Sitting in her car, Monica took one last look before backing out of the driveway. For years she'd avoided turning down the street where this house sat. She searched for that familiar emotion, but she no longer felt it. The pain had vanished like the summer dew.

Just as she was about to put the car in reverse, her phone chirped, and a text message appeared on the screen from Dustin. She smiled.

"I'd like you and dad to meet the girl I'm dating. Are you in town this weekend?"

That same morning, Markus sat on a couch in the newly-remodeled missionary home of Green Street Baptist Church. Boxes and furniture were scattered everywhere. He knew several days would be required to get everything situated, but that didn't bother him in the least. Shirley was with him now. If she'd left everything in Florida to join him in an empty house, it would still feel like a little piece of paradise.

Their frequent separations on account of his travelling schedule were now a thing of the past, at least for the foreseeable future. The time-consuming ordeal of relocating was now behind them. Now he was ready to focus on implementing the new ministry plan. Before heading out to the church, he took a few moments to update his blog.

Dear Friends: The night Gary Lovejoy spoke to the leaders of our church was a major turning point. He and I discussed at length what he planned to say. While he was truly grateful for my input, I must confess I underestimated the impact his words would carry. God's hand was upon him that night in ways that can only be described as mysterious and rare.

He told the funny story about sneaking into a movie theater when he was just a little boy. He didn't have his mother's permission, nor did he pay for a ticket. Unfortunately, he ended up in a horror flick called White Zombie, *which just so happened to be the very first zombie movie ever made.*

"No one had ever seen anything like that before," he explained. "All those dead people running around with menacing eyeballs frightened me so much I had nightmares for weeks."

When his mother found out what he'd done, she said, "It serves you right." Then she asked, "What happened to all those zombies in the end?"

"They died," he sniffled.

She replied, "Well, good. If they're dead, they can't hurt you, so stop dreamin' about 'em!"

Then Gary looked over the congregation and said, "We have too many zombie ministries from the past. Stop dreaming about yesterday and give them a proper burial. Slay the zombies," he thundered, "or you'll soon become one yourself. It's time for our church to walk among the living."

Markus stopped typing when his cellphone rang.

"Hello. Markus speaking."

"This is Monica. Sorry to call so early on your first day back."

"No, I'm glad you did. Shirley loved the flowers you left for her in the entryway. Pete said you got the ball rolling on the remodeling project. How do we ever thank you?"

"Markus…" There was a long pause.

"Is something wrong?"

"Gary Lovejoy passed away early this morning. Pete's resting after a long night at the hospital. He'd want you to know before the word gets out."

Markus processed the news in silence for a moment. "I wasn't expecting this to happen so soon."

"I know. It came as a shock to us too."

"How are you and Pete doing? And don't feed me the standard answer."

"Everything is beginning to make sense now, Markus. I believe Gary finally let go when he was convinced our church was healing. He missed Gail so much. I could see it in his eyes. It's been fifteen years. She's been waiting for him. God…"

Monica choked up again. Markus waited for her to finish. It took several seconds.

"God makes everything beautiful in His time."

Dear Friends: As I finished typing my last entry, I received an unexpected phone call from Monica Blackman. She just informed me that Gary Lovejoy, the last charter member of Green Street Baptist Church, died in his sleep early this morning. We didn't expect this for several months.

In all my travels, I've never met a layman who did more for his church over such a long period of time. His legacy will be remembered as a founder who never stopped founding, as a man from the past who launched a new future, as someone who had one last thing to accomplish before he took his first step in eternity.

Well done! Rest in peace, my friend.

Several miles away, Bender sat at a table waiting for Buck Simpson to arrive. They'd been trying to connect for some time now. They played phone tag for a few rounds. Then they juggled some conflicts in their schedules. Afterwards, there was a last-minute cancellation on account of something unexpected happening. Today, however, they were clear to launch.

Bender reflected on the events of the last few weeks while he waited. Not long ago, he sat at this same table and asked Pete to consider making him a third partner. As Bender presented the strategy to overhaul the discipleship ministry of Green Street Baptist Church, Pete was spellbound. Markus, Gary, and Bender cheered when Pete announced, "Let's go for it!"

The first step had to do with merging his growing house-church network with Green Street's flagging Sunday school program. He knew there'd be significant advantages to both groups if the plan succeeded. He also understood there were serious risks involved. All across the landscape of American Christianity, rarely had something like this ever worked. Both groups would have to give a tremendous amount of support. Bender needed a catalyst to start a chain reaction. He had Buck in his crosshairs.

When Buck finally appeared in the doorway, Bender gave his best shot at imitating the secret battle cry of the Imaginators, "Aaaoooooahhhhhh!" Nearly everyone in the coffee shop stopped what they were doing and gave him a curious look.

"You'll need help with that, son." Buck pulled up a chair and grinned.

"The inimitable Mr. Imaginator himself. I'm honored to finally get some face time. My top barista is preparing one of our signature coffees just for you. If I can pump enough caffeine in your veins, maybe you'll treat my customers to the real-deal secret cry."

"It's not much of a secret anymore. Ever since I gave my testimony at the Crossroads Mall Church, it's gone viral."

Buck's coffee arrived. He tasted it. "This is fantastic! It's doesn't have anything illegal in it, does it?"

"No, not anything that a Baptist would need to confess at the altar next Sunday."

"That's funny. If it did, I'd drag you down to the front of the church with me."

"Right. That would be a memorable way to start my new role at Green Street. I can almost hear Pete announcing my decision to the flock, 'Bender's rededicating his life and will no longer spike the coffee from this point forward.'"

"Speaking of public announcements," Buck chuckled, "I was inspired by what Gary had to say about you at the leadership meeting six weeks ago. It's the main reason I wanted to meet with you."

"Do you mean the part where he said, 'This is Bender. He plants house churches. That's how this church started. Why we stopped meeting in homes never made any sense to me.'"

"That would be it." Buck reminisced. "I also remember him saying, 'Get in on it!' He's one of the few men I know who can make a point without making enemies. Gary never ran over someone who didn't thank him for it in the end. He's a deep well of convictions."

"Agreed. He's like a spiritual father to me. He taught me the plan of salvation in a third-grade Sunday school class. When he told the story of how Green Street started in a home two blocks down the road, it planted a seed in my young mind. What I'm doing now reaches all the way back to that moment. My salvation and calling are linked to his influence."

Buck took another sip of coffee. He pondered the friendship he and Gary had shared over the last several decades. When Buck's wife died of a sudden heart attack, Gary was the first to appear at the hospital. The words he spoke back then were still clear in Buck's memory.

"It's been ten years for me, Buck, and I still miss Gail every day. I never understood what was so special about heaven until she ended up going there first. One day we'll see our ladies again. It's in the Book!"

Buck's eyes shifted from the coffee mug to Bender in a flash. "Sign me up. I'm in!"

His announcement was so unexpected that Bender looked stunned, a rare thing indeed. He was just about to share the proposal and ask Buck to pray about it when he jumped the gun. God had already prepared the way. *Who could ask for anything more?* he thought to himself.

"You need some people to help sell this new idea," Buck continued. "The Imaginators will be there to make sure everything goes according to plan. God's moving again. Let's not get left behind."

Bender's face lit up. "I was hoping you'd say that." He stood to his feet and reached for Buck's hand. "Let's shake on it."

"Are you ready for the secret cry of the Imaginators now?"

"Absolutely. Let 'er roar."

Buck obliged. Everyone looked their direction. Some looked up from their Bibles and smiled. They came to pray after Bender sent out an email to his house church leaders about "the strategic meeting with Buck Simpson." Most were also readers of Markus' blog and were eager to hear the secret cry. That they weren't disappointed made the whole trip worthwhile. The noise he made was just something you had to hear for yourself to really believe.

Buck gave Bender a manly slap on the back. "With a little imagination, a few sacred arrows, and a battle cry to frighten the enemy, we'll rock the houses of Ft. Worth for Jesus."

Bender was deliriously happy and nearly speechless. He just looked at Buck and said, "Right."

"Let's continue this discussion later. Fanny Mae left a message on my answering machine after I went to bed. Gary's in the hospital. I need to go see our old friend."

As Buck turned toward the door, his cellphone rang. It was Frank Sanders. In two seconds all the color drained from Buck's face. He turned back around.

"Something wrong?" Bender asked.

Chapter 48

I speak to sensible people; judge for yourselves what I say
(1 Corinthians 10:15, NIV).

The Saturday morning was beautiful. The sky was clear. The parking lots and the streets that surrounded them were full.

Pete Blackman was asked to officiate. First and foremost, he wanted to honor the legacy of a man who'd traveled through every season in the lifecycle of a church—his church, a place he called home for more than sixty years. The cycle all began under the same roof he shared with the bride of his youth and the children they raised together, a place where his friends gathered to chase after a God-sized dream.

As the years passed, so did the knowledge that Green Street Baptist Church began in Gary Lovejoy's very own living room. "How did that happen?" many wondered. After they thought for a while, it didn't seem so strange that people had forgotten. The other charter members were long gone by now. For more than half a century, thousands of people had come and gone. Only Gary knew, and he decided a long time ago to keep this part of the story quiet.

"The house is gone," he was known to say, "but the church still stands." Now he was gone. And through no small effort on his part, the church was standing stronger than ever. Another movement was taking shape under the leadership of Pete, Markus, and Bender.

Despite all this, Pete had a difficult time preparing the message for Gary's funeral. Their relationship over the past five years had traveled a peculiar path. Gary had introduced the Blackman family to the church on the Sunday Pete preached his first sermon. He was the one who shared the results of the congregation's vote. Then there was that painful meeting in 212b. Pete's mind raced from one event to the next: the bonfire, the plea for forgiveness, the leadership meeting where he was last seen in public, and that final visit to the emergency room. What to say?

Last night he talked with Monica about the memories and emotions swirling through his mind. Her perspective always seemed to clarify things for him, mostly because her worldview wasn't all that complicated. She believed everything always had something to do with the sovereignty of God.

"Pete, you can't tame God," she'd said to him. "All you can do is walk in His wild ways. The things in life that feel savage today have a way of taming our hearts tomorrow."

He liked what she had to say so much that he developed the message for Gary's funeral around the theme of "Walking with God," focusing on the life of Enoch. His text was taken from Genesis, Chapter 5, and Hebrews, Chapter 11. After the obituary was read and several of Gary's favorite hymns were sung, Pete took his place behind the pulpit.

"There's a man in Scripture who reminds me of Gary Lovejoy. You can read about him in both the Old and the New Testaments. He's only mentioned a few times and very briefly at that. His name was Enoch.

Who Killed My Church?

"Way back in Genesis, Chapter 5, we discover that Enoch lived on the earth for 365 years. That's a long time by any standard of measurement. For three hundred of those years, he walked with God. But that brings up an interesting question. What happened after his sixty-fifth birthday that caused him to start walking with God all of a sudden?

"There's one clue to be found if you know what to look for. That was the same year his wife delivered his firstborn son. Methuselah must have been a very hardy baby because he outlived his father by 604 years. In fact, he lived longer than anyone else on record. And like most babies, he emerged kicking and screaming, perhaps even harder and louder than most.

"This grabbed Enoch's attention in a very big way. The entire course of his life changed. He realized he'd better start walking with God. And he did this faithfully for the next three hundred years. If you ever want to see a picture of what real dedication looks like, start here.

"Now flash forward with me a few thousand years later. The writer of Hebrews had something else to say about Enoch: He was commended as one who pleased God. Here's the big idea of the story: Walking with God faithfully over a long period of time pleases Him. The Christian life doesn't get any simpler than that.

"Enoch's story has a lot in common with our story. There comes a moment in each of our lives when God sends out a personal invitation. A wise man or woman doesn't ignore the invitation, or even worse, casually throw it away. Open the envelope. Read the words. God is asking you a simple but life-changing question: How would you like to begin a new journey today?

"Watching someone decline an invitation from God is heartbreaking. Maybe they believe a better offer will come from someone else. Perhaps they've grown comfortable following the same worn-out path leading to nowhere. That's not the choice Enoch made. Neither did Gary Lovejoy.

"As I met with the family over the last few days, they let me borrow a journal that Gary kept on the founding of Green Street Baptist Church. No one knew the book existed outside of the family. Let me read a few sections that describe how Gary walked with God:

December 25th: I have spent the whole day thinking about the Incarnation of Jesus Christ. Was there ever a time in history that God opened the heavens wider than he did on that little town of Bethlehem? Sometimes I wonder if God put me here for a special plan. As I walk up and down the streets of my neighborhood, I notice so many new homes with new families moving in. I often wonder how many of those people know Jesus. What are their lives like behind those curtained windows? Have they found true joy? Are their children learning the great Bible stories from the Old and New Testaments? Has anyone ever told them about Moses or Daniel in the lion's den? What do they know about my Lord? God always visits the people who cry out to Him. I wonder if these souls will ever cry out. I believe what this community needs is a new work down the street. I'm praying for that door to open.

January 26th: Some of my neighbors are interested in the notion of starting a new work. I'm not sure how to make it happen. I haven't obtained the worldly means to buy a building and hire a preacher. God, I'm asking for your wisdom. Let your provision come like a mighty rushing stream. There must to be an easier way to start a church. I read Acts, chapter 20, today. Paul started churches in homes. I wonder if Gail would fancy that idea. Lord, please go before me as you did with Moses. May your timing be perfect and her heart receptive.

February 10th: Gail let me know that all I ever talk about is "starting a new work." I thought she was lecturing me at first, but then she surprised me by saying, "Just invite them over here next Sunday. Help me get the house ready the night before. We'll read the Bible, pray, and have lunch in the backyard." Thank you, righteous Father. I didn't know the door You planned to open would be the one to my own home.

February 19th: Heaven came down and glory filled my soul. Today we had our first church service. The new work has begun. Fifteen neighbors attended not including their children. We had a little portion of the service set aside especially for them. I told the story about Daniel in the lion's den. They sat quietly and listened with great intent. When I described the lion's teeth, one little girl opened her eyes so wide that she dared not blink. After the children left to play in the backyard, their parents beseeched me to study the same passage. Time slipped away before we had a chance to study John, chapter 1. I believe the Holy Ghost descended upon us in our living room. How many other homes could we reach by doing the same thing?

Pete carefully closed the journal. "I spent several hours reading Gary's Green Street journal. He wrote over a hundred pages in all. I wish we had all day for me to read the early history of our church. I'll make sure a copy of this record is placed in our historical archives. You can read the rest of it for yourself later on.

"For now, let me focus your thoughts back on Enoch. The Bible says that after 365 years he was translated into heaven. He walked with God and then 'he was no more.'

"Here's the way I picture that happening. Enoch walked with God every day of his life. God came to him in the morning and said, 'Get up Enoch. It's time to go walking.' In the evening God would take him home and say, 'You can rest now; we'll walk more tomorrow.' Enoch did that every day faithfully for three hundred years.

"On the last day God said to Enoch, 'We have walked a great distance today, farther than ever before. The way back to your house is so long, and you look so very tired. Let's face it, Enoch. You're not a young man anymore. But I have good news for you. Tonight we're closer to My home than yours. Why don't you come and stay at My house tonight?'

"All it takes is one night in the house of the Lord and you never want to go back to your old home again. I was with Gary when that decision was made. He came to the end of a long journey with God. When the heart monitor sounded the alarm, a lot of people came charging into the room. I knew in my heart what had happened. Gary walked with God, and then he was no more, for God took him home."

Gary had requested that an invitation be given at his funeral. Pete shared with the congregation how to walk with Jesus Christ by faith. There were many that day who made a decision to begin a new journey.

Buck Simpson came up with an idea to begin a new ministry called "The Walkabout 300." Of course, the ministry was in memory of Gary Lovejoy, a modern-day Enoch who walked with God. The big idea was to recruit three hundred people to go on a walkabout through their communities for three hours a week. The only requirement to be part of the ministry was to remain faithful. The purpose was to keep one's eyes open and seize opportunities to connect people with the growing house-church movement being organized by Bender and Buck's team of mighty Imaginators.

Markus got a kick over what one person had to say about this on his blog.

From Mowan in Australia: *We've been doing walkabouts for years in our church. When we realized all the miracles performed by Jesus happened during a walkabout, we decided to do the same. The problem with most churches is that there's too much "learn about," "sing about," "sit about," "complain about," and "gossip about." We have a saying here: "As you walkabout, talk about the One you know about." Come visit us in the land down under. We'll show you how it's done.*

Buck wasn't the kind of guy to let the grass grow beneath his feet. He was in Australia within a few months with a quiver full of sacred arrows. Frank Sanders made sure Bender was able to go as well. Before very long, the strategies employed in the 'land down under' were implemented in the land up above.

Chapter 49

Jesus did many other things as well. If every one of them were written down, I suppose that even the whole world would not have room for the books that would be written (John 21:25, NIV).

As they say, all stories must come to an end. That this story ended well was nothing short of a miracle. Rarely do people and circumstances line up in such a way that disasters are averted and the supernatural rules the day. But that's exactly what happened at Green Street Baptist Church.

Over the months and years that followed, so many lives were transformed that word of what was happening began to circulate far and wide. People kept buzzing about how God was on the move in an old church that dared to do ministry in a new way. Following is a brief description of some of the noteworthy things that happened.

The wedding was held at the pool hall. Kittens actually wore a tuxedo. On account of his size, the suit had to be custom-made. Cindy's two little girls were flower girls. Fanny Mae, Kate Shoemaker, and Georgette Freeman were the matrons of honor. Bob Freeman was the best man. Pastor Pete performed the ceremony.

One of the more interesting things that Pete said was, "Kittens, if you don't take care of this little girl, I'll have Nails, Bleeder, and Hater ride you down. That's not a threat. It's a promise." Kittens laughed until he turned red in the face. Shortly after that he said "I do" and cried like a baby. Cindy stood on her tippy toes to kiss her one big hunk-a-man. He made her feel safe and special. She treated him like a king.

Not too long afterwards, she changed his name to Simba. "I like that name better than Kittens," she said. So he became her lion king, and as the story goes, they lived happily ever after.

Though she remained an active member, Fanny Mae chose to resign her position as the administrative assistant to the pastor of Green Street Baptist Church. She finally came to terms with the reality that computers and technology annoyed her something fierce. When Markus and Bender revamped the church communication process from top to bottom, Fanny Mae decided to cut loose. "Life is just too short to let technology get under a woman's skin," she said.

Her new dream was to get a job at the Hog Barn. Everyone there had gotten to know her so well she didn't even need to fill out an application. What she enjoyed so much about her new vocation was the opportunity to be a "Gospel Granny." In fact, she coined that phrase herself. She tried to come up with something clever like "Grannyator," but no one understood what she meant when they heard that name the first time. She grew tired of trying to explain the name to everybody and just settled for Gospel Granny.

On occasion someone she witnessed to was baptized at the pool hall or at Green Street Baptist Church. She was loved for the unusual things she said and did. One was something she repeated often, which went something like this: "God does crazy stuff through old ladies. Think

Sarah. It's in the Book!"

Dr. Pat Sheets invited Pete Blackman, Shawn Davis, aka Bender, Jim Jake, and Markus Cunningham to lead a church-growth conference for the seminary students. Each had a unique perspective on the subject. Pete's message was entitled, "Don't Waste the Pain." Bender talked about "The Changing Landscape of Discipleship." Jim spoke on the subject of "What's in the Book about Church Growth." Markus stole the show, however, with his message on "Sometimes You Need to Stare into the Abyss and Look at the Grim Ripper."

During the event, Dr. Sheets announced that anyone who went to the Jan-Kay Ranch to study for their finals would receive extra credit. John Dewayne let them stay free of charge. He figured some would be back in a few years with their church groups.

Buck Simpson became an internet sensation. Then he became a frequent speaker at conferences all across the nation. Everyone seemed to want to hear him perform the secret battle cry of the Imaginators. He could never explain the sensation himself. The yell was a crazy thing, but people loved it. When he talked about how Green Street allowed sanctified imagination to revitalize the entire church's ministry structure from top to bottom, people sat spellbound. Everywhere he went, he sold sacred arrows at cost. People took them back to their home church and told the story of Buck and his mighty Imaginators.

Markus kept his word and gave Pete a full year. They had so much fun working together that their jobs didn't feel like work at all. After the first year was over, Markus signed up for another. And as Pete hired

Markus, so Markus hired Pete.

"I get so many phone calls now I can't operate as a solo act anymore," Marcus confessed. "I need a sidekick to blow in, blow up, and blow out with me. You're the only guy I know who's more messed up than me. Deal?"

"Let me run it by Monica and my leadership team first," Pete said. "I need to get their blessing before I start moonlighting with a guy who's fixated on zombies and the Grim Ripper."

The decision was easy. Green Street was gracious enough to share Pete as they had Pastor Jake. Both benefited and the kingdom was blessed.

Frank Sanders called Pete one day. "Can you meet me for lunch?"

They met at Bender's coffee shop. Both ordered the special for the day—iced chai tea lattes with warm egg salad croissants. Pete started the conversation after they found a seat.

"I've been doing a whole lot of thinking lately."

"Me too. That's why I wanted to see you today. But please, I'd like to hear what you have to say first."

Pete took a sip of tea and nodded. "Okay. The only reason I'm still here today is because you met me in the parking lot on that chilly November morning."

"Pastor, I think you're giving me too much credit."

"No. Not at all. Anything of great significance can be traced back to a defining moment. If you hadn't given me advance notice that something was wrong, I'd have walked into that finance committee meeting without Markus' business card."

"That was God's doing, not mine."

"I know His hand was guiding us that day, but you responded in a

302

big way. You paid for Markus to come out of your own pocket. I don't know that I've ever thanked you properly."

"You're welcome, Pete. Now I'd like to do something else for you."

Pete studied his friend for a moment. He knew Frank's heart was bigger than the Metroplex. "Please, Frank. You've done so much already. All our needs are being met."

"Pastor, hear me out, please. I'll pay for you to write the story of Green Street and to find a way to get it published. I want everything to be in the book—all the people, the Jan-Kay Ranch, Ripper, Gary, Markus, even Pastor Jake and Monica. Make sure you explain the lifecycle of a church. Don't leave anything out."

Pete paused for a moment before answering. "That's an amazing offer, my friend but I don't know that everyone involved here wants their name written in a book. Some of the things we've dealt with are pretty sensitive issues."

"I've already thought about that. Change the names, the place, and a few of the circumstances. Call it a fictional work. The story's so compelling that people will want to read it."

Pete spent the next few days thinking about the offer. Then he called Frank with a response. "Find a decent writer, someone who can help me tell the story, and I'll do it."

Frank was a smart businessman. He knew exactly how to pull the right strings and make things happen. The ball got rolling after he made a few phone calls.

Frequently, people have asked Pete if the book you're reading now is the story of his church. He just smiles and says, "No, but I will say this. The book tells the story of every church. Every church I've ever known started as a movement, became a monument, struggled as a museum, and then had to make a decision over whether or not to become a morgue."

As you've read, Monica finally met the "bright-eyed" girl who fell in love with Dustin. The fact that she was the granddaughter of Gary Lovejoy was one of those ironies that could only be explained by the sovereignty of God. After a short while, Gari Lovejoy became part of the Blackman family. Monica approved wholeheartedly and started thinking about the reality that she would be a grandmother one day.

The invitation Monica issued to the ladies of the church at the Jan-Kay Ranch was not forgotten. She frequently met with the "Soprano section" at Bender's coffee shop. They exchanged funny stories and laughed until the tears flowed freely. Women often dropped by the house to help make cakes for people who came to Green Street's version of Furniture with a Cause. Every chair, table, bed, and couch given to a young couple or any person in need included a delicious treat made by loving hands from an old family recipe. The church nursery was soon filled to overflowing on Sunday mornings.

Each night before they went to sleep, Monica took Pete by the hand and walked him into the living room. Standing before the old wooden cross they repeated these words together: "Love, joy, peace, patience, kindness, goodness, faithfulness, gentleness, and self-control. Against such there is no law. It's in the Book."

For the joy and the crown set before him, Pete ran hard and fast after God. Monica cheered for her husband from the bleachers, the pews, the hallways, and anywhere else she saw him reaching for a second wind. She was at peace. He found joy. They were both very much in love.

One evening Monica lay on the bed meditating. Pete stopped in the open doorway of their bedroom when he noticed her staring at the ceiling.

"I've been thinking," she said.

"About…?"

"I've just realized something."

"What's that?"

"Did you know God never wastes a tear?"

Epilogue

*And a vision appeared to Paul in the night: a certain man of Macedonia
was standing and appealing to him, and saying, "Come over to
Macedonia and help us"*
(Acts 16:9, NASB).

The day was another Monday morning in a cold November.

Cindy buzzed Pete in his office. After graduating from the local community college, she'd replaced Fanny Mae in Green Street's office. Her "one big hunk-a-man" was the one who encouraged her to train as an executive assistant.

"There's another pastor on line three who needs to talk with you."

Pete picked up the phone.

"Is this Pete Blackman?"

"Yes, it is. How can I help you?"

"You don't know me, but I met Markus Cunningham at a church growth conference several years ago. He asked me to call you. My church is falling apart. Everyone's asking the question, 'Who killed my church?' They think I'm to blame. I've just been asked to resign."

Pete thought for a moment. "What's your name?"

"Terry Kennedy."

"Where do you live?"

"San Antonio."

"I'll be there in six hours."

Topics for Discussion

Part 1

1. How would you describe Pete and Monica's marriage in terms of strengths and weaknesses?

2. What emotions did you feel as Green Street faced some of its challenges? Did they remind you of anything you have experienced personally?

3. In what ways could God use you to play a positive role in your church?

Part 2

1. Of all the things taught or experienced at the Jan-Kay Ranch, what interested you most?

2. When Monica made her surprise visit and spoke to the leaders,

what emotions did the people in the room experience? Did you experience any?

3. Which team would you serve on at Green Street Baptist Church: Frank's Guardians of Salt and Light, Buck's mighty Imaginators, Kate's handsome Man of Peace search team, or Monica's Sopranos?

Part 3

1. Which relationship is the most interesting to you: Pete and Monica, Markus and Pete, Gary and Bender, or Kate and Fanny Mae?

2. Had you been personal friends with Bob and Georgette Freeman and they invited you to meet Mike Murdock at Hands and Feet Ministry, would you go?

3. Which ministry would you have chosen to be part of during the month of December: Bender's house-church network, The Crossroads Mall Church, Furniture with a Cause, Hands and Feet Ministries, or hanging out with Nails, Bleeder, Hater, and Kittens?

Part 4

1. In your opinion, which character developed the most throughout the story?

2. What emotions connected with you personally?

3. What have you learned that has challenged you most and is most likely to result in positive change?

Frank's Big Yellow Notebook

Frank Sanders was rarely seen without his big yellow notebook. He carried the book with him nearly everywhere he went. He started the practice when the leaders of Green Street Baptist Church met for the retreat at the Jan-Kay Ranch. As a successful businessman, Frank was passionate about a number of things—like words and ideas—and how they possessed the ability to transform culture in positive ways, whether for a church or a business.

Not long after Frank placed the wheels into motion for *Who Killed My Church* to be written, the first draft of the manuscript landed in his inbox. After reading through the pages word by word, he fell in love with the story, mostly because he lived through the experience himself, but he felt something important was missing. So he made an appointment to talk to Markus Cunningham about the matter.

"I believe the more technical discussions we had on 'The Lifecycle of a Church' were some of the most beneficial aspects of our whole journey," Frank asserted. "I wrote some things down here in my notebook, but I couldn't write fast enough to catch everything. Could you help me fill in the missing information? I want to make a case with our publisher about including some of this information as well."

"Frank, I can do better than that. Why don't you come along with me as I speak at conferences and consult with other churches in need? I've been developing the concept more fully, and I believe you'd have a better understanding if we spent some time together."

"I'd love that, Markus. When do we start?"

"How about right now? I've developed a spreadsheet that lists the thirty-two characteristics in the lifecycle of a church. The spreadsheet shows what the climate of a church transitioning from the movement phase to the morgue phase looks like. Why don't you take a look for yourself and tell me what you think?"

Frank studied the chart Markus handed him for several minutes. In fact, he lost all sense of space and time—even the fact that he was sitting in another man's office. He studied with the wheels spinning in his mind until Markus' voice unlocked the grip the spreadsheet held on him.

The Four Seasons in the Lifecycle of a Church

Movement	Monument	Museum	Morgue
Revolutionary	Evolutionary	Stationary	Reactionary
Passion	Profession	Paycheck	Poverty
Creativity	Mimicry	Hypersensitivity	Sterility
Spiritual Vitality	Spiritual Inertia	Spiritual Frustration	Spiritual Death
Imagination	Determination	Exasperation	Stagnation
Life Change	Life Support	Life Draining	Lifeless
Multiplication	Addition	Equilibrium	Division
Status Change	Status Symbol	Status-Quo	Status Offline
Flexible	Fatigued	Fragile	Frozen
Catalytic	Analytic	Paralytic	Apocalyptic
Vision	Strategy	Structure	Decay
Sacrifice	Commitment	Obligation	Contempt

"Frank, what do you think?"

"Simply brilliant. I want to know more."

"Thank you. That's the best compliment I've had all week—except from my wife, of course."

"Have you defined these thirty-two characteristics?"

"Absolutely. In fact, my plan is to develop a survey from these characteristics that churches will be able to access online. This will make the process of diagnosing where a church falls in the lifecycle easier for the leadership. If the entire membership took the survey, the data could be crunched according to age, gender, spiritual maturity, even by how long they've been a member of their church. To a discerning leader, the information would be invaluable. The possibilities are endless."

"Markus, send me your itinerary. I want to be in every place where you elaborate on these characteristics. And don't worry. You won't have to entertain me along the way. I'll just sit in the back of the room and observe."

"No, you'll do more than that," Markus insisted. "You'll help me teach some of the sessions once you get the hang of it."

"I couldn't do that."

"Oh, my Guardian of Salt and Light, where is your faith? 'You can do all things through Christ who strengthens you.' Do I need to tell you where that comes from?"

"No. It's in the Book."

Markus slapped Frank on the shoulder. "That's perfect. Here are some of my typed notes on each of the thirty-two characteristics. You can add them to that big yellow thing you carry around with you. Start studying now. My throat's feeling scratchy. I might need you to replace me in Cleveland next week."

In Cleveland, Ohio, Frank sat in a small conference room with Markus and the leaders of Bethany Hills Episcopal Church. The pained looks on their faces appeared strangely familiar to him. A few years ago, his face pretty much looked the same. And on that chilly November morning when he caught Pete in the parking lot just before the finance committee meeting, the same expression was on his pastor's face too.

Markus took a sip of water and softly cleared his throat. Somber eyes lifted from the table or the floor and shifted in his direction. Their faces brightened a little when they took in the generous smile the consultant offered in return.

Markus launched the meeting with his trademark enthusiasm. "I'm glad to be meeting with you today. I'm here because Jesus loves your church."

A few smiles emerged. Frank marveled over the soothing effect the words had on the people sitting in the room. They were exactly what this group needed to hear most. *Jesus loves your church.*

"I've brought my assistant, Frank Sanders, with me. He's lived through the same problems you're facing today at Bethany Hills. He'll be a resource for you in the future. Are we ready to begin?"

Everyone nodded their heads in affirmation.

"Please allow me to get to the point quickly. Here's what my due diligence has uncovered: Your church is dying."

Markus paused to let the words sink in. Frank half expected to see some push-back in their body language, but they didn't even flinch. Most of the men and women in the room nodded in affirmation to what he'd said. After scanning the room, Markus continued.

"You've made a bold decision and invited me to help you turn this ship around. Before I climb onboard, we need to be in agreement about where we go from here. I plan to show you how to do three things well: Create an attractional environment, extend an irresistible invitation, and live out your mission effectively. What I won't do is help you do a better

316

job at what no longer works."

He offered a smile before asking, "Do I still have a job?"

The awkward silence in the room continued. Several people shifted uncomfortably in their chairs. Frank had grown accustomed to Markus' way of getting to the point quickly, but he'd almost forgotten how brutally honesty Markus was when he first arrived at Green Street.

The chairman spoke up. "I'm pretty sure you don't need this job. Everything we've heard and read about you indicates you know your business. We may not like hearing what you have to say, but we have no other options. Everything we've done has failed."

"Thank you for your honesty," Markus said. "With that attitude, we'll overcome these struggles together. Please hear what I have to say. With all my heart and every truth I hold dear, I believe the Spirit of God is ready to launch a new movement at Bethany Hills."

Without delay Markus tapped a key on his laptop. Suddenly the LCD projector came to life and displayed a chart on the screen behind him. "What you see before you are the four seasons in the lifecycle of a typical church. Notice each one carefully, and make a mental note of where you believe Bethany Hills to be. Each and every church can either be classified as a movement, a monument, a museum, or a morgue."

The Four Seasons in the Lifecycle of a Church

	Movement (Spring)	Monument (Summer)	Museum (Fall)	Morgue (Winter)
Attractional	Revolutionary	Evolutionary	Stationary	Reactionary
	Passion	Profession	Paycheck	Poverty
	Creativity	Mimicry	Hypersensitivity	Sterility
	Spiritual Vitality	Spiritual Inertia	Spiritual Frustration	Spiritual Death

"Follow the next set of words from left to right. They explain the attractional qualities as they move throughout the lifecycle of a church. Movements attract *revolutionaries*. These men and women function as change agents who readily embrace innovative ideas. Excitement runs high as they create a new culture to replace the old. The members picture themselves as living on the cutting edge of what God is doing to transform their world.

"As the revolutionary atmosphere fades, however, change becomes less radical and more incremental. The movement is now a monument-class church. *Evolutionary* change over extended periods of time becomes the norm. This phase attracts a new class of church members who are more like consumers than reformers.

"The museum-class church is entirely *stationary*. Change is nonexistent and avoided at all cost. Policies and procedures are designed to tame any change agents that may still exist within the church. The balance of power tips in their favor. Feeling that they're no longer needed or appreciated, the revolutionaries abandon the cause to seek out the next movement on the horizon.

"When a church becomes a morgue, a *reactionary* breed of followers is attracted. They demonstrate amazing similarities to the original revolutionaries who founded the movement. The major difference is that they lack optimism and hope in the future. They protect their culture against the influx of any new change agents and often react negatively in their presence, sometimes resorting to public shame when threatened.

"Take a look at the second line. When movements first begin, they attract *passionate* people. High levels of energy and enthusiasm exist within the hearts of the early adopters. In the next phase, passion fades somewhat. Still dedicated but now weary, the volunteers attract *professionals* to do the work that once was done freely. In a museum-class church, the professionals grow frustrated at the lack of movement but hang around for the *paycheck*. They'd rather have a rewarding life but settle for making a living instead. A church enters the morgue phase when the institution becomes *impoverished* and struggles to meet its payroll. Layoffs become inevitable.

"When a shepherd is dismissed, the sheep take the loss hard."

Markus surveyed the pained expressions emerging on the faces of the men and women in the room. Unfortunately, their pastor had recently been terminated. The leadership believed moving in another direction would solve all their problems. Their actions made matters far worse. Markus was brought in to lead the disaster-relief efforts. After a few moments of awkward silence, Markus drove the point home.

"Sheep attach themselves to shepherds. You've heard the saying, 'Strike the shepherd, scatter the sheep.' In Matthew 9:36, Jesus noted that sheep without a shepherd appear harassed and helpless. Morgue-class churches are a wrecking ground for the dreams of shepherds and sheep alike. Don't make this mistake again.

"Follow me on the third line. Movements attract *creative* people. They bring their imagination and ideation skills to serve the cause. Monument-class churches often send their staff members to conferences where they learn to *mimic* the innovative ideas fueling movement-class churches. Museums are *hypersensitive* and very effective at stonewalling innovation. Fear that members may abandon the fellowship prevents them from embracing anything that might advance their ministry. Morgues are *sterile* and, as such, cannot reproduce or create anything new. Here, death overshadows the church like the sword of Damocles.

"Notice on the fourth line that movements generate *spiritual vitality*. People are attracted to promising environments where they may grow personally. In this culture, Christians will give testimony to what God is doing in them and around them, present tense. The focus is fixed on discipling new converts. Learning leads to doing. Faith produces works. The abundant life is in no short supply.

"However, spiritual vitality yields to *spiritual inertia* in the monument-class church. Here the church concentrates on meeting the needs of the saints at the expense of outreach. The saints nourish themselves more readily than providing for the hungry souls around them.

"In a museum, people have a high degree of *spiritual frustration*. They blame leadership for their malaise. They complain about not being fed. They yearn for the vitality of the old days and become highly frustrated.

"Members of morgue-class churches suffer under a climate of *spiritual death*. Their spiritual condition is nearly identical to the world outside their door, perhaps even a little worse at times. Sheep and goats, wheat and tares all occupy the same real estate. Since the majority of churches in America are declining, this is quickly becoming the norm."

After Markus finished explaining the handout, he asked, "Are you ready to dance with Quasimodo?"

"Dance with Quasimodo?" the chairman asked. "You've lost me now."

One of the ladies in the room responded, "I believe the consultant's question is a curious reference to *The Hunchback of Notre Dame*— cryptic but interesting."

"You want us to dance with a hunchback?" the chairman fired back. "What's that supposed to mean?"

Markus flash a devious grin. "You don't need to know what my words mean right now. I just need to know whether you're ready."

On another occasion, Frank flew from DFW to PHX to meet up with Markus. The consultant had been invited to deliver the keynote message at the Arizona Pastors' Conference. Nearly one thousand ministers and church leaders from a five-state region had gathered at the Phoenix Convention Center. As Frank walked with Markus through the concourse, he was surprised to discover how enormously popular his friend had become. He overheard more than one pastor confess to Markus that "The Blog" was bookmarked on their internet browser.

What surprised Frank even more was that a few people knew something about him too. One comment, however, left him feeling a little chagrined. "You must be Frank, the 'Guardian of Salt and Light.' I've read about your big yellow notebook. Did you bring that thing with you? I haven't seen one of those in years. Rock on, Dude!"

Frank also noticed how many people stood in line to greet Markus after he spoke. Most walked away with the consultant's card in hand. He wondered how many were like Pete—they would simply place the card in their billfold or Bible. Ultimately it would land in a desk drawer. Occasionally it would be searched for, and a cry for help would be issued.

In Phoenix, Markus was in rare form. He stirred up the convention hall and lit a fire beneath the pastors' feet. Unfortunately, the house recording system experienced technical difficulties and failed to record his message. Frank was unaware of this at the time, but his Big Yellow Notebook came to the rescue and has provided the material for what Markus had to say.

"My topic is both simple and complex," began Markus. "Some of you theologians out there believe that I just contradicted myself."

Note: Laughter

"I'm comfortable with paradoxes. You can't survive long in the ministry and not be comfortable with them yourself. Take a lesson from Jesus. Lose your life to save it because the first shall be last, and the least the greatest, and every adult should become a child to enter the kingdom. Those are paradoxes, my friends, and if you can't handle them, go be a brain surgeon somewhere."

Note: More laughter.

"My topic tonight is entitled 'Creating an Invitational Culture.' My first objective is to describe what this means for your congregation. Then I need to show you how this culture thrives or dives across the lifecycle of a church. Are you with me tonight? If you are, let me hear your voices."

Note: Pastor's conventions are filled with gifted people who possess genetically-superior vocal cords.

"Consider how important a simple invitation is to the stuff of life. A shy boy invites a pretty girl to go out on a date. Years later, he gains the confidence to invite her to become his wife. As a newlywed couple, they invite their friends to hang out together. One of these friends invites the husband to apply for a new position being created at his growing company. They become coworkers, and next, church members at the same house of worship. Each of these relationships was formed because society is built on this thing we do called inviting.

"How good is your church at inviting? In other words, do you have an invitational culture growing in your church? The characteristics I'm going to share with you tonight determine whether or not your church will do this successfully or poorly. So let's get started.

	Movement (Spring)	Monument (Summer)	Museum (Fall)	Morgue (Winter)
Invitational	Imagination	Determination	Exasperation	Stagnation
	Life Change	Life Support	Life Draining	Lifeless
	Multiplication	Addition	Equilibrium	Division
	Status Change	Status Symbol	Status-Quo	Status Offline

"Follow me on the first line. The presence of *imagination* is one of the driving forces in a movement. When old methodologies have lost their appeal, *imagination* fills the empty spaces. Such an atmosphere allows people to think freely, dream, and even speak out loud. This leads to a whole host of other things vital to a movement, like ownership, creativity, and passion for the cause. Every church needs a team of Imaginators who will draw a line in the sand and protect this as their sacred ground.

Note: Spontaneous applause broke out. This had become Markus' trademark word. He claimed that the word simply materialized out of the thin blue air when he met with the leaders of Green Street at the Jan-Kay Ranch.

"Where imagination flourishes, there will be buzz. You know what I mean by that. People can't stop talking about what keeps blowing their mind. They'll tell others who will tell others and others until the word spreads like a box of tissues in a chick flick.

Note: There were mostly men in the room, and they all laughed.

"I challenge you to let imagination roam freely throughout your church. Sadly enough, when a church keeps repeating the same strategies that were successful year after year, imagination has lost the battle to *determination*. Now you're a monument.

Determination is only good when you're committed to doing the best things, not just anything. There's no reward in repeating what God's no longer blessing. That's a recipe for *exasperation*, the museum phase. Exasperation leads to *stagnation* after imagination has completely flat-lined. In other words, the morgue phase has arrived.

"When's the last time you got invited to a morgue? That's probably never happened to you, and I hope you don't go to one for years. What you need to understand is that your members won't invite people to see what isn't living. They're not going to say to their close friends, 'I attend a really lame church that needs money all the time. All the people have sour looks on their faces. I don't know why I go there myself, maybe out of guilt, but since you're my special friend, will you go with me?'

"Yikes! Run away. That's what I'd call a scary friend.

"So let's talk about movements once again. Look at the second line on the chart behind me. Movements are places where people experience *life change*. Those are called healthy, growing churches. How does this invitation strike you? 'The church I attend is phenomenal. People give up booze, partying, and Twinkies all the time.'

"You say, 'They give up Twinkies?'

"Yeah. We're committed to a sin-free, gluten-free, devil-free, carb-free, animal-fat-free life in Christ. We don't eat at all. We just fast all the time. I think you need to lose some weight too. Want to join us?'"

Note: Markus had people rolling in the aisles.

"Run away—as fast as you can. That's not the kind of life change that invites people to come to your church. So what does? Imagine your church members showing up at work on Monday morning empowered by the Spirit of God. They have a positive attitude where they once spewed poison. Even the boss notices the life change because there's a big change in their work ethic. His workforce is now enthusiastic about what they do on the job because they're doing their work as unto the Lord. Genuine life change is an invitation in and of itself. This is the stuff that movements are made of.

"Whenever life change slows to a crawl," Markus stated in somber tones, a noted contrast to the giddy atmosphere permeating the conference, "the monument phase has arrived. Sickness enters the body. Now the focus is on *life support*, or merely sustaining those whose lives were changed. The work of life support is less exciting than life change and becomes *life-draining* over time. You can only sap so much life out of a church until the church becomes *lifeless*. Church leaders and members alike will encounter little success when inviting people to join a lifeless fellowship.

"Now turn your attention to the third line. The early church did more than add to the number of disciples. They *multiplied* disciples.

"Acts, Chapter 6." Markus paused.

"It's in the Book!" the crowd called back.

"Cheers to Jim Jake," he replied.

Note: Jim was actually present and smiled like a friendly pumpkin at a church harvest festival. He'd spoken earlier that day but hung around to hear Markus.

"You have a few hundred souls on any given Sunday. Imagine the shockwaves that would spread throughout your community if the Spirit of God moved in a way that your numbers doubled every Sunday. Where would you put all the new members after just one month? You'd have to start new churches everywhere. I believe Spirit-enabled multiplication is still possible. When this happens, people invite themselves to join the movement. At Pentecost, they cried out, 'What must we do to be saved?'

"Do you remember William Carey? Among Baptists, he's considered the father of International Missions. He preached a sermon in eighteenth-century England that challenged his colleagues to 'expect great things *from* God and attempt great things *for* God.' His message planted the seeds that led to a worldwide mission's movement. If he were alive today, I believe Mr. Carey would tell you our churches are small because our dreams are small. Most churches do well just to *add* a few more members than they lose throughout the year.

"Sadly, the statistics reveal that eighty-five percent of all churches in America are at *equilibrium* or in a state of *division*. And times are not getting any better; they're only getting worse.

"Take a look at the final line. Facebook has popularized the phrase *status change.* Recently I watched a popular wedding video on YouTube. After exchanging rings, the groom whipped out his cellphone and changed his status from 'in a relationship' to 'married.' Then he surprised the bride by pulling her phone out of his pocket. She did the same. They kissed, and the crowd cheered.

"People experience many status changes throughout life. They may go from single to married, miserable to divorced, childless to child-bearing, and child-rearing to empty-nesters. Our calling is simple. We invite people to experience an eternal status change. There's no greater change than moving from lost to saved.

"Movements create radical change in the lives of people who get involved. They go from empty to full, from meaninglessness to significance, and from uninvolved to involved. When you invite people to join the new movement that will launch in your church, God willing, you're offering them the possibility of an abundant life in Christ.

"The main reason you're a church has little to do with buildings, budgets, or bylaws. Church is really not about all the nickels and noses you count either. Churches exist because they're about Jesus—the body of Christ for a broken world. Be His hands and feet today, and you'll help people change all their tomorrows.

"Many churches, unfortunately, allow their emphasis to shift from this simple truth. They begin focusing on themselves instead of beyond their stained glass windows. Creating a country-club atmosphere where church membership becomes a *status symbol* happens all too often. Pride joins the club. Given time, the church will plant its feet in the wet cement of the *status-quo*. That's when it becomes a museum class church.

"Social media websites have tried to solve the problem of what to do when someone dies, even though their account remains active. The phrase *status offline* defines this reality—a morgue class church. Sometimes friends and family continue to post comments on the message boards of the deceased. But be very afraid if the deceased respond. When a church is offline, being in touch with the living is impossible."

Markus paused momentarily to let the words find their mark. Then he drove the point home. "The only invitation that matters, the only invitation of any consequence in eternity, and the only invitation that will take back what the enemy has stolen, is the invitation to life."

Reader Note: People stood to their feet and cheered as Markus left the stage.

After the conference in Phoenix concluded, Markus invited Frank to his room at the Palomar hotel for a late-night snack. He wanted to catch up on how Frank's project was progressing and offer whatever assistance might be necessary.

Frank had some things on his mind too. As the meeting progressed, he was determined to unleash a big idea of his own for the consultant to consider. Markus later confessed to him, "Frank, your big idea was the *pièce de résistance* that tied all the loose ends together."

Markus answered when he heard knocking on the door. "Hello, Frank. Come on in. I believe Phoenix arose from the ashes tonight. The crowd was alive."

"You were on fire, Markus—and funny too, I might add."

"Thanks, my friend. Here, try some of Shirley's cookies."

Frank remembered his lack of restraint when eating Sparky Girl's crumb cakes and decided to take just one. After the first bite, his eyes lit up with surprise, "Wow, you are a blessed man! How do you maintain that girlish figure of yours?"

"Girlish! Are you flirting with me, Frank?"

Frank had thought himself to be funny, but now he was slightly embarrassed. He stopped chewing momentarily and mumbled, "No, I..."

Markus smiled as he slid the bag of cookies closer. "Loosen up, Frank. Here, have another one."

Frank obliged.

"I'm on a diet myself. But I can't fly back to Ft. Worth with a pile of uneaten cookies. That might hurt Shirley's feelings."

Frank went to work on the second cookie.

"As you knock off that bag of cookies, let me get to the point of why I asked you to come."

Frank nodded affirmatively and kept chewing.

"If you had one question about all you've seen, both at Green Street and on the road with me, and if you knew I could answer this question to your complete satisfaction, what would you want to know?"

Frank swallowed then said, "You'd have made an exceptional businessman. Success and failure are determined by knowing the right questions to ask. Yours was almost as good as this cookie."

"Almost? I'll take that as a compliment anyway. Keep inflating my ego, and I'll be impossible for Shirley to live with."

Frank swallowed the last bite of his second cookie. "Right. Poor girl. I suspect that's happened already."

"You may be right." Markus laughed. "So what's your question?"

Frank leaned back in his chair and thought for a moment. He'd already planned to talk to Markus about what was on his mind. After wiping his mouth with a napkin, he responded.

"Here's the question, but I need to begin with an observation first. Over the last two years, we've experienced sweeping changes at Green Street. We had one foot in the morgue when our pastor called you. What God did was nothing short of a miracle."

"I would agree with that," Markus affirmed.

"So how do we take these thirty-two characteristics in the lifecycle of a church and equip pastors to start movements within their own congregations? In other words, if you're not there to guide the process, how can we equip the people who can? One movement in one church is one thing, but a simultaneous movement in many churches is called an awakening."

Frank leaned forward. "Markus, are you ready to launch an awakening?"

For one of the very few times in Markus's life, he was speechless. But his humor soon found a way to mask how truly dumbfounded he was at the moment. "I was prepared to answer your questions about Higgs bosons and string theory, but you've kind of caught me off guard, Frank."

Frank picked up a third cookie and pointed it in his friend's direction. "Markus, who teaches you?" Then he took a bite.

"Excuse me?"

Frank swallowed. "Who mentors the great mentor?"

"That's a good question. You want to know who pokes around in my life."

"Precisely."

"Shirley's got the poker."

"No. Shirley wants to make you a better man, but who makes you a better leader? Let me show you something and I think you'll understand what I mean. Do you have your laptop?"

"Got it right here." Markus opened up his aging laptop, typed in the password "Ripper," and handed the laptop to his friend.

Frank went to YouTube and found a video he'd viewed several times over the last few days. As the video began to stream, he showed it to Markus and asked what he observed.

"This is hilarious," Markus exclaimed.

A young guy on a crowded beach was dancing as though all the lights of Broadway were shining in his direction. Markus felt the poor guy should have been embarrassed. He wore no shirt, sported a skinny body with few muscles to brag about, had no tan, and wore the tightest short-shorts Markus had ever seen on a dude. Making matters worse, every dance move that followed the last was nerdier than the one before. But he danced away, uninhibited and free—all without music or even a partner.

Frank paused the video and reached for his fourth cookie. "Tell me what you see here, Pastor."

"I see a white guy who's got no swag. He needs to stop. Seriously, I want to rescue him from his shame. Everyone in the crowd is looking at him like, 'Please stay away.'"

Frank started the video again. For the next thirty seconds or so the beach dancer carried on as the crowd slowly gained interest. Sometimes his moves looked like a man swinging at flies while walking on a tight rope, and in other moments, like he was experiencing a seizure or had waited too long to find a restroom.

But then... Markus' eyes widened when he saw what happened next. Someone on the crowded beach jumped from his towel and joined the nerdy dancer. Not only did he dance with him, but he mimicked his strange moves as well.

Frank pushed "pause" again and reached for the last cookie, reflexively. "Tell me what you see now, Markus."

"Two dorks on a beach, which inspires me to jump into my car and drive a few miles down the seashore."

"Right," Frank said. "That's the comment I knew you'd make. I felt that way too, until I realized something profound."

"And what would that be?"

"The second guy is the first follower of the leader. The leader has modeled some strange dance to the onlookers. Most just sit and try to pretend they don't care, but they're watching nonetheless. When the second guy embraces the same dance, people become intrigued. The first dancer has now gained some credibility in the eyes of the crowd. This is the gift that every first follower gives to a leader."

Frank pushed "play," and the video started back up. "What do you see now?"

Markus noticed the second dancer looking over his shoulder. Then he waved to his friends in a way that suggested, "Come join us." In a few moments there were five dancers, all engaged in the same odd rhythmic gyrations.

Frank stopped the video again and swallowed the last bite of Shirley's cookies.

"I see what we're looking at now," Markus said. "The nerdy guy isn't so much of a nerd anymore. He's just emerged as a leader."

"Brilliant, Markus."

"Simple deduction, my dear Watson."

Frank caught the allusion. He loved reading Sir Arthur Conan Doyle when he was growing up. So he decided a little banter was appropriate. "'The game is afoot,' right, Sherlock?"

Markus laughed. "You're pretty clever too. That reminds me of conversations I had with Pete awhile back. 'I'm the superhero, you're the sidekick,' he'd say."

"You'll have to fill me in on those details later." Frank smiled back. "I want you to focus your skills of observation on what you see next."

Frank restarted the video. The beach now erupted with people abandoning their towels and rushing to the guy who once danced alone. Soon there were so many that the first dancer could no longer be seen. He was lost somewhere among the throngs of people who rushed to his side. Now everyone jumped and twisted and turned as they sought to imitate their leader.

Frank paused the video again. "What do you see now?"

"I see a modern-day leadership parable. One guy's dancing moves on that beach launched a dancing movement."

"Markus, do you mind if I offend you a little bit?"

"Bring it, Frank! I can eat what I dish out."

Frank smiled at Markus. This night was turning out to be a real treat for him. As a business leader, he always wanted to use the talents God gave him to help his church. But for some reason, he also felt these skills were looked upon with suspicion in the house of God. "Give us your money, and we'll let you know when to give us your opinion." No one ever said that to him directly, but he assumed as much.

"This is what you did for Green Street, Markus. You were our nerdy dancer."

"That's awesome!"

"You taught us how to dance. Your gyrations were crazy at first. In fact, if I were to put a name on your dance moves, I'd call them things like 'The Ripper Two-Step,' 'The Zombie Tango,' and 'The Death Kiss Slow Dance.'"

"Stop!" Markus was laughing out loud now. "You're killing me. You can't repeat that to anyone. I'll lose my reputation as the consultant who's got swag."

Frank laughed and decided to play along. "Embrace the pain. You showed us how to bust a move and tear up the dance floor. Pete was the first one to dance with you. He signaled others. Pretty soon everyone left their liturgical beach towels and joined you in the hustle.

"What you need to help me with next is how to reproduce this on other beach fronts, or in other churches. Do you get my drift?"

Markus got his laughing under control as he gazed thoughtfully at his friend. As far as he was concerned, Frank was the man with swag. He always invested in things that mattered so the right things might happen. But the night was still young, and Markus wasn't quite finished having fun yet.

"You want to clone me? That's awesome. Do you need hair, blood, or spit?"

"If you don't get serious, I'll ask you for a pound of each."

"Look at me, where am I going to get a pound of hair?"

"Would you prefer Kittens or Fanny Mae to help you figure that out?"

"That was so wrong, Frank."

Frank snorted and both men roared with laughter. Conversation couldn't resume for several minutes. Frank clutched his side and confessed to eating too many cookies. Then Markus claimed he was hungry now and wished there'd been just one cookie left for him. That started another round of laughter.

Finally, Frank wiped the tears from his eyes. "You have an ability to get people excited, Markus. You demonstrated that tonight here in Phoenix. But what are those pastors going to do when they get back home?"

"They're—"

Frank interrupted. "Let me answer that question for you. They're going to do what Pete did. They'll stick your card in a drawer and call you when the emergency arises. Then you'll fly down and walk them through the crisis. But what if you'd taught those men in the convention center how to dance tonight? That's how awakenings begin. Can you see what I'm saying?"

"Teach them how to dance…" Markus' eyes drifted out the window of the Palomar hotel overlooking the city's lights. The Cityscape shopping district was glowing with activity. He journeyed back to the day when he first met Monica and Pete in the airport. Frank was right. He flew to Ft. Worth to teach a desperate pastor and his wounded wife how to dance. Or perhaps he helped them realize they'd stopped dancing and needed to believe they still knew how.

"Frank, how would you teach people how to dance?"

Frank didn't even hesitate. "I'd do what you've taught me. Not in the same way, of course. I know Pete is helping you some. But Markus, there's a whole church that's already been taught how to dance along with you. Send us out too. Send Buck and Bender and Kate, and for crying out loud, unleash Fanny Mae with her pink wave and leather jacket.

"Let the pastors know there's an army ready to invade the pulpits and pews anywhere and anytime a crisis is brewing. You taught us the bride of Christ is something that matters to the heart of God and that she's worth our best efforts. You can't do this alone. You've awakened us. Send us out to awaken others."

Markus took Frank's advice. In fact, Shirley made certain that he did. While her husband was bedridden with a bad bug, she put her foot down and refused to let him travel until he was well.

"You are not leaving Ft. Worth. You will stay in this bed or I will call Kittens to come and sit on you!"

Markus laughed and claimed that Kittens was no match for him, but he knew Shirley was right. He called Frank at the last minute.

"Are you still planning to meet me in Orange County, California?"

"Have my ticket ready and looking at it right now."

"Great, you're ready to dance alone."

"Excuse me, but are you asking me to lead the meeting at Mt. Zion?"

"Frank. I believe you're ready. Just remember to be yourself."

Frank took Markus' advice and made the trip without incident. He was thrilled to be given an opportunity to help a struggling church. But even more so, he was honored that Markus trusted him enough to take his place.

"Hello. My name is Frank Sanders. I'm here for two reasons. First,

Markus was ill and couldn't be with us today. And second, I guess I cared enough about my pastor to help save his ministry one day. God has called me to be a guardian. I understand that now."

Frank showed them the chart in a handout and asked them a few simple questions about what they saw. He was a business man, not a preacher. He would describe the process to Markus later as simple and intuitive. Looking at the words in each column and having a candid discussion about where they were falling short seemed to make a lot of sense.

	Movement (Spring)	Monument (Summer)	Museum (Fall)	Morgue (Winter)
Missional	Flexible	Fatigued	Fragile	Frozen
	Catalytic	Analytic	Paralytic	Apocalyptic
	Vision	Strategy	Structure	Decay
	Sacrifice	Commitment	Obligation	Contempt

Then Frank popped the question: "Are you ready to dance with Quasimodo?"

The responses reminded him of the ones he'd heard at Bethany Hills Episcopal Church when Markus posed the same question. But Frank decided to go ahead and explain what the question meant, which was an obvious departure from the way his mentor carried on.

"The hunchback had a terrible deformity," Frank explained. "His life was miserable, and people treated him as the outcast. All around you are people who've been disfigured spiritually, sometimes by all the sin in the world, sometimes by religion itself, perhaps even the actions of your own church. One thing I know to be true is this: God loves them, and they matter to Him.

"Go find them.

"Take some music with you.

"And just dance."

Topics for Discussion

1. Have you been taught to dance?
2. Where are you dancing?
3. When was the last time you invited someone to dance with you?

41819736R00187

Made in the USA
Lexington, KY
28 May 2015